THE SEGONTIUM SWORD

ELLE DUNPHY AND CERIS THOMSON

Also by

Elle Dunphy and Ceris Thomson

The Seer and The Stargazer

The Sibyls' Secrets

This is a work of fiction. In some cases, real life names, events and places appear but their use and reference within this book is entirely fictitious. All other characters, events and locations are the product of the authors' imagination.

First published in England 2024
This edition published in 2024

ISBN (paperback) 978-1-7395748-3-3

Printed and bound in Great Britain

For more information visit
https://www.newmoontarot.co.uk/

Sometimes,
for author and reader,
a story can wield
an invisible shield.

Prologue

The sweeping rain slanted in the freezing afternoon. The light was fading fast when Allan and Jim sighed simultaneously, exhausted and disappointed. Cold seeped into their bones. For hours they had been metal detecting through a waterlogged field within the Conwy Valley, in the grounds of the ruined Ancient Roman Fort of Segontium.

"Even the sheep are sheltering" Jim said as his fingers, bitten blue by the raw wind, clutched a metal detector. "I know we are new to this Allan, as it's only the second time we have been here, but I think we should call it a day. There isn't anything to be found on this land."

Allan lifted his sodden parka hood, blue eyes glittering, and objected. "I have a funny sensation about this place Jim. I can feel its energy. The Roman baths are to our right, and a small temple was found hidden under the riverbank to our left. I'm sure Roman legionaries would have made offerings around here. Let's keep trying for a little while longer. Rome wasn't built in a day."

Jim grimaced. Allan shoved his metal detector down onto the claggy earth for one last try. It began to ping loudly as a signal registered. Falling to the wet ground, both men grasped at the thick mud with their hands. A grubby, aged leather strap was exposed, followed by the top of a faded lapis lazuli embellished pot. Jim carefully tugged at the worn strap whilst Allan held the blue pot in place, careful not to damage it. Five minutes of gentle manoeuvring revealed a faded leather pouch inside the pot. Jim stared at Allan.

"Open it then," shouted Allan.

Hands shaking, Jim slowly unravelled the little bag to reveal a hoard of green, corroded Ancient Roman coins. He stared at Allan and whispered, "Welcome to 2023 ancient coins. You are in one of the most beautiful and mysterious places on earth. Wonder who you once belonged to? See Allan, I told you that truth is stranger than fiction."

***

November 2023

Chapter 1 – Collective Subconscious

Our energy is interconnected.

"Nain[1], you're not going to believe this. I've conjured someone out of thin air!" shouted Seren as she burst into the kitchen of her grandmother's newly built home, Beudy Bryn Gosol.

"Well, that's novel!" laughed nain. "Even though you're a white witch Seren, you can't magic someone to appear. Although there is something magnetic and enchanted about the collective subconscious" replied nain good-naturedly as she turned from a bubbling pot.

"What's collective subconscious?" asked Seren as she helped herself to a cup of nettle tea from the teapot which her nain had christened Niwbwrch.

"Have you ever thought of someone, and they've messaged you out of the blue, or remembered somebody you've not seen for a long time, and then met them unexpectedly?" enquired nain as she blended lavender pods and bee pollen together.

Seren answered, "Yes, of course. That happens to everyone doesn't it? But I don't mean someone messaged me and it was a surprise, or that I bumped into somebody I already know. What I mean is, I've just encountered a man that I've never met before *in this life* but who I think appeared in my *past life regression.* Remember Magpie?"

Nain said, "Now you *have* piqued my curiosity. You mean the Ancient Roman Centurion who was based at Segontium in the Conwy Valley and had skills as an Augur?[2] The one who became

---

[1] Grandmother

[2] Person who says they can see past, present and future.

known as Magpie because of his name from the raven family, and who had an image of two magpies tattooed on his neck?"

"Yes. Him! Wait" demanded Seren, "before I say any more, please explain to me what you understand to be *collective subconscious.*"

Nain's obsidian eyes shone as they held Seren's attention. "It's simple really" she responded, "we can communicate with others telepathically which means we are all interconnected. We link across space and time, through different dimensions, because the energy within and around us collects our thoughts and feelings and transfers them as information to other people. But there are only certain individuals who are receptive to sending and receiving telepathic messages since their minds are open to a life of possibilities."

Nain stopped to stir her concoction in a clockwise direction, '*to bring in good things*' she would say. She added the contents to two cups of panad[3] then placed the fingers of her right hand on her forehead in between her closed eyes, as if searching for something within her. After a few minutes she faced Seren.

"We all have the option to turn on our psychic abilities, but most people choose to ignore signs and symbols. Sometimes this is because they can't believe what they are seeing, or feeling, or hearing, or dreaming. Have you ever felt as if someone is around you, but they can't be seen?" nain asked.

"Yes. Doesn't everyone have that sensation?"

"They do, but most explain it away as '*just a daft feeling*' or '*just imagining things*' and even though what they are experiencing might not fit with received wisdom, it is real."

"You believe that because Magpie appeared in the past life regression Madoc and I had with you in the Temple of Mithras,

---

[3] Tea.

he has now materialised for he sensed this as a psychic message from Madoc and me?"

"Yes" nain replied. "When your minds stepped back to Ancient Roman life in 52BCE your thoughts would have attuned to Magpie, in this life. He could have intuitively sensed your existence in this time dimension. Serendipity and so-called *coincidences* may have led him here, to the Conwy Valley. Destiny has played her part."

Seren's brow raised to her hairline. This was a movement she had learned from her photographer husband Madoc who was an eyebrow raising master.

"Wow" was all she could marshal.

A kelpy sea breeze gently drifted around the kitchen, swelled through an open window before racing back to tease the rills on the Irish Sea.

"Our subconscious mind extends beyond our brain. For ease, let's call it our seventh sense. As you and Madoc have a strong emotional bond with Magpie, forged throughout different lifetimes, your thoughts and emotions will resonate with him across vast distances and dimensions. Thus, we are all interlinked."

"Go on" urged Seren.

"This type of communication works at the quantum level. The universe consists of dark matter and dark energy which provides a conundrum for scientists. Most want to have clearly defined evidence, to *quantify* if you will, why quantum particles can affect other quantum particles and even when they are millions of miles apart, they appear to be connected to each other. Entangled so to speak. You see, different time dimensions and telepathy are possible. These elements have been tricky to verify for scientists and yet, no single quantum theory has been found to explain the fundamental forces of life."

Seren pondered for a while until nain spoke again.

"It seems strange that millions of people believe in deities that they haven't seen, but have faith, without proof. And, unless something can be established by scientists, it's considered pseudoscience. Our psychic abilities would be dismissed by many as simply the foolish thoughts of old women. Old women like me, and women like you, Seren. Those named Seers, Prophetesses, Sybils[4] or *witches* in bygone ages."

"Hey nain I'm only twenty-seven and that's not old! My past life regressions showed me to be a Sybil in Ancient Rome and I'm a white witch now, in 2023" exclaimed Seren, her thoughts tripping over themselves. "Nain, how do you know these things?"

Nain smiled, pleased to share her wisdom, and gently touched her granddaughter's cinnamon coloured cheek.

"Many people are wiser than they allow themselves to admit. It's all a question of thinking for oneself and not following the crowd. It's about learning the lessons from past lives and this life. Besides, when people are over sixty years of age cariad[5] tlws[6], they still engage in life you know."

"I know nain." Seren smiled.

"Listen Seren. I have vim, vigour, and lots of adventures to experience, even though taid[7] is no longer in this life to share them with me. See" she said twirling around her kitchen "I've moved into my converted cowshed on Bryn Gosol farmland. Who would have thought that I could start a fresh chapter of life … at my age! Besides, I sense taid is always around me."

Silence dangled between them like an ethereal silvery cobweb.

"Is it annoying nain, that people might think we are silly to live our lives through the magic and power of prophecy? That we live

---

[4] Seer/Prophetess/Sibyl/Augur person who says they can see past, present and future.
[5] Beautiful.
[6] Love.
[7] Grandfather.

in the tiny Welsh village of Llanrhos where nothing much happens, but we are Seers and know much more than people would ever believe?"

Nain's determined voice reverberated around the kitchen of Beudy Bryn Gosol. A sonorous sound that Seren considered Madoc might have heard as it carried through the open window and across the field which divided nain's cottage from their farmhouse.

"No cariad tlws. Not at all. Over the years you've seen the number of people who have visited me to be *read* when I lived at Bryn Gosol Farm, or those who see you for readings and past life regression at your room in Benarth Beach. Some people, especially the younger generation, are more in tune with spirituality. Their thinking is evolving, and, thankfully, we are all free to choose our beliefs in this country. Not like in ancient times in some countries when women like us would have been burned at the stake. Many people judge it impossible to be psychic, but others know that life is full of infinite potential. It won't be long before what you and I do Seren is accepted as *normal* practice."

"Isn't there anyone in the scientific world who comprehends what we do?" asked Seren "and who can authenticate our psychic abilities?"

"Oh yes. There are some erudite scientists who are trying to grasp our type of communication. By that I mean interaction through space and time. Entanglement. Until enough of them do though, we will quietly go about the business of helping other people to aspire to be their highest self. Remember Seren, that not everything can be seen and any tangible item which illustrates that prophecy is real, must be kept under lock and key. You know what has happened throughout history when the wrong people get hold of prophetic writings?"

"I understand. The ancient mystery of the grimoires[8], the Sibylline books should remain secret."

"Indeed. Now. Tell me about Magpie. What's he doing *in this life?*"

"Walk home with me nain. I've made a cheese pie for you and Madoc. Rhubarb crumble for dessert. Madoc is home. When I left the farmhouse, he was busy researching for the Historical Society about the Ancient Roman Segontium Sword. I'd like you to explain collective subconscious to him and if you don't blow his mind, I'll be able to tell you both about Magpie after dinner. Does that sound enticing?" Seren questioned.

"It does. We can check on the apiary as we pass. The bee pollen is particularly good this year."

A stripped Devil's Tree, Saint Hilary's church and the two sodden, uneven hills of the Vardre lay in the distance before them. Nain and Seren strolled arm in arm towards Bryn Gosol Farm where Madoc waited impatiently for their arrival. He could not wait to tell them about a local news item he had just heard. Two metal detectorists had made a huge find of antique coins at the Ancient Roman Fort of Segontium and he knew who had buried them there more than two thousand years ago.

---

[8] Textbook of prophecies, spells and magic.

November 2023

Chapter 2 – A Wreck

Two for joy.

"The rhubarb crumble was delicious Seren" praised nain. "So good I'll take some home with me for tomorrow."

"Great. I'm pleased you enjoyed it nain."

"Tell me Madoc, how's your friend Gareth and what did the two of you get up to today?" asked nain.

"He's fine. Still working at Bangor University. I met him there after I'd popped into the Bangor Museum. I'll tell you about that little escapade shortly. The weather was clear today, we decided to drive over to Anglesey, and scuba-dive near Moelfre Beach."

Nain's interest piqued. "We have relatives there. Were you able to dive to any of the wrecks? There are plenty of them around the area. When the north-westerly winds blow, and the tide is in the opposite direction, an unwholesome concoction is brewed by the moon and the wind. The swell on the Irish Sea can be treacherous. I've seen such turbulent waves, and a ship is no match for their ferocity. I imagine if a vessel is caught in a violent storm, it's a little like a fish being chewed then gulped down the throat of a sea-serpent. It usually ends with the craft's battered wood being spat out like splintered bones."

Seren and Madoc locked eyes, with expressions that could not be read, then stared at nain. She said the most peculiar things sometimes.

Madoc shook his head and replied, "We dived to the wreck of the Royal Treasure. It's quite a straightforward dive as the ruin lies in cold and clear shallow waters."

"My mother told me about the steam clipper, the Royal Treasure" revealed nain. "It sank and about five hundred people lost their lives. The Irish Sea has irascibly and greedily consumed many souls."

"Indeed" replied Madoc, exasperated that nain had interrupted his story.

"Did anyone survive?" questioned Seren.

"The story in Anglesey is that a Maltese seaman swam ashore with a rope and the people of Moelfre risked their own lives by forming a human chain to help him, other passengers, and crew. Only forty-one people were known to have survived. The dead whose bodies were washed ashore were buried in churches along the Anglesey coast and there's a memorial in Moelfre to commemorate them. Did you know that a large gold nugget was recently found on the seabed at Moelfre?"

Now it was Madoc's turn to have his interest stirred.

"Was that the ship's cargo nain?" asked Madoc. "Gold?"

"Yes. And Anglesey is awash with rumours that gold still lies along the coastline, especially near Moelfre Beach" replied nain.

"This weekend, we'll take our metal detector there Seren. We can have a little trip out" stated Madoc, eyes bright as ingots.

"Whatever you find will be covered in barnacles" said nain darkly "and certainly wouldn't bring positivity to anyone in this family."

Madoc's eyebrows rose up his crinkled forehead. To change the mood in the back dining room Madoc hastily cleared the dessert plates from the oak table and said, "I've been waiting to tell you both about three fragments of information I've received today. The first piece of news is that the Segontium Sword has disappeared from the Bangor Museum."

Seren sighed, "It can't just disappear Madoc. It's a fragile piece of metal forged two thousand years ago, encased in a sealed glass cabinet."

"Who would be in a position to remove it from the Museum in the first place?" queried nain "and why?"

Madoc pressed on. "That's just it. I visited the Museum this morning to take photographs of the Segontium Sword. Well, it's actually an Ancient Roman gladius, but let's not be pedantic. I had planned to include it in the photographic display about Ancient Roman Wales that I'm organising for the Historical Society. And it wasn't in its case. The Segontium Sword was missing."

"Strange" announced Seren.

"Very odd" agreed nain.

"It wasn't out to be cleaned, or for maintenance work, was it? You didn't think to ask the Museum's Curator where the Sword was, did you?" asked Seren.

Madoc raised his eyebrows almost to infinity. In a low and deliberate voice, he replied, "Seren, of course I asked the Curator. She didn't know. She said she'd find out for me and let me know what's happened to it. I gave her my mobile number but haven't heard anything from her."

"Maybe these things take time" assuaged nain "since it's not every day that an Ancient Roman gladius goes absent without leave, is it?" Seren, who caught Nain's eye, smiled. "Perhaps the Curator has asked the Military Police to search the Museum. Or maybe Interpol are on to the problem?"

"What? In case the sword's slashed a hole in the glass case and taken a stab at strolling outside for a breath of twenty-first Century fresh air. It'd cut quite a dash in Bangor, wouldn't it?" Madoc replied sarcastically.

Seren shot him a warning glance. He could speak sharply without thinking sometimes. The air fizzled around frustrated Madoc.

"What was the second piece of news you were going to tell us?" soothed Seren.

"Word is within the Historical Society, that a skeleton has been discovered in the Temple of Artemis, in Greece.

Archaeologists are hoping to uncover the secrets held within the bones. There's speculation that the frame belongs to a woman, possibly the ambitious half-sister of Cleopatra. Arsinoë IV."

"No!" exclaimed Seren. "I thought Cleopatra and Arsinoë were Egyptian. Why would Arsinoë be buried in Greece? That doesn't make sense."

"Didn't Arsinoë appear in your past life regression?" asked nain.

"Only briefly. Yes" replied an astonished Seren.

"Wasn't she one of the prisoners paraded in the Triumph alongside Vercingetorix, when Caesar returned to Rome from Gaul?" persisted nain.

"She was in our past life regression" agreed Madoc. "The teenager entered the Circus Maximus, and the audience of Roman citizens expected her to be murdered in the Arena but when they called for clemency, surprisingly Julius Caesar acquiesced. Much to Cleopatra's fury. Instead of having her slain, Caesar supposedly exiled her to the Temple of Artemis in the large Roman province of Ephesus in Greece. But that's debatable" explained Madoc.

"Our past life regression showed that to be a momentous day in 46BCE" recalled Seren. "I shudder when I remember it. Why might Julius Caesar choose the Temple of Artemis nain to exile Arsinoë IV, why not have her killed?"

"Like the Ancient Romans, the Ancient Egyptians worshipped many Gods who represented nature's subtle mechanisms of air, fire, water, and earth. The Goddess Artemis was linked to the moon, hunting and fertility. Her twin brother Apollo was linked to the sun, healing, and prophecy. Both twins delivered prophecies through Sibyls and Julius Caesar often consulted Prophetesses before making huge decisions. Perhaps it was a prophecy in one of the Sibylline books that Caesar must save Arsinoë IV. Or she may have reminded him of his beloved daughter Julia, who had died. Or perhaps he wanted to remove her from Cleopatra's withering gaze. Maybe Caesar knew there was something extraordinary about Arsinoë."

"Interesting" responded Seren.

"And the last piece of news" interrupted Madoc, keen to move away from discussion about Arsinoë, "is that two metal detectorists have found a hoard of Ancient Roman coins at Segontium."

"Oh, my goodness" gasped nain. "Have they been verified?"

"Yes. Today they've been declared as Welsh treasure. There were almost 3,000 coins found. If we do another past life regression to Ancient Roman times, I'm sure it will reveal …".

"MADOC" shouted nain, her face pale and pinched "this discovery might lead to people snooping around Bryn Gosol farmhouse, discovering the secret Temple of Mithras or an ancient grimoire. We cannot have that. No. We cannot possibly have that. It was bad enough when busybodies excavated one of the farm's fields years ago. They asked too many questions. Taid managed to focus their attention away from the farm. We were happy when all they found were bric-a-brac. You will have to do the same as taid, Madoc. We cannot let them know about the Temple of Mithras deep under Saint Hilary's church or our ancient books of prophecy."

The air crackled. Madoc was stunned into silence for nain's gentle temperament rarely changed. He had never seen her agitated.

A shaking nain eyed Seren and delicately changed the subject. "You wanted to tell Madoc and me some news Seren. What is it?"

In a steady voice Seren replied "I've read a man today that I've never met before in this life but who I think appeared in my past life regression. I used your Tarocchi tarot cards nain because he is Italian."

Madoc checked for a moment. His lovat coloured eyes observed Seren. She could feel his curiosity brimming but no word was spoken for several minutes.

"Your friend Gareth sent him to me" announced Seren as she steadily returned Madoc's gaze.

"You mean the scientist he works with at Bangor University?" questioned Madoc.

"Yes" she confirmed.

"We don't know him" stated Madoc frowning. "I'm sure Gareth said we'd never met him before."

"Gareth was right. We haven't met him before in this life, but he was a friend in a past life."

"Who?" demanded Madoc.

Nain quietly observed the interaction between Seren and Madoc.

"Well …" responded Seren tantalisingly "you'll never guess. He said I could tell you about his reading. His full name is Gaius Romeo Cangini, but he prefers Romeo."

Unwittingly Madoc lifted an eyebrow and maintained his contemplation of Seren.

"Go on" he insisted.

"He was full of energy and admired your photography. Do you know what he said when he saw the panoramic view you'd taken from the Vardre, Madoc? The one which shows Conwy, the Irish Sea and three Welsh mountain ranges?"

"Enlighten me" replied Madoc.

'*Is he a little bit jealous*?' thought nain.

Seren ploughed on "He said '*we live in the picture*!' And he's right. We do! You, me, nain, him. We live in that picture. Romeo had the biggest smile. It could light up any room. His collar-length hair had the dark colouring of a nuummite crystal, and his eyes held the shimmer of obsidian. Like nain's eyes" offered Seren as she pointed at nain.

"He sounds delicious" replied nain.

"He's not something to eat nain" retorted Madoc huffily.

Nain's lips twitched into a half-smile.

"He said *I* was famous" announced Seren. "Imagine! Me? Famous? Well, I just laughed at that. Because I'm not, really, famous."

'*What she is though, is a little bit giggly*' deliberated a half-annoyed Madoc.

"I feel giddy Madoc. And you will too when you realise who he is" admitted Seren.

'*Goodness. It's as if that woman can read my thoughts*' pondered Madoc and shook his head. '*That's the price to pay if you're involved with a white witch I suppose.*'

"He said he wanted to meet me because, although he's a scientist and usually needs proof of everything, since he was a small boy, he's experienced visions, images, dreams. Sometimes an event will happen, and he's known beforehand that it will occur. Presentiment. He finds it unsettling."

'*Try being married to a witch, then you'll know the true meaning of unsettling, Mr Gorgeous Gaius Romeo Cangini*' thought Madoc.

"He's a physicist. He's trying to find answers to the unknown but hasn't solved his own conundrum yet. He's hoping I'll be able to help him. Oh, and I spotted his blue aura" Seren confessed.

"What does that mean? A blue aura? Have I got one? What colour's mine?" demanded Madoc. "I'm sure you've told me this before, but I can't quite recall" he conceded.

Seren took out her mobile phone and searched the Internet for instances of auras.

"Madoc, here's a good example. Look at this energetic painting by Tintoretto. It's called Il Paradiso and is a large-scale narrative which has a path of light at its centre known as the Empyrean Domain which details the element of fire. Tintoretto depicted that this is where souls reside. There are more than five hundred characters within this piece of art. Look at the two central figures with rayed, golden glows of light around them. The glows represent how auras look."

"Wow. Yes, I've seen auras in paintings. But forgive me. I'm new to witchy ways. What is the Empyrean Domain and what is a real aura?" insisted Madoc.

Seeing Madoc this belligerent was unusual. Nain stepped in.

"I can understand your frustration Madoc. We can sometimes take things for granted and forget other people aren't always acquainted with our idiosyncrasies. There is much to absorb about a witch's life. The Empyrean Domain is a dimension in the universe inhabited by beings with the highest energy, beings of pure white light known as light beings or star seeds."

"And they are what exactly?" asked Madoc.

"Simply put it's a person who has a high dimensional light. Someone you might call a good soul. They light up others' lives" replied nain.

"Ok. I understand that. And an aura?"

"Ah. An aura is a unique electromagnetic field of light, an energy which surrounds your whole body and radiates from you. The aura emits different colours depending upon your feelings and level of spirituality. Gwrachod gwyn[9] like Seren and I, can see a person's aura. Intuitively most people can feel others' aura even if they are unaware of its existence and colour" explained nain.

"Ah. I recollect now. It's when you've met people that you're drawn to and others that repel you" stated Madoc. "It's their aura which is sending out messages about them. What colour is my aura?" he asked of nain who regarded him intently.

"It's orange Madoc."

---

[9] White witches.

"Tell me what that means" he demanded "as it sounds zingy."

Nain responded, "That you are action-focused, optimistic and creative."

"May I get on with my story now Madoc please?" asked Seren. Placated, Madoc nodded, his moss-green eyes bright.

"There was so much positive energy in my room that it sparkled" gushed Seren.

Madoc tutted. Seren continued unabashed.

"Romeo was surrounded by birds."

"Who is this man? Damon bloody Albarn?" retorted Madoc.

Nain looked flummoxed.

"Damon Albarn is a musician. The front man of Blur. A bird watcher" replied Madoc.

Seren ignored nain's discombobulated expression.

"Madoc, like you, Romeo is a stargazer. I've invited him to watch the Leonids this month when we're next stargazing on the Vardre. He said '*yes*'."

"That'll be a delight for us all wont it?" replied Madoc.

Nain wondered if he was being a little sarcastic but said nothing.

"He's incredibly handsome but hasn't yet met his soulmate. I told him that he had the choice of plenty of women, but that they want him for the wrong reasons. He keeps picking inappropriate types of women. To meet his soulmate, he needs to start looking away from bars, and clubs. He needs a woman who will happily look at the stars with him. Nain, he knew that nurture of the soul was important."

"It is Seren. And never underestimate the power of love either" nain said as sagely as any Sibyl might.

"I can't work out who he was, from our past life regression Seren" divulged Madoc.

"You will when I tell you that he has two tattoos. One on his left forearm with the words carpe diem and another on his neck, of two magpies."

"Magpie?" shrieked Madoc. "You've met Magpie? In this life? Well. Why didn't you say before? When can I meet him?"

"That's what I've been trying to tell you" replied an exasperated Seren. "I'm sure that Romeo is Magpie from our past life in Ancient Rome. But guess what? He doesn't know that he knows us. What I mean is, he doesn't know that he knew us in a previous life, and I can't be certain it's him."

"Why not?" demanded Madoc.

"Nain will explain it later Madoc" placated Seren. She paused for a few minutes before saying "let's move into the front sitting room. It's cosier in there. I'll make a panad and bring some bara brith[10] for us as I think this is going to be a long night."

Madoc suggested that nain's tangy homemade dandelion wine, which flowed down the throat with a refreshing trickle, might be more appropriate. He found it wasn't easy dealing with gwrachod gwyn. There were many stories to be told, lessons to be learned and above all, a need to observe and embrace the challenging frontier of irrational thought, to gain a richer understanding of life.

[10] Welsh tea bread.

November 2023

Chapter 3 – Is it crazy?

What appears ordinary can lead to the extraordinary.

"Romeo asked me if the mysterious essence of time linked with his visions. He said that he thinks time is emergent."

"What does that mean? Time is emergent?" questioned Madoc.

Seren considered for a while how she would explain this to Madoc and nain, mindful she did not fully understand it herself, sighed, then said:

"Time is real in the sense that it emerges from events and processes. We can't see, hear, feel, smell, taste, or touch time … but it dominates our lives."

"Go on" Madoc urged. "I agree with that."

"We are living mortal lives. We think that time passes in chunks because we have allocated it to seconds, minutes, days, weeks, months, seasons, years" continued Seren.

"I blame Julius Caesar for that because he returned from Egypt with an understanding of how time was measured and thus created a calendar linked to the moon's phases," said Madoc.

"I was just about to tell you that Romeo blamed Julius Caesar for the formal measurement of time!" exclaimed Seren. "What he also said was that time in our body is finite as we witness ourselves, and others, getting older."

With a ripple of approval Madoc uttered, "Very profound but everybody knows that".

Seren continued. "Through the passage of time we witness decay and new growth, but time for our souls is infinite."

"That's what nain believes too!" exclaimed Madoc.

"Romeo asked if it was possible that mortals could experience different lives or different dimensions of time. He wondered if some people, those who are like nain and me, can encounter events randomly and concurrently so that we access the past, present, and future because for us time is experienced in a different way. He said that he was trying to work out the mysteries of time and how that linked to his life."

"What did you say?" asked nain and Madoc in unison.

Her eyes refulgent, Seren said "I asked him if he'd ever had a past life regression."

Nain and Madoc, again in harmony asked, "What did he say?"

"He replied *'you think our time, our life, isn't ephemeral? carpe diem*!'"

With surprise on his face Madoc said, "What does that mean?"

"Let's enjoy ourselves while we have the chance!"

"Now what happens?" asked Madoc.

Seren laughed. "He's having a past life regression with me next week."

Madoc punctured the air with a question. "Magpie. How has he come back into our lives then?" he asked of nain and Seren.

"Nain has a theory about that Madoc."

"Which is?" challenged Madoc.

Nain sat beside the inglenook fire and stared into the orange twirling flames watching the wood charring and scorching, as it cracked. Cosily enveloped by the soft gold velvet cushions on the sofa, Seren and Madoc keenly watched nain's bright face.

"Go on nain" urged Seren. "Tell Madoc about collective subconscious."

Nain repeated what she had previously told Seren. "What appears to be irrational Madoc only reveals that we need to learn more. You know there isn't one truth, and that no one person has total knowledge. No-one really understands how the universe works but what I do know is that collective subconscious communication operates at the quantum level."

"I grasp that nain. But how does that link with Romeo being here in Conwy?"

Nain continued. "Our subconscious mind extends beyond our brain. For ease, let's call it our seventh sense. As you both have a strong emotional bond with people from past lives who are currently in this life, your thoughts and emotions will resonate with Romeo across vast distances and dimensions. We are all interlinked. Let's call it entangled. It works through quantum particles which can affect other quantum particles. Even when quantum particles are separated by millions of miles, they appear to be connected to each other. So, you see, subconsciously we are emitting energy all the time. Not everything can be viewed simultaneously unless you use your seventh sense.

It's likely that Magpie will have attuned to your energy when you and Seren were immersed in your past life regression in Ancient Rome. Subliminally, he will have felt your existence. Destiny, or Fate, will have engineered serendipitous moments to lead Magpie here to North Wales."

"So, he doesn't know why he's here? He's been led here by Destiny and when Seren takes him on his past life regression, he will realise what Seren, and I meant to him?"

"Not exactly" answered nain. "It all depends upon which past life door he opens when he regresses."

"Can't we merely tell him who we are?" queried Madoc.

"It's not that simple Madoc. He's got to have the past life experience himself to realise the lessons he still needs to learn before he recognises how you were linked in his past life" explained nain.

"Carpe diem, Romeo" whispered Madoc as Seren met his gaze and shuddered.

The universe stopped spinning. tempora tempore.[11]

Mother Gaia gently placed the universe back on its axis. Was she enabling time to march on towards the past life regression of gorgeous Gaius Romeo Cangini?

---

[11] Time stood still.

April 2002

Chapter 4 – Polignano

Dragons and worms.

It was midday in Polignano as Romeo and Alessandro ran their fingers clumsily through the hot, soft sand to dig for crabs. The water's edge glittered like fairy dust as the children gathered buckets of warm briny sea to mix with sand and create sandcastles in which crabs could live. The ten-year-old boys were twins; one robust and hearty like a bourgeoning oak tree, the other thin and stringy as a fading sapling. Their mother, Cinzia wore a broad brimmed hat covering her delicate Mediterranean features as she ceaselessly surveyed the boys' activities. At her feet the cerulean-blue Adriatic Sea delicately curved as it tiptoed into the harbour, which lay sheltered between two craggy limestone cliffs.

Cinzia called out to the boys who sprang like foals to a loving, sinewy mare.

"Let's go and cut some aloe vera from the rocks" she instructed.

"Why do we need aloe vera mamma?" asked Romeo.

He laughed when she made a face and kissed his cheek.

"The spiky leaves have a gel which we can use to create medicine. We can wash in it and make potions to treat any wounds we might have."

"The leaves are like razors mamma" exclaimed Alessandro seriously. "Be careful or you might cut yourself and I'll have to put gel on your arms" he advised.

Cinzia hugged her spindly son and kissed his cheek.

"You're right. We will all have to be especially cautious Alessandro, but the potions will be useful at home."

"Will papà help us make potions?" asked Alessandro excitedly.

"I'm sure he will when we ask him" Cinzia answered. "Come, let's take the leaves home. The sun is high. Soon it will be too hot to be outside. You can play in the garden, under the shade of our olive trees."

The trio skipped from the beach, and the boys chased each other up the Volare stairs. At the top of the cliffs, together they strolled through the old city gate, The Marchesale Arch, along the labyrinth of narrow winding alleyways to their charming house with its terracotta pots of oregano, parsley, thyme, and marjoram on the downstairs windowsills. The boys had vied to carry the bag containing the aloe vera cuttings. Cinzia negotiated a truce. They could each carry the bag for five minutes, but an argument broke out about who would be the first to transport the spoils. Spying sadness in his mother's grey eyes, Romeo relented, mindful his brother was a sickly child.

At their white-washed building, Cinzia opened the front door. Romeo and Alessandro ran through the kaleidoscopic living room towards the back of the house.

"Come into the garden Alessandro" ordered Romeo.

His brother smiled.

"Let's catch worms and spiders" Alessandro suggested "but don't eat any Romeo. You make my stomach churn when you do that."

"They're tasty" teased Romeo. "Yum."

In the verdant garden, enterprising Cinzia had cultivated anemones, mulberries, roses, lavender, and lotus flowers. From these she created natural beauty products and sold them from her tiny shop in the village. Her olive trees provided olive oil for moisturising serum and lip scrub, and along with the bee pollen she sold in small jars, had proved to be best sellers. Cinzia's innovative husband, Fausto encouraged her to use organic packaging and advertise widely. Fausto had been right when he assured her it would widen her customer-base.

"Make sure you excavate at the bottom of the garden boys. Please avoid digging up the flowers this time" instructed Cinzia. "Enjoy being with the worms. I know how much you love them."

It was true that most of all Romeo prized worms, dragons, and glittering stars. Licking toads and eating spiders were also enjoyable pastimes. Watching worms wriggle as they burrowed their way through the thick, damp soil which lay underneath the toads until the worms were lost in darkness, inventing stories about dragons with his brother and imagining missions for the two of them to distant stars caused Romeo the most excitement. Alessandro shared Romeo's obsessions but refused to eat worms. Together in the garden the boys knelt on the earth, heads touching, hands dragging at the fertile black soil.

"Look Alessandro" tormented Romeo as he placed a pink wriggling worm near his mouth.

"Don't eat it! It's unkind" replied his brother with a shudder.

"I won't" replied Romeo "I promised I wouldn't. But tonight, Alessandro we will summon dragons and watch the stars dance."

As his brother quivered with excitement, the olive trees whispered to each other in the wisteria fragranced air and the dipping flowers bowed their approval. Romeo detected the back door open as their father stepped out of the house.

"Papà" he called. "Come and help us."

"What are you two doing?"

"We are making a wormery for mamma so that her flowers grow rich and lush" replied Alessandro.

"Good. Good" replied Fausto as he brushed away his unruly greying hair from his round-rimmed black glasses and knelt beside his children. "When you've done, would you like to paint with me?" he asked. "I have finished at the hospital for today."

"Yes please," shouted Romeo.

"Shall we paint outside papà?" asked Alessandro. "We can use the table under the olive trees so that we have some shade."

"Great idea. As mamma fashions her potions, we will be able to create as much mess as we like out here" suggested their father mischievously.

Fausto tickled both boys who giggled. They would have been surprised to learn that anyone outside the family had to be brave to get to know Fausto Cangini. A fiercely protective, quiet man he managed to keep strangers at bay with his direct speech, assertive demeanour, and acerbic wit. There was a fault line which could not be breached between his position as a surgeon and his role as a family man. Fausto was indeed a contradiction.

Aided by their father, Romeo and Alessandro covered the azure-coloured metal table with tubes of watercolour paints, various paintbrushes, three palettes, finely tipped pencils, micron pens, three containers of water, and three bars of soap. The thick sheets of white watercolour paper were placed on a chair held in place by a modest sculpture of two magpies which their nonno[12] had crafted when playing for Newcastle United. The boys knew it was in honour of the Club's emblem and his time in England. They treasured it.

"What are we painting today papà?" asked Alessandro.

"Something to amuse mamma" he replied furtively.

Both boys were intrigued. Their father's crinkly eyes smiled.

"Come with me to my study" he instructed. We are each going to create a painting which tricks Mamma. "Look" he said, "here are some examples of what we will try to do."

Fausto referred to two books he had bought in Milan to show three paintings to Romeo and Alessandro.

"Look at this image. It has the illusion that the ceiling is open to the sky. Can you see here?" Fausto pointed to the page.

---

[12] Grandfather.

"There are artists such as Salvador Dali and René Magritte who like to play tricks on the eyes and mind with their paintings."

On one page Fausto showed a picture entitled Metamorphosis of Narcissus by Salvador Dali.

"Look at the painting. Close your eyes. Look again at the image. Tell me what you think you see" he instructed.

In a handful of minutes Romeo answered, "On the left of the picture I see a muscular man, created from stone, kneeling in water papà staring at his own reflection".

"And you Alessandro? What do you see at the forefront on the right?" asked his father.

"I see a thumb, holding up a broken egg, which is held in place by two bony fingers" he answered.

"The artist, Dali enjoyed presenting double images. There are multiple figures which can appear as different things depending upon how you look at the painting. Look at it again. Now do you see two men side by side?"

"Yes" both boys agreed excitedly.

"You see boys, perception isn't simply relying on our five senses. We have extra senses which are part of you. Look deeply into what is presented to you and try not to accept anything at face value."

Breezily sweeping through his books, Fausto showed another idiosyncratic image.

"Now look at this picture" he ordered as Magritte's painting appeared.

"What do the words mean papà?" asked Alessandro.

"This is not a pipe" answered Fausto.

"But it is a pipe papà, isn't it?" asked Romeo.

"Can you touch it?" asked Fausto.

"I can touch the page of the book" replied Romeo, "but not the pipe."

"So, is it a pipe?" asked Fausto.

Alessandro responded, "No papà."

"No Alessandro? Why?"

"Magritte is correct papà. It is not a pipe."

"Why isn't it a pipe?" queried Romeo.

"It is a painting of a pipe" answered Alessandro joyfully. "It is Magritte's interpretation of a pipe and also, what we have been taught a pipe should look like."

"Correct" said their father. "The painting represents what we believe to be a pipe. Magritte's work offers a paradox. Images that are simple, but which provoke us to think. These images might deceive the eye" he explained. "We can't see everything with our eyes."

"What do we see with?" asked Romeo, puzzled.

"All of our five senses. Which are?" Fausto questioned.

"Sight. Sound. Taste. Smell. Touch. And our sixth sense. Our intuition" said Romeo gravely.

"An image can change our perception, and our extra senses are incredibly important boys. Always remember that."

For three hours the boys painted with their father until it was time to eat their evening meal. It was an encounter that would have a lasting impression on Romeo. When they had finished their work, Fausto instructed:

"Show your paintings to Mamma and ask her what she thinks of them."

The two boys marched to the kitchen, held their artwork aloft to present to Cinzia. Alessandro instructed, "Mamma look at these paintings. What do you think they are?"

"Romeo's is a black and white feather. Yours is a lemon tree" responded Cinzia.

"You're wrong" announced Romeo.

"They're very realistic" replied Cinzia "I think I'm correct. Why am I not?"

"They are paintings mamma of a feather and a tree. They aren't really a feather and tree. Not real ones. Not ones you can touch" said Alessandro spiritedly.

With a conspiratorial grin, Fausto pressed his lips to his wife's forehead and squeezed her waist.

"You two boys and your father. Always playing tricks on me. I'll place your artwork on the fridge door. Now go and wash before our meal. We will eat in the garden. Fausto, please will you clear the table?"

"Certainly" he agreed.

"You are a wonderful father" she whispered to him. "Making the children think deeply about the world around them. It's an important life lesson."

As they stepped out of the house onto the edge of the garden, Fausto kissed Cinzia again before setting up the metal table for dinner. Their two boys joined them. As they watched their two children appear from the house, bringing with them home-made cicchetti of creamed cod of polenta, and boiled egg with anchovies, Fausto and Cinzia cherished this incomparably beautiful moment. Below them, the spectacular cerulean-blue sea washed away their anxieties, just for today.

April 2002

Chapter 5 – Weird Little Boys

Diorama of dragons.

Wide-eyed and spent Alessandro hid among the olive trees his mother had lovingly cultivated. He was being chased by a red fire-eating dragon. With perennial obsession, his brother Romeo had achieved a highly polished interpretation of this magical, legendary creature by painting his face scarlet and wearing a crimson bath sheet expertly tied around his shoulders. Romeo ran at full pelt around the garden, flapping his arms as if in flight.

"Each day I slay three hundred men" shouted Romeo as he pressed on a cigarette lighter which emitted a long flame.

In between deep breaths Alessandro answered defiantly, "You shall not slay me you evil dragon. My sword will strike your breast and render you dead". A wooden sword, which he had constructed with his mother, was held tightly in his left hand.

"I will not die" replied Romeo "as I am immortal."

"I will bind your mouth with red ribbon, and seal it. Then I shall enchant you and remove your venom."

"You will be swallowed whole before you have the chance to touch me" shouted Romeo as the cigarette lighter again released a long flame.

How many times does a mother interrupt the marvellous imagination of her children? This is precisely what Cinzia did just as Alessandro sprang from behind a tree, grappled his flame-throwing brother to the ground and sat on him.

"Mamma!" shouted Alessandro in indignation. "We are enacting one of the Golden Legends and you arrived just when the dragon was about to be slayed. I am the knight in shining armour who needed to rescue the princess held captive in the tower, patrolled by the dragon!"

Conflicted, Cinzia curtsied and replied, "I'm sorry knight in shining armour. I apologise fire-eating dragon but papà will be home shortly and we need to get ready. Am I the princess being rescued?"

"No mamma. *She* has cobalt blue eyes, lots of black hair and black skin. Not at all like you. The princess is beautiful. Romeo saw her in a dream" replied Alessandro innocently.

Cinzia paused, smiled at the naïve barb, stared at Alessandro, and asked, "How have you strapped that enormous metal pan to your chest and the two small pan lids to your knees?"

Alessandro turned around to show his mother elastic ropes wound through the pan handles, tied around his back and legs which held the pots in place. Cinzia laughed.

"Just one more minute mamma please" appealed Alessandro.

"One more minute. That's all" replied Cinzia.

"Thank you, mamma," shouted Alessandro "I love you."

Romeo roughly pushed his brother off his chest and onto the sloping earth. The knight in shining armour and the dragon gripped each other tightly. The dragon slipped on the incline. The knight in shining armour seized the moment, lunged his wooden sword to the dragon's red chest, looked up to the sky and shouted, "Please Goddess of the Moon, bring me the dragon's potion. I am here waiting for it and am ready. I will harm none, other than the dragon, as I am doing this."

The warm air lay still. A gentle waft of jasmine filled the crepuscular night. All was silent until Alessandro shouted, "Yield dragon. Yield."

"I yield but I'm only doing so because papà is coming home" conceded Romeo.

"I accept your surrender dragon" said Alessandro as he helped his brother from the soft ground, lumpily cross-stitched with tree roots.

Their father appeared in the gloaming.

"Am I entering the diorama of dragons?" he asked elaborately.

"Papà" they cried in unison.

"I see Romeo you are the fire-eating dragon and Alessandro is the knight in shining armour" said Fausto in the flickering early-evening orange light. "I love your outfits."

"Papà I slayed the dragon this time" said Alessandro proudly, his handsome wide eyes bright with joy. "Usually the dragon eats me!"

"Well done, Alessandro." Fausto hugged both boys and ruffled their hair. "What's new today with you two?"

"Papà a quite extraordinary thing has happened. Today Romeo had another vision" stated Alessandro pragmatically.

"You have little man? Come and sit with me under the olive trees. What have you seen?" asked Fausto tenderly.

Romeo helped Alessandro divest himself of his pan and lids before both boys sat on a hand-carved acacia bench either side of their father.

"He saw a flood and a volcano" stated Alessandro "in Italy."

"Tell me about it, Romeo" encouraged his father.

With black eyes bright with tears Romeo quietly said, "I saw a volcano erupting papà and the flooding of a village."

"What happened?" his father probed. "Start from the beginning."

"I saw an island. A small island just off the bottom of the Italian coast. It had a volcano. At first all was calm then suddenly I saw gas and lava spewing out of the top of the volcano. Later I saw the sides of the volcano collapse. The land slid into the sea and created huge waves which engulfed part of the island. That's what I saw papà. It frightened me" said Romeo as he began to cry. Alessandro moved position and hugged his brother tightly.

"Don't cry Romeo" whispered Alessandro into his brother's ear and rubbed his back. "Papà's here with us. It'll be ok. See papà" said Alessandro "I told you he'd had another vision."

With composure, his father asked, "Do you know when these events will happen Romeo? Was there any indication?"

"It will begin in May papà when the cherry blossom falls and be at its height in December when the air becomes cold," revealed Romeo.

The sun smudged the horizon as Fausto thrust his fingers through his spikey hair. He was pensive for a long time.

"Thank you for telling me, Romeo. Come inside boys" he instructed. "Who wants to play chess with me?"

Already a Chess Master, Alessandro readily volunteered. Romeo chose to help his mother make potions.

Later that evening, when the children were in bed Cinzia settled at the azure garden table appreciating the incandescent exquisiteness of the night sky.

"First Romeo and now you" she said lightly into the cool evening air.

"What do you mean?" replied Fausto as he joined her.

"You've both been preoccupied all evening" she stated.

Her husband deliberated for a long while before responding.

"Today Romeo told me of another vision. And the last few he's revealed have come true."

"You mean the earthquakes which struck the Umbria region five years ago?" asked Cinzia.

"Yes, and he clearly predicted the deaths of Princess Diana and Dodi Al Fayad in the same year. Then he foresaw the September 11 terrorist attacks last year" replied Fausto effortfully. "I had a look at a map of Italy and the terrain of the islands. I think he's referring to an island off Sicily. He may have predicted a volcanic eruption and a tsunami on Stomboli. There is an incredibly volatile volcano there which spews fountains of molten rock."

"What can we do Fausto? He's a little boy. It's frightening. Should we tell someone in authority about his ability to visualise things, that others may not be able to see?" asked Cinzia.

"I've been seeking a scientific explanation about this Cinzia" replied Fausto forcefully. "I've searched through the medical encyclopaedia in the library at work. I have thought, and contemplated, and considered, and measured each argument. Let's not draw any outside attention to him."

Unusually agitated, Cinzia said, "I know you have examined different avenues. Did the medical books reveal anything we can hang our hope upon? Can we help Romeo?"

Fausto placed a comforting arm around his wife.

"I can't work out what it is exactly that is happening to him. I've read about remote viewing, clairvoyance and something which might be similar in the Indian Yogic system called Divya Drishti."

"Oh" responded Cinzia forlornly, "I am familiar with the term clairvoyance but not the other two. I don't know what those are" she confessed.

"It may not be any of those phenomena. I may be searching in the wrong place for answers."

"Describe them to me, then we can decide together if we think any of the explanations fit our son's visions" encouraged Cinzia ardently.

Fausto sighed. A deep, soulful, melancholy breath. Cinzia rubbed his hand reassuringly.

"Ok. Remote viewing is visualising information and images of people, places and objects that may be unknown to the viewer. It's meditating to access something known as the third eye which is between the eyebrows and linked to the brain's pineal gland. Some say it plays a part in our metaphysical and spiritual dimension. By focusing on the pineal gland and using the third eye, Romeo may see an event or person in his subconscious mind which is transferred to his conscious mind. Remote viewing is purported to be utilised by government intelligence agencies for spying but obviously I don't know how true that is, as I'm not a spy. At least, I'm not telling you if I am" he teased.

Cinzia was thoughtful for a while. "Hmm. Does that mean Romeo could be able to see what is happening here and now with people and the environment in different parts of the world? But that doesn't answer how he can see what happens in the future or how he can look back into the distant past."

"I know" replied her husband. "But, as far as I can make out, remote viewing is associated with clairvoyance, which is also known as second sight. Knowing something is true without understanding how you believe it is so. Being psychically receptive to receiving communication from somewhere, but I don't know where that *somewhere* might be. I know that physicists are grappling to understand the dimension of time and, whilst we are aware of the three classical dimensions, length, width, height, currently physicists are speculating about another six dimensions which are invisible to us. From what I can gather, Romeo may be able to use extra senses which scan time in the future and possibly the past."

"Are clairvoyance, remote viewing and second sight the same?" probed Cinzia.

"Well. Clairvoyance is knowing information, or events are going to happen in the future using a sense beyond our five usual senses."

"Is that what people call a sixth sense?" asked Cinzia.

"I think so."

"And second sight is the same thing?"

Fausto rubbed a hand over his stubbly chin. "Yes. Possibly" he answered.

"And Divya Drishti? What have you found out about that?"

"It's the practice of yoga where people meditate. A calmness overtakes them, and they can peer into the future using their third eye. I think meditation is the key. Switching off the mind, breathing deeply, allowing images and words to seep through into the conscious mind. That's about all I know."

"This method is practised by people who follow yoga?" asked Cinzia.

"Yes, but I don't know much about yoga. Perhaps we could learn about it together?" he suggested.

Lost in a whirlpool of anxiety, Cinzia tried to grasp hold of reality instead of trying to grab onto thin air. She asked Fausto if there was a medical explanation for her son's revelations.

"Insanity?" he joked.

"Don't joke Fausto. That's cruel. Our son is normal. He has a gift which many others have shared over the years. Look at Nostradamus" directed his wife.

"Yes, let's look at Nostradamus! Some of his prophecies appear to have been fulfilled but people still do not believe in his predictions. Our son will become the collateral damage for all kinds of spooks if we draw attention to his abilities. Any idea of him living a normal life will evaporate Cinzia. We can't allow that to happen to him, or to Alessandro. I will speak to both boys tomorrow and tell Romeo that he must only share his visions with us, his family."

Cinzia had never seen Fausto so frustrated, so animated, so afraid.

"But what if his premonitions can help others? Can save lives?"

"We can't stop natural disasters Cinzia. They will occur no matter what. And as for people harming others, well, perhaps they are living their Destiny, and we cannot interfere with what is fated."

"But …"

"No Cinzia. I have given this a lot of thought. I'll speak to the boys in the morning. We will encourage them both to put their energies into studying and working hard. Perhaps these visions will disappear over time. I read an article in one of the medical journals about psychic readings which stated that all people can be psychic, that children are psychic until their parents tell them not to be silly and then most people turn away from their visions."

"I think that Romeo is not being silly at all" replied Cinzia "in fact I think he's clear, articulate and insightful."

"The trouble is Cinzia, I agree with you. History is peppered with people who claim to have had visions. The English poet William Blake was beset by them, and he was recognised as a genius, a visionary but only after his death."

"Exactly. See. Divine inspiration" stated Cinzia.

"Divine inspirations make other people think you're mad! Look, I promise not to impose limits on Romeo's thinking, unlike Blake's Urizen who put chains around the mind to hinder the imagination. I do believe we need to keep this information within the family until Romeo becomes an adult. Then, he can decide himself what he wants to do with his prophecies. It's not our place to try and protect the world. We are not Superman and Superwoman, but we can shield our son from those whose thinking is inflexible."

"You're saying we will not enslave his thoughts?"

"We will not" reassured Fausto. "Absolutely not. We will still hold the ladder to help both boys climb to the stars."

Cinzia looked up to the sky, the colour of deep blue lapis lazuli lined with golden speckles, and smiled.

"Thank you. Let's try and be a typical family. Well, as normal as any family might appear to be."

***

His parents knew that Romeo's sixth sense never failed him. Later that evening it rudely interrupted everyone's slumber with a stomach-churning, brutal scream. The boys' bedroom light was switched on by Fausto. Romeo nimbly ran across the arthritic wooden floor to his father.

"What's wrong Romeo?" asked Fausto.

"It's Alessandro, papà. I think he's gravely ill."

Fausto moved to Alessandro's bed and tried to wake him. Delicate, rapid shallow breaths escaped Alessandro's mouth. He felt cold, clammy to touch. Immediately Fausto slipped into the cloak of being a medic. Cinzia appeared at the bedroom door.

"Grab the blood pressure monitor Cinzia" Fausto ordered.

With little time to think, she did as commanded.

"Romeo, grab the thermometer. Stick it in Alessandro's ear. Press the button. When the alarm sounds, say aloud the number on the screen."

"Which ear papà?" asked Romeo who was determined to help his fragile brother.

"It doesn't matter Romeo" replied his father calmly. "When the measure beeps, tell me what the reading says on the machine's screen."

At the same time as issuing instructions, Fausto was dialling 118 for an emergency ambulance and walking to the kitchen. He opened the fridge door, removed a box of medication and two large, medical needles which were in an airtight plastic container. Cinzia could hear her husband on the telephone.

"It's Doctor Fausto Cangini. Please may I have an ambulance sent to Via Barcisol, 70044 Polignano a Mare? Yes, my ten-year-old son Alessandro is having an Addisonian Crisis. Thank you. I appreciate that. Yes, I'm going to inject him with Cortisol. See you as soon as possible."

In the dark alleyway of her mind Cinzia flayed herself. '*Was there anything I missed today that would have prevented this situation? Could*

I have done more? How can I support Fausto to help Alessandro? What will I do with Romeo? How will we get to the hospital? What if . . .'

"Cinzia" her husband said guardedly. "We need to help Alessandro now. Take his blood pressure. Tell me what it is."

"It's 80/50. That's low. It signifies hypotension."

"Cinzia the ambulance will be here shortly. Stay calm. Speak to Alessandro. Even though he's unconscious he will still be able to hear you. Speak of happy times to him Cinzia."

"Papà his temperature is 35.2" reported Romeo anxiously as he huddled beside his terrified mother.

"Thank you, son. I'm going to inject him with Cortisol to try and stimulate his adrenal glands until we get him to hospital. You've both seen me do this before."

"Yes papà. Shall I get into bed with Alessandro to keep him warm?"

"Yes son. Once I've injected Alessandro you can get in with him until the ambulance arrives. You hold him. Let mamma speak to him. I'll listen out for the ambulance."

Within minutes the benevolent sound of shrieking sirens came within earshot. Fausto ran to the front of the house and spoke to the paramedics. In monotone Fausto reported, "Alessandro is pale, cold, clammy to touch. His temperature is 35.2 and his blood pressure is 80/50. His breathing is rapid and shallow. He appears to be unconscious."

"Ok Doctor Cangini. We can take it from here. Will you travel in the ambulance with Alessandro?"

"Yes. My wife will follow in the car with Romeo, his twin brother."

"Tell Mrs Cangini that we will put on the blue light and race to the hospital, but she is not to rush. We don't want her to have an accident."

"My wife understands that. We have been in this situation before with Alessandro" replied Fausto.

He stalked into the boys' bedroom.

"The ambulance is here Cinzia. You take Romeo to the hospital. Drive slowly as it will take us some time before Alessandro is in the ambulance. Wait for us there. Take the bag of change for the car park. Grab something for us all to drink. Pack a change of clothes for both boys. It'll be at least an overnight stay. Remember. We must be practical now. There will be time for emotions later."

Fausto bent and kissed his trembling wife.

"Romeo. Leave Alessandro now. Look after mamma for me. Be brave, son."

Romeo hugged his brother, kissed his cheek but not before saying "I love you Alessandro. You know that. I will always love you."

"Papà please may I put nonno's figurine of two magpies next to Alessandro?"

"Yes son. Do that before you leave" replied Fausto as he hugged Romeo.

Trying not to weep as she watched the paramedics placing needles in Alessandro's arms, Cinzia took Romeo's hand. They both blew a kiss to Alessandro and Fausto as they walked away from their normal life, into a diorama of dragons and the malevolent, cloying arms of Urizen.

February 2003

Chapter 6 – The Time Is Now

Let's make this moment last.

Their bedroom looked different: darker, emptier. The floorboards sighed with effortful breath and creaked like the bones of an aged relative. Romeo's eyes adjusted to the sombre, yellow-bruised darkness as his twin flickered into view, a bitter taste of fear filled his throat, his chest heaved. Romeo forced his tense limbs to shuffle up the bed and threw back the bedcovers. A hissed terror filled his ears.

"Alessandro. Alessandro" he whispered anxiously into the cool night air.

"Don't worry" was the reply "I'm here. No need to be afraid now."

Alessandro sat on the edge of Romeo's bed, on the crumpled cover near to the pillows.

"It was the same dream again Alessandro. In anxious dread I was running through a sacred grove of olive and fig trees under cover of darkness stemming the life force of Vercingetorix's men with my gladius. Hearing the soldiers' fearful breath, listening to their screams, seeing blood oozing from their skin, watching death grasp hungrily at their souls. It was frightening but exhilarating at the same time. I was ready to fight to the death for my Legate, Titus, and our leader Julius Caesar."

"We are at home Romeo. In our bedroom. You're not an Ancient Roman legionary. There's nothing to be afraid of now" soothed Alessandro.

Romeo trembled. "The striking lady was there on the edge of the grove, beneath the crisp branches of a wish tree. The lady who wore the amber ring. She was just beyond my reach as I tried to clutch her. Remember, I told you about Ceres?" questioned Romeo. "The woman who was kind to me?"

Yes. I recall" murmured Alessandro. "Think about what mamma taught us Romeo. When we are afraid, we close our eyes, breathe in deeply. Come on" urged Alessandro "let's do this together. In through your nose to the count of four, hold your breath for four and breathe out to the count of five" directed Alessandro.

Shivering with cold and fear Romeo meekly followed his brother's instructions and breathed mindfully to quell the terror in his thumping heart. Five minutes passed in silence apart from the hushed whisper of invisible, untouchable air gently being breathed.

Alessandro murmured into the still of night, "Are you feeling calmer Romeo?"

"Yes. Thank you" replied Romeo gratefully as he examined the dimness where delicate air and a slightly open curtain exposed dust and moonbeams gambolling.

"Shall we look for the Big Bear Alessandro?" asked Romeo tentatively.

Alessandro challenged his brother. "Let's see who is the first to spot the Big Bear and the Little Bear". Deftly he moved across the room. "Come to the window. Tell me what you can see. Come and stand beside me Romeo, please" he ordered "as the air is chilly."

Romeo quivered, got out of bed, pulled on his small dressing gown, and moved in a bid to be closer to the brother he revered. He fully drew back the curtains. Against the background of a dark, guiltless universe, Romeo's perception was that a blue light skittered around the room. He observed Alessandro who spoke confidently.

"Remember papà telling us that the Greek astronomer Claudius Ptolemy discovered the constellation of Ursa Major?"

Romeo was embarrassed to reply. "Alessandro. I remember Ptolemy but don't recall all the legend papà told us. My memory is not as far-reaching as yours."

Importantly, Alessandro stuck out his chest and recounted to his brother the legend of Ursa Major and Ursa Minor.

"Papà said that the king of all gods, Zeus was married to Hera. Zeus fell in love with the Goddess Calisto who had sworn a vow to the Goddess Artemis that she would not fall in love, but she had a baby with Zeus. They named him Arcas. When Hera found out, she wanted to stop Zeus from loving Callisto so turned her into a bear who wandered the woods.

One day in the woods, Arcas met a bear and tried to kill it. Zeus knew the bear was Callisto, so he sent a whirlwind which carried Callisto and Arcas into the sky. To protect them both from further harm, Zeus turned his son into the Little Bear and Callisto into the Great Bear so that they would be together for eternity."

Fizzing with gentle excitement, like a newly poured glass of champagne Romeo stated giddily "I remember now. Every twenty-four hours the Great Bear rotates around the North Star, which is confusingly also called Polaris. We can use the Great Bear to help with navigation on clear evenings because of its position in relation to the North Star."

Alessandro confirmed that Romeo's explanation was correct.

"You are my North Star Alessandro. I will always follow your direction" divulged Romeo, in a straightforward way, his huge black eyes looked straight at his twin.

Alessandro expelled a tinkling, joyous laugh as he ruffled Romeo's thick brown hair streaked with iridescent gold. "I love you, Romeo. You are my Little Bear. We can see each other every clear night, in the dark sky. Promise you'll look for me when we are not together, and I'll seek you too."

"I promise Great Bear" assured Romeo smoothly. "When I look up at the marbled blue sky, you will be with me, wherever I am in the world. I will follow you and make you proud. Always."

Their conversation was disturbed by a quiet knock on the bedroom door before it opened slightly. Like a magician's disappearance trick, Alessandro dissipated into the sparkling blue night air.

"Romeo. May I come in?" whispered papà.

"Yes."

"Who were you talking to?"

"Alessandro."

"Ah. Were you looking at the stars?"

"Yes papà. Alessandro was telling me the legend of the Great Bear and the Little Bear."

"Ok Little Bear. Show me where the North Star is and then I'll tuck you up in bed."

Twenty minutes passed before Fausto returned to Cinzia in their bedroom.

Spectacularly concerned, stomach knotted, Cinzia asked, "Is he ok?"

"Romeo was speaking to Alessandro and looking at the constellation Ursa Major and Ursa Minor. He asked me to read to him Tennyson's poem about Ulysses. Did you know there's a line he can recite verbatim? '*Made weak by time and fate, but strong in will. To strive, to seek, to find, and not to yield.*' Our boy is a tough character. Like Ulysses, his intellectual brilliance and versatility means he will not yield in this life Cinzia" said Fausto reassuringly.

Her lips trembled slightly before she answered. "Unlike his brother who was made weak by time and fate but whose will was very strong. Right until the end" she murmured. "I do believe in Destiny Fausto. That our fate is pre-determined, but how will our hearts ever know peace and harmony again?" she asked sadly. "How will our little boy face life without his twin? He's an odd little thing with his visions and premonitions. If people find out about them, we might lose him too Fausto. He's only eleven. What if someone were to come along, take him away from us and place him into an asylum? I'm terrified."

"Our son isn't insane Cinzia" stated Fausto irritably. "His insight was correct last year when he spoke about the spewing fountains of molten rock from the volcano on Stromboli. The volcanic activity increased in May and climaxed in December leading to large rocks crashing into the sea which created a tsunami on the island. Just as he prophesised."

It took some time for Fausto to regain his composure. He was acutely aware that Romeo's prognostications overwhelmed him and that Cinzia was fearful of their future.

Eventually he whispered "Why don't the two of you pick some sumptuous peonies from the garden in the morning? Later, when my shift has ended, we can take Romeo to visit Alessandro's grave. I've had a copy made of nonno's figurine of two magpies. I'd like Romeo to have it, since the original was buried with Alessandro. Please will you give it to him at Alessandro's graveside?"

As fear rose within her like stampeding thunderbolts she answered, "Romeo sees his dead brother and speaks to him as if he were in the same room. Is that not madness Fausto? Have we been placed on a path where we are heading for a seminal cultural collision?"

"He sees what others cannot, Cinzia. His mind is open to possibilities that we can't even begin to dream about. That's all" her husband replied reassuringly.

A taciturn man, Fausto felt a fearful black whirlpool opening within him. As he gently placed his arms around his wife, he kissed her head and tenderly rubbed her back as if trying to erase the fault lines which had appeared, heavy and disruptive as railway tracks. He took a deep breath. Cinzia smelled of freshly hand-picked pomegranates. As the juicy apricot sun began to climb in the sky, Fausto and Cinzia clung to each other. Perfectly aware that they were two tortured souls entwined, but totally oblivious to the three obstinate Fates which curled malevolently around them.

May 2010

Chapter 7 – Dante, Ducati and Dionysus

It's only a matter of time.

The second major destination Romeo Cangini ever drove to independently was Bologna when, at the age of almost nineteen he went to read Astrophysics at the oldest university in Italy. Surprisingly, even now this feudal city is off the tourist map despite possessing miles of intricately detailed porticoes and boasting two gravity-defying leaning towers, the Asinelli and the Garisenda. The latter having been favourably compared to a giant by the poet, author, and philosopher Dante.

An archaeologist's dig beneath the medieval houses in Bologna would reveal that this tumultuous metropolis was forged upon the foundations of the Ancient Roman city, Bononia. Sited in the Po Valley, this agricultural area has been invaded, occupied, coerced, and thus metamorphosed into its current stunning, walled splendour. Despite its turbid history, Bologna is a congenial city except if you use the gargantuan railway station. Before he left home at the beginning of the summer, Cinzia had advised Romeo to take care if he travelled through the main train station because of the deft pickpockets whose frenetic activity distracted unsuspecting travellers.

Without hubris, in its recent history, Bologna could lay claim to spawning brilliant inhabitants, such as Guglielmo Marconi who invented the radio. The city was also home to other daring engineers, like the three brothers who created the world-famous Ducati and whose factory produced the shiny red Multistrada 1200S motorbike which Romeo Cangini received from his parents the summer following his eighteenth birthday. His passport to freedom.

Before he moved to university life in Bologna, Romeo had planned his first lone adventure, riding the Ducati from his hometown of Polignano to the Bay of Naples where he intended to spend the summer. Romeo had never visited the area but often when he meditated or dreamed, an Ancient Roman Centurion appeared to him, laughing, swimming, and dancing in a city close to the sea around Naples. Romeo tried to imagine why this vision, which rose from his unconscious memory, would purposefully share knowledge from the past. Was it to taunt or help him? Whatever the reason, open-minded Romeo intended to follow the spirited footsteps and visit Naples where he intuitively believed that the answer might reside.

The morning he left home at the end of May, Romeo bade arrivederci to his parents, cockily turned on the Ducati's engine, flicked the riding mode system to Sport and rode out of Polignano. Speedily. Very speedily. Reminiscent of a black spot delicately balanced on the wing of a vivid, deep-red peacock butterfly he was gone, unaware that his mother's heart was still fluttering too quickly an hour after she waved him goodbye.

It took Romeo three hours, fifteen minutes to navigate across Italy from the Adriatic Sea to the Tyrrhenian Sea where, resembling a crazed lion, the Ducati roared its arrival in the soul-stirring city of Naples. Had she known the rapid speed of his journey, Cinzia would have suffered a heart-attack or at the very least a panic attack, either of which his father would have dealt with calmly.

As he dismounted his motorbike in Mergellina, Romeo smiled broadly to himself. Although his heart too was beating rapidly, a sixth sense reassured him that this would be a memorable summer. He was in Naples to do as he pleased. As smooth as his mother's home-grown lotus flower wine, Romeo streamed across the road and into the artful hands of Giovanni, tatuatore straordinario[13].

Only a handful of tattoo artists win international recognition. Giovanni was one of those few. He created unique jewellery pieces at his shop in the centre of Naples and designed then inked black and grey tattoos like no other. Nulli secundus.[14] An extraordinary sight to unworldly Romeo, Giovanni's half-shaven head, adorned with tattoos of legionaries on horseback, a wolf and two ravens coupled with a long blond beard with a black pearl knitted at the end of it, reminded Romeo of images of Odin, the striking Viking God of wisdom, war, and death, before he exchanged his physical eye for the wisdom exposed through the third eye. Adroitly Giovanni set to work on Romeo, this muscular stranger who watchfully peered at the arched mirror opposite him and observed without flinching, every miniscule stroke and scratch made by the artist.

The two young Italian men had much to discuss and plenty of time to do so. Their love of international football heralded a common bond, an interest in the sea another, and a desire to take the world by storm, a third. They discussed the forthcoming football World Cup and who, in their opinion was the best Italian footballer ever chosen to represent his country. Giovanni favoured the recently retired L'Ottavo Re di Roma,[15] Francesco Totti, but Romeo argued that the midfield playmaker Pirlo was the world's best as he was the most influential on the pitch. It was a discussion which would be kicked and bounced around the whole summer and one which spawned a deep and lasting friendship. Football. It's a funny old game.

---

[13] Tattooist extraordinaire.

[14] Second to none.

[15] The Eighth King of Rome.

Around the walls of the tattoo parlour were black and white photographs of world-famous sportsmen and women whose bodies were adorned with the unique artwork created by Giovanni, the master. Romeo was in exalted company. Glass cabinets displayed exquisite necklaces, rings, bracelets, and earrings hand-crafted from silver. Romeo found himself drawn to a blue leather case which held a startling array of jewellery.

"Those pieces are they a set Giovanni?" asked Romeo as he pointed to a small glass display cabinet held on the wall.

Without looking up Giovanni replied, "They are parures which means the jewellery is designed to be interchangeable. The pieces don't need to be bought as a set."

"The torque necklace" Romeo paused "the one with the asp's head on either side of it, who made that?"

"I did" replied Giovanni.

"It's a stunning piece."

"You have good taste" complimented Giovanni.

"What are the asps' eyes made from?"

"I used sapphires. Stunning, aren't they?"

"Why an asp's head Giovanni? It's an Egyptian symbol, isn't it, not Roman?"

Giovanni was silent for an age before he responded to Romeo's question.

"The asp was a symbol of royalty in Ancient Rome, Ancient Egypt, and Ancient Greece. It represents wisdom as the asp can transform itself easily. It's a symbol of temptation and power but conversely, also fragility. It links with water and protection. This necklace was made to curl around the neck of someone who encompasses these qualities. Do you have anyone in mind that you would give it to?"

"Not yet" replied Romeo "but I'll buy it anyway, just in case I meet the woman of my dreams. She sounds deadly."

Both men laughed.

"You're a charmer Romeo. Planning is an excellent trait. I'll wrap the necklace for you when we've finished. What about if I bind the necklace in blue silk and pop it into a silver box with a blue wire tied in a bow. That might attract her attention."

"Thanks Giovanni. You're obviously an enchanter yourself."

Both men smiled broadly. A reflection of their even, pearlescent teeth skimmed the gilt mirror's surface. Romeo bit his bottom lip and held his breath a little as he watched the intricate design being worked upon on his neck by Giovanni. He tried to keep as still as possible. After a while Romeo said, "I've got the summer off before I go to university in Bologna. For the first time in my life, I'm free from studying and on leave of absence from being a dutiful son. As I'm in a place where I'm unknown, I plan to be a free spirit. To release the shackles until I'm bound tightly again in September, perhaps compelled for the rest of my days by duty and obligation."

"That sounds like you've felt suffocated" replied Giovanni.

"No not suffocated. Just tried to be the best son I can be. My parents are good people who've had horrible things to cope with. They're both driven by their careers. Hugely successful. I feel the pressure of never wanting to let them down. I know that they will expect me to reach the usual milestones" Romeo held up his hand and pointed to each finger as he said, "y'know get a good degree, buy a house in the suburbs, get married, have children, get old, die, life over." He sighed. "But I'm not sure who I am, or what I am, or what I want. I know that I'm looking for an adventure before my life is totally mapped out for me."

"That's fair enough. You wanna go a little wild?" responded Giovanni. "Life doesn't have to be mapped out Romeo. You always have the choice of what to do."

"Perhaps. I would like to explore the unknown. See things I've never seen. One of the adventures I'd like, is go out into the Bay of Naples and learn how to scuba dive. I'm planning to be here for the whole summer. Any recommendations of who could teach me?"

"If you're willing to travel west to the Bay of Pozzuoli, then yes, I know someone."

"Where's Pozzuoli?"

"It's not too far away, in an area called Campei Flegrei, which is made up of a collection of volcanic craters, known as caldera which spreads over seven miles. The super volcano is still active but it's mostly underwater. That's probably why it's so deadly as no-one knows for certain when it will blow and when it does, what will happen. There have been many tremors felt recently! The area is beautiful and it's a stunning journey. The Ancient Roman underwater city of Baiae is in this part of the world. Read about the district if you can. Have you got a car so you can explore?"

"A bike. A Ducati" Romeo replied proudly.

Giovanni was enthusiastic. The beginning of their friendship was sealed when he said, "When I've finished, I'd like to see your Ducati. It'd better be red!"

"Do you drive Giovanni?" asked a naïve Romeo.

"I do. I drive a Prancing Horse."

"A Prancing Horse?" replied Romeo with intense interest.

"See the red Ferrari across the road?"

"Of course. It's unmissable."

"That's mine" replied Giovanni, his chest puffing out.

Romeo looked half stunned, half disbelieving but found the words to say, "Which model is it?"

"Ferrari LaFerrari. A V12, 6.3-litre engine, with a total of 950bhp and 663lb-ft of torque."

Romeo gulped. "Wow. When you've finished. I'd like to see your Ferrari and at least sit in it please."

"Deal" replied Giovanni, who looked up from his work and flashed another broad smile at Romeo.

"When we were kids my brother Alessandro and I used to watch James Bond movies together and vowed that we'd buy an Aston Martin, but we did deliberate upon a Ferrari" confessed Romeo.

"You can't buy a British car instead of an Italian Ferrari" argued Giovanni. "You're Italian!"

"That's what our discussion was about but, of course, I resolved that I could have an Aston Martin. When I buy one, it's going to be red. A red Volante" said Romeo firmly.

"We could debate cars, their engines and quality all day long" replied Giovanni.

"And footballers" chided Romeo.

"And footballers" agreed Giovanni. "And women. Is your brother here with you on this summer adventure?" asked Giovanni.

"No" stated Romeo firmly.

"Do you see much of him?"

"From time to time" responded Romeo non-committedly in a way that meant Giovanni sensed not to ask any more questions about Alessandro.

Giovanni paused from floating the needle and looked up at Romeo.

"That trip to Pozzuoli, it's a bit fiddly to get out of Naples, but once you do, it's a straightforward journey. Head for the Interno Lido Montenuovo Beach. Look for a boat called Il Sole.[16] Tell the Captain that Giovanni sent you. I'll write out the instructions for you on my card as a way of introduction."

"Great. What's the Captain's name?"

"Hell."

"Hell? Uh oh. Sounds like I'm in for a tough time."

---

[16] The Sun.

Giovanni laughed. "Yep. Now" Giovanni paused for effect "what do you think of your tattoo?"

Romeo stared unblinkingly into the mirror.

On his neck was an intricately detailed black and grey image of two intertwined magpies.

"These symbolise bravery and offer protection but having them on my neck also acts as a warning to people, that I'm no pushover and know whom to trust. It's in honour of my grandfather who played football for Newcastle United. Their emblem is magpies."

"Perfect choice for you then Romeo. It's apotropaic, to ward off evil. What do you think of it?"

"It's superb Giovanni. Thank you. I'm proud of it."

"Keep this dressing on for a day. If you're going swimming in the sea the salt water will heal it within a moon's cycle."

"Now you're sounding like my mother."

Giovanni laughed again. "I ain't no mother. Give me a ride on your Ducati."

"Only if you take me for a spin in your Ferrari. Please."

"Deal."

"Why don't we go out and paint the town red tonight, Romeo? Let me introduce you to the night life of Naples. Wine and women. Something tells me that you're a hell-raiser. Like Dionysus."

"Is he a footballer?"

Giovanni laughed heartily and explained, "In Greek mythology the God Dionysus was used to link the Gods with humans. He was known as the bad boy of Mount Olympus, wild and dangerous, clever, but kind. He enabled people to transcend themselves, he liberated them and brought about ecstasy using intoxication, but it meant people risked losing control of their behaviour. Dionysus was accompanied by many female hangers-on. Nymphs. Women reached a state of delirium under his influence. He had the reputation of driving people insane probably because he plied them with too much mind-altering wine, herbs and plants. Any Ancient Roman festival in his honour became riotous. You may be familiar with his Roman name, Bacchus. Wild rituals became known as Bacchanalian. There were plenty of them in this Bay. Right here in the Bay of Naples. In Baiae. Where Ancient Romans partied."

Romeo looked intrigued.

"I like the sound of Baiae … and Dionysus. Is the area still a wild getaway for Romans?"

"Ask Captain Hell when you meet. Tonight, we can paint this town red … Dionysus."

"Giovanni that sounds like a perfect introduction to Napoli."

For a few moments Romeo considered what he had heard.

"Did Dionysus ever find true love?" he wasn't embarrassed to ask Giovanni.

"Much later in life. With a Goddess called Ariadne. When she was free. But that's a tale for another time. Right now, Destiny is calling, and she has the sweet voice of a siren, or maybe a few."

The Bay of Naples. Under the long dark shadow of the throbbing volcano of Mount Vesuvius, with imposing palaces around the Bay, its narrow streets, ancient golden stone churches, unique underground landscapes, exquisite cuisine, alluring sea, a thousand colours and a million contradictions, Naples could turn out to be the perfect fit for Gorgeous Gaius Romeo Cangini with his newly *made in Napoli* magpie tattoo.

Mad. Bad. Dangerous to know.

Dante. Ducati. Dionysus.

O Sole Mio![17]

---

[17] My Sunshine.

June 2010

Chapter 8 – Masche[18]

The present and an irresistible gift.

Romeo stayed in Naples longer than anticipated.

The mysterious, intimidating, shady, narrow alleyways of Naples closed in tightly around Romeo. His hands trembled a little, his lips dry from the briny air, parted. He gulped for breath, as if in a storm-surge, and spotted a large sparkling silver crescent moon pinned above a narrow doorway. Guide to a safe harbour possibly. Through the tiny window, a powerful yellow-red glow around an elderly woman was eye-catching surrounded as she was by knick-knacks, curios, and jumble. Inside, the shop was dusky, the air wafted sickly with boggy meadowsweet blended with dried seeds of ignatia bubbling in a glass pot, but Romeo felt compelled to enter. Bright as gold, her eagle eyes spotted him immediately. Lithely she moved forward.

"Want some?" she asked. Greying, long curly hair bobbed around her crinkled face.

Romeo stared at the woman, then at the bony, red painted finger she used to point at the thin brown liquid steeped in creamy-yellow frothy cymes.

"It stinks" she admitted. "It's got wonderful pain killing properties, but it won't cure heartache." Her red lips turned upwards. "You're surprised that I know you've got heartache giovanotto"[19] she said kindly and paused briefly "but it covers you from head to toe like a soggy fishing net. Your aura is brown. That tells me you're sad."

---

[18] White witches.

[19] Young man.

Holding an aged wooden spoon, she returned to the back of the shop and used it to stir the pot clockwise. Silently Romeo moved towards her and waited. He instinctively knew she would not stop speaking and waited for her silky voice to coil around him.

"Forgive me. I haven't introduced myself. I'm Stella Maris.[20] This is my shop. I was born in Paroldo, a region famous for Masche.[21] It was there that I learned the art of using magic to heal. The gift was transferred to me by my nonna.[22] Only the Gods know how I ended up by the sea in Naples. Nevertheless, here I am with my shop of magical things."

"My mother makes potions," stated Romeo casually. "I have learned the art from her."

"Ah but you use herbs, spices, flowers, and fruit for intoxication. To deaden the pain. It won't go ... yet."

Her words lashed Romeo.

"Here. Drink this." Stella passed a crystal glass of meadowsweet to Romeo who lifted it to his lips. Before drinking he asked, "Will this turn me into an ass?"

"I'm not Circe" she laughed. "This won't cure your heartbreak, but it will ease it. And you don't have to look like an ass to behave like one."

Romeo winced. Stella looked deep into his soul.

"You've lived before. In a past life, you married a queen. You loved her deeply. She loved you too. With all her heart. It was a sentiment that embraced the spiritual, emotional, and intellectual essences of you both. Three fragments of each soul. That love never died. You'll meet her again. Your soulmate. In this life. But not yet. Not until the time is right."

---

[20] Star of the sea.

[21] Shaman women believed to possess healing powers.

[22] Grandmother.

"How will I know when the time is right?" Romeo was curious.

"You'll know. When you are with her, you will feel whole."

Since losing Alessandro, knowing how whole felt had become a fuzzy recollection, except when his brother visited him in dreams or through meditation, then Romeo felt complete. But it was only a fleeting emotion. He was jolted out of that drifting thought when Stella said, "Perhaps you and your lady will both consummate the union this time."

'Bloody hell. She's direct' he thought and shook his head in disbelief.

Stella continued, "You're predominantly driven by personal pleasures offered by the senses. Sex. You enjoy sex, but making love is different. It's better. You'll see."

Romeo's black eyes widened.

"You've not moved on from focusing upon your sacral chakra. When you activate the energy of your sacral chakra and unite it with your crown chakra, that's when you'll understand that sex becomes love."

Understanding nothing of a white witch's craft he was bemused and did not know how to respond. Romeo breathed deeply then said, "What is a chakra?"

Stella smiled. "Everybody has energy running through them. There are seven focal points of psychic vibrational energy which run from the base of the spine to the top of the head and enable the body to receive and emit energies. Chakras or Prana as some people say. These points, which are circular in shape can be open or blocked and influence our physical, emotional, and intellectual wellbeing."

His mind chaotic, Romeo recalled his own psychic experiences. No-one had discussed his abilities since he was eleven, lest he be considered mad.

"Psychic vibrational energy? That's something only a Masche is concerned with?" he asked innocently.

Stella laughed and replied, "We all can be psychic. Most choose to ignore their inner senses. Let me explain chakras to you." This unbridled woman took a deep breath. "The first," she turned around and pointed to her bottom "our root chakra is at the base of the spine. Imagine it as a red circle. It represents the need for survival: food, shelter."

"Those needs must be met before anything else can be achieved, that's clear" he stated. "Why red?"

"It's the colour of energy. A healthy root chakra enables us to face challenges, if it's less energetic we feel anxious and indecisive" she clarified.

"And the other chakras?"

Stella's eyes fixed firmly upon Romeo. "You focus on the passionate chakra, the orange sacral chakra, located in the lower abdomen. An overactive sacral chakra means addictions dominate your life. If you have an underactive sacral chakra, you feel as if your emotions are jumbled. You have a strong creative centre but the lust for gratification may overwhelm you" she warned.

Romeo blew out air from deep within his lungs. This encounter was proving to be challenging. "Go on" he urged, returning Stella's gaze, for he needed to learn more.

"You already know about these things but cannot name them."

Confidently he said, "I am interested to hear what you have to say Stella."

"The yellow solar plexus chakra is the third one. Here, above the belly button. It is the source of physical and mental power. It feeds the ego. If it's open, you will enjoy participating in group activities. If it's blocked, you will feel adrift at sea without your North Star to guide you. A little lost soul.

Romeo's eyes narrowed.

"Most people focus on sex, power, ego?" he asked ominously brushing aside her direct observation of him.

Stella nodded and continued, "The fourth chakra is the colour of renewal. Green. It indicates the heart and emotion chakra which offers emotional intelligence, compassion. If it's open then it's possible to feel healthy emotions but in extreme cases, a person may not experience genuine reactions if this chakra is blocked."

"A psychopath ... or sociopath ... or narcissist, those people labelled as such are likely to have a blocked heart chakra?"

"Absolutely" agreed Stella. "The blue, fifth chakra is in the throat. It concerns speech and communication. An open throat chakra means being able to convey feelings about important matters in an appropriate way. The converse is true if the throat chakra is blocked. That's why we sometimes use the word 'choke' when we cannot convey what we mean. Words become stuck in the throat."

"Is one of the chakras concerned with something known as the third eye? I heard my parents speaking about it when I was younger. They were frightened by my psychic abilities especially when I predicted disasters."

"Awareness. The purple sixth chakra, known as the third eye, is the source of intuitive and psychic knowledge" she responded, "and is found at the forehead between the eyebrows. It links to the pineal gland deep within the brain. An open third eye chakra means you may know that something will happen beforehand. Foresight. Or you might be empathic and understand the feelings, motives and possibly thoughts of those around you. A blocked third eye makes it difficult to use your spiritual gifts. You could also be forgetful and find it challenging to learn new things."

Romeo absorbed this information and confessed, "I have visions of my twin brother Alessandro. He died when we were eleven. He visits me still and I communicate with him. I promised my parents that I would not reveal my gift of insight outside of our family. Now I have told you."

"Forgive your parents. Most people are afraid of such abilities" replied Stella in a low voice. "Loss of a child can be a crushing burden."

"Is it true that other people have psychic visions?" Romeo asked incredulously "because I heard my father say so to my mother. I believed it was a lie therefore my mother would not worry about me."

"Your father told the truth. Your parents did not wish to draw attention to you. However, you will not be able to hide from your gift because you practise it. You communicate with your brother through the third eye. You have unwittingly kept your gift at the forefront of your mind so to speak."

Tension hung eagle-like in the air.

"And the seventh chakra. What is that?"

"By now you will realise that each chakra links with an individual's consciousness."

Romeo stared at Stella and nodded.

"The chakras represent the soul's progress. The seventh one is located just above the head and is known as the Crown chakra. It symbolises the potential to receive universal energy. The highest intelligence. This white chakra is only open during limited occasions when we enter what is known as bliss, usually through meditation. We progress through each life with the aim of our soul learning lessons, if it does, we can enter the state of unified consciousness, if it doesn't, we must live another life. When all our lessons have been learned we can join with our soulmate to become whole."

"Both of us have to learn lessons?"

"Yes."

"What if we don't learn them in the same life?"

"You each have to live another life until you have *both* learned lessons, then you can join together and become complete."

"How can I find my soulmate?" he asked.

"You may not recognise her when she arrives in your life" Stella replied. "All I can advise is that you meditate, and your soul will slowly reveal itself. You will find her. You will feel a spiritual bond with this woman. You will not understand why you connect, but it will be at a deep level. Follow the star. Concentrate on learning your own lessons."

"Have I been cursed?" Romeo asked, ignoring this last piece of advice.

"Not cursed. You have lessons to learn which may take a long time for you. You're an old soul. You have been here many times and if you don't learn your lessons, you'll return many times still. Be warned."

"Old soul? Been here many times? What do you mean?"

"It means your soul has been reborn repeatedly. Our past, present, and future endure in different dimensions of time, and we can access them when we meditate, or through people who have a gift. The Masche gift. We are all guided by others from a different dimension. I see that you have a great Roman warrior as your guide. He didn't listen when he was warned by a Seer, and he ended up dead before his time. The genius of prophecy has been bestowed upon you, but you choose to hide it. Let's see how long the pledge to your parents holds true. Here. Take these Tarocchi cards."

Stella offered a pack of cards to Romeo, her thin face shining as a perigean moon. "Keep them safe giovanotto. They're yours."

Romeo was quizzical as he handled the pack. "What are these?"

"These will support you along your path. They are cards which will help you to foresee the past, analyse the present, foretell the future, perform rituals, and interpret dreams. For your use only. Keep them safe."

"Thank you but how do I use them?"

"You'll learn."

"From whom?" he questioned.

"You'll just learn" Stella replied forcefully. "Here, sit with me and I'll show them to you."

Stella took her time to lay bare the extravagantly illustrated tarot cards, one by one. The refined images were copper engraved, created without precedent. Romeo delicately ran his fingers over each card. When she had finished, Stella announced, "The designs are fanciful."

"They're exquisite. Thank you. How much do I owe you?"

Stella looked offended. "They're a gift to you for visiting my shop. I've enjoyed meeting you."

"Nevertheless, I must pay for them."

"No. But thank you" she said with grace.

"Stella, when I've learned my life lessons, and am one with my soulmate, then what happens?"

"You get to choose. You could become a deity, a God with powers greater than those of ordinary humans. You may want to help others on their soul's journey. Be wise in the use of your psychic abilities."

Stella grabbed Romeo's left hand and pressed the pack of Tarocchi cards into it.

"Take them. From time to time think about our encounter when you see a crescent moon. Control your chakras."

Romeo closed his eyes briefly, inhaled deeply and imagined the coloured chakra circles spinning along his body, then exhaled. As he walked out of the shop the wind skirled around the tightly packed buildings, the way Cliodhna, Queen of the Banshees[23] wails before a death, as if angrily rapping on each door and window. Despite the afternoon heat, Romeo shuddered. '*An ass or a God*?' he mused. '*Universal life energy*? *Where does that come from*? *How am I going to learn how to control my chakras*?' He assailed his mind with questions before suggesting to himself '*Perhaps her message meant I need to search out lovers, like Dionysus with his nymphs. I can certainly take control of my sacral chakra*!'

Possibly it was the yellow-red aura which disrupted his thinking. Or perchance sometimes people hear what they wish to hear and see what they choose to see. Or maybe a young man does not heed Fate's warning signs and must learn from his own mistakes.

After all, this was Romeo's first encounter with a white witch, but it was unlikely to be his last.

---

[23] Female spirit who heralds a death.

July 2010

Chapter 9 – Flying In The Face Of An Archaeological Dig

Any old iron?

Panic gripped Romeo as he stood at the cliff edge and peered forward into vast empty space. Below lay the glittering azure Bay of Naples. Above beckoned an infinity of sapphire. To his left was the stratovolcano, Mount Vesuvius. To his right, an image of Alessandro encouraged him to leap. Romeo felt as if a million hardened cylindrical pupa wriggled mercilessly to tickle his stomach, but he did not laugh. Fearfully he shouted, "I might fall". Into the wind Alessandro whispered Apollinaire's words, '*so he came, and he pushed him …*' Romeo yelled violently when his feet launched from the ragged layered ground of dust and ash. He heard Alessandro yell … '*and he flew*'.

"I'm flying. Look at me. I'm flying" Romeo called to the air and the birds and the sea. Below him lay the verdant valleys of Accero and the restless volcano, Vesuvius as he bobbled on the wind. In his tummy, pupa exploded into a million exotic dipping Mazarine butterflies. This is what giddy freedom felt like. Riding the adrenalin rush on an invisible carpet of air.

"Ok Romeo. Take-off was just as planned. Control the glider. Hold tightly. Pull to the left. Ride the thermal lift" invited his daredevil paragliding instructor, Fillipo. "Don't let the glider go too far forward or it'll collapse."

"Push, push, push, push, push forward" screamed Romeo more to himself than Fillipo.

"Go for it, Romeo" encouraged his instructor.

Romeo's breath burned hot as smelted magma; his face wobbled in the rippling air. Gliding wildly and soundlessly as a magpie feather, he looked across at Mount Vesuvius and imagined the disturbingly intense raging orange-red lava spewing out of its vicious mouth. Saw the hot liquid mud, and ash heading towards the towns of Pompeii, Stabiae, Lapilli, Oplontis and Herculaneum, greedily devouring everything on the mountainside. Witnessed inexplicable strange periwinkle blue lightning flashes streaked low against a darkened sky. Heard human screams and cries for help. Smelled burning flesh, hair, and noxious gases. Felt the soul-deep destruction.

"Concentrate" blasted Fillipo as the glider lunged forward.

After a momentary pause Romeo responded, "Let's use the thermal columns to rise and fall" as he tried to erase the ugly image from his mind's eye. His third eye.

Although they applied simple physics to pull on the left and right controls and manoeuvre the direction of the paraglider, it was challenging to hold as they wobbled in the air stream.

Fillipo reminded Romeo, "Keep your hands on the control hoops, that way we can ridge soar".

With a bird's eye view, Romeo imagined himself on the metallic coloured wings of a mythical Sirin with its curvaceous womanly top half and owl-like body, revealing mantic truths through her exquisite singing. He wished to feel unshackled, like this, forever. Weightless. Captivated by musical notes. Held aloft, like a God, but then the God Icharus sprang to mind, whose hubris engineered his own demise when he flew too close to the sun. Romeo coaxed his mind back to focus on flying.

"I'm going to pull the left brake. The glider will yaw to the left Fillipo. Be prepared."

"Stay out of the turbulence Romeo otherwise the glider will stall. Now, is there any wind drift? Look at the trees to see which way they're blowing and which direction the waves are rippling in the Bay. That should help."

Romeo looked at the sea below and felt an acidic swell of choking fear at the back of his throat. It banished abruptly when he gulped a tonic of refreshing cold air.

"Ok let's line ourselves up. We are NOT landing on water. Use your knees to line up our landing zone."

Romeo lifted his knees. The earth below quavered then steadied.

"We're aligned, Fillipo."

"Get your legs down now Romeo" ordered Fillipo. "Land into the wind. Hold onto the brakes but don't brake too early otherwise we will lose steering control. Remember to flare up."

"Flare up. Bloody hell I've forgotten what that is. Remind me Fillipo" shouted Romeo trying not to panic.

"Apply both brakes fully. NOW."

Romeo and Fillipo landed on the soft grass and ran for twenty metres before the paraglider pulled them to a halt.

"That was the most exhilarating feeling ever" shouted Romeo breathlessly. He laughed and placed a trembling hand on Fillipo's shoulder. "Thanks for teaching me. These have been the best weeks of my holiday so far. Amazing. Thanks."

"You're welcome, Romeo. See you back here soon I hope."

Romeo's bronzed face glowed, his eyes sparkled. One more thing ticked off his bucket list. Flying like a bird. A rare Sirin to be exact.

"What are your plans for the rest of the summer?" asked Fillipo as they walked back to the cabin.

"I'm going to visit Herculaneum, the haunt of the God Hercules, and possibly Pompeii. There's also an archaeological dig at Capua which I've signed up to join."

"Isn't that where the slave leader, Spartacus began his revolt?"

"Yes. There's an amphitheatre where Spartacus fought as a Gladiator, and the Temple of Mithras is supposed to be worth viewing."

"Then what do you plan to do?"

"I'll climb Mount Vesuvius, have loose plans to learn scuba diving, and explore the sinful city of Baiae."

Fillipo laughed. "You'll find it difficult to settle to life at university after this trip. Although you've got time enough to feel the weight of the world on your shoulders."

A pained expression flittered across Romeo's face as if the weight of the world was already hammered into his sinews and muscles, hidden deep inside. An observer could not witness the subterranean scars of sadness scored into his soul.

"I'm living life for two people" he replied breezily. "I've got to pack in lots of experiences." With that parting shot, he was gone, like a thief in the night holding on grimly to his secret freight.

***

The next day, in his red prancing horse, Giovanni collected Romeo from his apartment, with its breathtaking views over the Palace of the Spirits, a place percolated with witchcraft, on the rocky peninsular of prosperous Posillipo. He brought with him a steady stream of frivolous laughter, and two women they had met in a bar the previous week. The car bolted away from the Bay of Naples, along the chaotic coastal road of Corso Giuseppe Garibaldi, past the lush vineyards and halted at the town of Ercolano. During the journey Giovanni entranced his passengers with tales about the Ancient Roman city of Herculaneum, sited below Ercolano.

"The city was supposedly named after the God Hercules, the God of protection! The Fates eventually outsmarted Hercules and were cruel to the wealthy Romans who lived in this vibrant seaside retreat. Innocent victims of a feud between the Gods. The Fates provoked Vesuvius until poisonous vapour ejected from every orifice, he roared and threw hot lava, mud, and ash down the mountain's flanks. The city was covered in roasting mud, its inhabitants boiled alive or choked to death on lethal gases. Recently there have been excavations of Herculaneum, and many of the buildings were found largely preserved intact. Most of it though remains buried, shrouding the stories of its dead." This was Giovanni's ominous introduction.

The Ferrari galloped into the car park.

"Here we are" announced Giovanni breezily.

"Is it safe to go in?" asked Romeo who felt weak as a jellyfish. He leaned against the pebbled city walls.

Perplexed, Giovanni replied, "Of course. At least I think so" he added doubtfully.

As they entered Herculaneum, Romeo wobbled, and made to sit down. Giovanni was alarmed. To distract unwanted attention, he said, "I've brought some sandwiches for our picnic, using sourdough bread my mother created using wild yeast. She calls it 'The Herculaneum' and claims it's an old recipe passed down through her family. You'll know that she made it since she pressed her initials about one centimetre deep into the dough. It's conceivable that it's an ancient recipe as there were bread ovens found during the excavations of the town. Even in those times people ate bread and pizza, likely made by their slaves. Tuck in."

"Look at you. Knowledgeable and domesticated. A catch for any woman" teased Romeo feebly.

Once the food had been eaten the four friends wandered the narrow marble-laid streets. They entered the Central Baths and admired the intricate black and white marine mosaic on the floor which depicted Cupid and Neptune surrounded by dolphins. In the Hall of the Augustales, with its impressive marble columns and arches, Romeo was convinced he saw a spirit in the room which depicted Hercules on Mount Olympus alongside the Ancient Romans' three most important Gods: Jupiter, Juno and Minerva. He said nothing.

When the group entered the Villa of the Papyri, a grand four-storey home with a clear view to the Bay of Naples, Romeo wandered through the atrium lined with marble columns which supported the upper floor. Among the bronze and marble statues found in the niches, it was the bronze figurine of wild Bacchus which drew his attention. He closed his eyes and felt the panic of the family who lived in the villa, turbulent as a violent storm. Helpless, perhaps against the Fates.

Romeo made his way along the covered walkway, into the garden beside the swimming pool, breathed deeply the fresh sea air, picked up a twig and ruffled the fertile volcanic ground beneath his feet. He knew exactly the spot. As he scraped at the soil and stones, he spied a glint of leather. Now on his hands and knees he gently moved the earth aside, picked up the item, removed the dirty gold from a leather pouch and wiped it clean to reveal an aureus, an Ancient Roman coin. Minted by the emperor Vespasian, it depicted him on one side and Minerva, the Roman Goddess of Justice on the other. Without thinking, Romeo quickly placed the aureus in his pocket. With barely a smile, he joined his giggling friends where Giovanni was entertaining the two women with tales of his follies. Romeo remained silent. Would it be folly to keep the aureus since it was his? From another life. Justice served? Or were the Fates tempting him?

July 2010

Chapter 10 - Villa of the Papyri

Dreams are like steam. They can scald, vanish but leave a scar.

When he looked at the coin held gingerly within his left hand, Romeo felt a tremor of excitement. He had polished it until the gold gleamed like the jewel it was. A priceless artefact, an unassailable link to a past life. Intuition told him where to search out the aureus and for two nights after the discovery he had paced the floor of his accommodation wondering what to do with his treasure. It was not possible to sell it. Obviously. That would draw attention to his theft. But could it be classed as stealing if the aureus originally belonged to him? A dream had revealed that his father had given him the coin a day before Mount Vesuvius had erupted in AD 79. A tangible link with his father, Romeo did not wish to hand over the aureus to archaeologists when it would have no emotional connection for them.

On the morning of his trip with Giovanni to Herculaneum, Romeo had woken with the clear impression that he had lived in a villa on the edge of the energetic city, despite knowing that he had never visited the place before. In this life. Weird. Disconcerting.

The previous evening his vision had depicted large flocks of screeching birds swarming around his parents' home in Herculaneum, creating strange patterns in the sky. He was woken when he felt the ground shake so violently that he heard some of the marble statues along the sprawling peristyle[24] falling. Once dressed, with one hand he held tightly to his golden bulla[25] hanging around his neck, with the other he touched a handful of shattered

---

[24] Covered garden walkway.

[25] Good luck charm to ward off evil spirits.

statues, then ran from the carefully excavated fourth terrace to his mother in the pine grove. He knew that Sosipatra would be in the underground Temple of Mithras, hidden as it was among the pine trees, a symbol of immortality and good fortune. This is where his mother usually practised her incantations.

A protective circle of pinecones lay at the entrance to the Temple; in its centre smoke rose from a golden urn which contained the burned embers of pine needles, resin and frankincense used to purify the sacred place and awaken the Divine light. He passed two pine trees planted either side of the open wooden door and descended worn stone steps. At the end of a long candlelit aisle, he spied Sosipatra kneeling at the central wooden nave, head bowed in front of an engraved stone statue of Mithras. She poured a libation of honey and elderberry wine. Upon hearing footsteps, Sosipatra turned and asked her son to kneel with her to invoke the presence of the God Hercules for protection and the Goddess Vesta, guardian of the family.

"What is wrong mother?" he asked.

"The Fates are angry Trebius."

"The Fates? What do you mean?" he asked.

"The Three Goddesses of Fate control life from birth to death. Collectively they are known as Destiny. Even the Gods fear them."

"Why?" questioned Trebius.

"They have immense power. The first Fate, Nona uses a spinning wheel to whirl the golden thread of life. She decides when souls are born. The second Fate, Decima measures with her rod the length of the thread of life for each soul. She decides upon the temptations and joys each soul will encounter during their life. The third Fate, Morta cuts the thread of life. She has the power to choose how and when a person dies. The Fates are plotting to unravel the golden skein of life on this mountainside and the Gods cannot stop their conspiracy."

Innocently Trebius asked, "What matter is that of ours?"

"The Fates are angry with the God Hercules. They asked him to cease his brother Bacchus' hellraising, stop him leading people into witlessness oblivion, along the wrong path through intoxication, but he has not intervened. The Gods say that the Fates have awakened a giant within the mountain to destroy Herculaneum and the towns of Pompeii, Stabiae, Lapilli, and Oplontis as punishment. They will extinguish all the people who live on the mountain."

"Last night I saw the birds heading for higher ground. The air now smells of decay, the rocks higher up the mountainside are hissing as if in anger. The Fates' destruction may have already begun mother."

"Quickly Trebius. We must speak with your father."

Together they ran through the pine forest, across the neat garden where Trebius could hear his twin brother Aelius and younger sister, Larentina, giggling in the swimming pool.

"Hey Trebius, join us" shouted Aelius "the water is warmer than usual and there are some strange waves in the pool which are pushing us from side to side. It's fun."

"Maybe later" called out Trebius.

When the earth violently tremored, Sosipatra grabbed Trebius' hand. They marched along the covered walkway lined with open heart-shaped shiny red anthurium to signify abundance, past the pretty nodding hellebores, breezed by the bizarrely shaped purple orchids, through the bright atrium and into the family's library. His father, who appeared surprised to see them, was leaning against a bronze table upon which lay numerous papyri scrolls. Sosipatra kissed her husband warmly on the cheek before saying:

"The tremors are making me feel extraordinarily anxious Lebiatus. We must move away from the mountainside by tonight."

"I am gathering the scrolls Sosipatra so that I can put them in a safe place. You're the theurgist my darling. A Sybil. What is it you have seen with your extraordinary psychic abilities?"

"Our son Trebius has noticed the birds in distress. A clear signal of impending disaster. The wind has gathered speed bringing with it an acrid smell from the water. The toads have disappeared from the fountain. There are strange blue lights in the sky. The Gods have spoken to me Lebiatus and advised that we return home to Rome."

"Many of these scrolls are yours Sosipatra. Your thoughts on nature. Your understanding of human limits and how our lives are influenced by the Gods. Your insightful visions which we follow, I treasure and wish to place the scrolls somewhere for safe keeping."

"Leave them Lebiatus" commanded Sosipatra. "We must return to Rome. I can re-write them. We must travel by sea."

"I understand your anxiety and share it, but the earliest we can leave is tomorrow morning Sosipatra."

Lebiatus turned to Trebius.

"My son, run to the boat stores. Inform the boat man that we will be leaving at daybreak. Have him prepare our ships for the journey to Rome. All the vessels are needed as we must take our friends and neighbours too."

Lebiatus turned to Sosipatra and asked her, "Where are Aelius and Larentina?"

"Playing happily in the swimming pool" she replied.

Considering his words carefully, Lebiatus said, "Leave them for the moment. No need to alarm them yet" he instructed. "Send word to our friends and neighbours. They are to meet at our boat houses at dawn. They must travel light. The vessels can accommodate about three hundred people. Nothing else. We will return to Rome, as you advise."

He paused and waited for his son to leave the library. Trebius closed the door quietly but remained on the other side of it so that he could hear his parents' conversation.

"You fear death my wife?"

"Our souls live numerous lives Lebiatus, which means we have faced death countless times. I fear the pain of death. I fear not being with you and our children. I fear the unknown of my next life. The Fates may allow us to flee."

"If we do not escape the mountainside and cannot travel to Rome, I wish you to know that I love and respect you Sosipatra and thank you for our beautiful life together."

Trebius moved away from the door when he heard his mother's intense sobs, ran to his bedroom, and carefully removed his treasured golden aureus from its brown leather pouch. His father had given it to him that very day for his eleventh birthday. Placing the coin back into its pouch and holding it tightly, Trebius walked through the atrium, past the swimming pool and knelt at the near corner where the marble path met the grass. He fell to his knees, pulled furiously at the rich earth with his hands and buried his aureus as an offering, pleading with the God Hercules and the Goddess Vesta to save his family. On his return to the villa, he spat in the face of the Bacchus statue. The Fates smiled.

***

On the day of his treasure find, Romeo had stood on the villa's top terrace, overlooking the bay which was backlit with steaked gold from the sun. Giovanni questioned him. "See the villa's boat stores down there by the water? Did you know that many skeletons have been excavated from that place? Up to now, no skeletons have been found in this villa, which is curious."

"The family who lived here tried to escape to Rome" answered Romeo steadfastly.

"No-one knows the name of the family who lived here when Mount Vesuvius erupted in AD79. The only clue could be the many papyri scrolls which were found intact in the library, but their content has not yet been exposed. That's why this place is known as the Villa of the Papyri. Why do you think the family escaped?"

"The woman who lived in the house was a Sibyl. A Prophetess whose predictions were circulated widely. It was known that she linked with the Gods. Her prognostications were written on the scrolls found in this villa."

"How would you know that?" asked a surprised Giovanni.

"I had a dream. It was shown to me in a dream" responded Romeo. "I'm sure it was just a dream, but I woke up this morning feeling rattled."

"In your dream, what happened to the family? Their friends? Their neighbours?"

"One of the sons, Trebius, whom I felt was me in the dream, was told by his father to escort his mother Sosipatra, sister Laurentina and other members of their extended family to Rome. They departed on the first ship to leave the harbour. The weather was stormy."

"And the rest of the family?"

"The father Lebiatus and Trebius' twin brother Aelius stayed and worked on the shoreline helping friends and neighbours to get onto the family's ships. Lebiatus would have viewed that as his duty. To take charge and help others."

"Did they make it? The father and son?"

"As they pulled away from the harbour, from the ship's deck, Trebius, Sosipatra and Laurentina waved goodbye. The weather was turbulent; there were long intervals between the earth rumbling tremors, so they believed the giant was calming. As the three of them watched their family, friends, and neighbours massed in the boat houses and along the seashore, they could not understand why some people suddenly fell to the floor" answered Romeo.

"We know now that they would have been overcome by invisible noxious fumes" responded Giovanni "which can lead to blackouts within minutes, followed by death."

"Not long afterwards, when the volcano blew his top, those fallen people were buried where they lay. The boat houses were covered by boiling mud, ash, and heart-stopping crimson lava. Trebius, Sosipatra and Laurentina watched helplessly as Lebiatus and Aelius, their friends and neighbours died. No-one on the shore stood a chance of escape."

"Those poor people. Agonisingly traumatic" whispered Giovanni. "The eyes cannot unsee. That scene would have stayed with the remaining family for the rest of their lives."

Romeo was silent for a long time.

"The Fates always put a condition on love" replied Romeo.

"A condition? What condition?" questioned Giovanni.

"That we endure pain when the Fates cruelly sever our ties with loved ones."

The air was hushed. Giovanni stared at Romeo. He found his new friend to be strange sometimes, and wondered if he was a necromancer. This tremulous thought flickered until he hurriedly extinguished it. Giovanni felt as though divination wrapped Romeo's soul in a clammy grey caul when instead he should glisten silver as a star, gliding across the raven sky. When he looked away from Romeo, and out across the Bay, Giovanni would swear that the golden sun bowed in assent before it was washed away by delicate, white-crested waves.

That is how Romeo came to know that the third eye can reveal both the beautiful and repulsive, that each life matters, and a heart is always broken when the Fates take someone we love.

August 2010

Chapter 11 – Antro Della Sibilia[26]

Send me forget-me-nots.

It may be easy to flatter an ego with a tender word here, a kind comment there, a gentle touch, or an irresistible song. Doubtless throughout history sirens have been illustrated as captivating their prey with their alluring ways. Like any siren, without qualm Gaius Romeo Cangini could be ruthlessly bewitching.

After leaving riotous Belledonne Alley the previous night they had danced together passionately on the crescent shaped beach as it blushed under the light of a full moon. The following morning, he slunk out of her waterside apartment in exclusive Chiaia as silently as any feral tom cat. Not that Romeo hadn't delighted in her voluptuous body, but there were too many days and too many other women eager for his attention for him to be tamed. He enjoyed most women's company. A lot. Maybe he would see this one again when he was next in Naples, but probably not. Like him, she would have moved on.

Before the holiday, Fausto had advised his son not to drive in Naples. Romeo relished each crazy moment of ignoring his wise father's counsel. Having ridden on the wing of every vice together, when Romeo left town with the sincere promise to return, Giovanni never doubted his word.

"Remember" shouted Giovanni as Romeo revved the Ducati's engine "the boat is moored at Porto di Pozzuoli. Look for a boat called Il Sole and tell Captain Hell that Giovanni sent you. Here's my card. Use it by way of introduction."

"I'll be back" called Romeo as the Ducati darted away.

---

[26] Cave of the Sibyl

On his way to meet Hell, leaving Naples on the wide, unmarked roads was a chaotic, twisting, adrenaline-inducing, gut-wrenching journey. Not unlike a journey into Hades, Romeo imagined. Still, he reassured himself with all the arrogance of an eighteen-year-old, the golden aureus would pay the blazing-eyed ferryman Charon for his passage to the Underworld if necessary. Preferably escorting him to the wonderland Elysian Fields[27] to join his brother Alessandro, rather than depositing him in the foul guts of Tartarus.[28]

Fifteen minutes before his arrival in Pozzuoli, Romeo stopped the Ducati, bought, and drank an espresso, rolled a cigarette, lit it, sucked heavily on the nicotine two or three times then flicked the remnants into the street. A long time ago his father had read to him Virgil's poem about the Cumaean Sibyl who acted as a guide to Aeneas in the terrifying Underworld so that he could seek advice about his Destiny from his dead father. Romeo felt curious about the Sibyl. A woman widely regarded in Ancient Rome as a Seer, a bridge between the Gods, the living, and the dead. His recent dream about the family in Herculaneum, when Sosipatra had been called a Sibyl by her husband, also captivated him. Romeo pulled his jacket closer around his chest. He could not decide if it was an ugly or illuminating thought which gnawed at his consciousness. '*Could he be a Seer, one who summons spirits for the purpose of revealing past, present and future*?' Romeo stood tall. He decided to make a short detour to visit the famous Antro Della Sibilia, in Monte di Cuma reputedly the cave of the Cumaean Sibyl.

***

[27] Paradise

[28] Abyss of the Underworld

A large octagonal brick temple to honour Proserpina, Daughter of the Goddess Ceres sat in decay at the slimy edge of sacred Lake Avernus where thermal springs gurgled, and sulphuric odours ran with the wind. A slinky red fox patrolled its broken outer walls. Romeo ambled along the fallow lake path, admired the crumbling stone archway he walked under, and breathed the sweet scent from the palms which lined the rocky passageway. He knew the yellow eyed pink and blue forget-me-nots growing on the tumbling slopes of the acropolis which encircled the Sibyl's cave, symbolised an enduring connection, challenging the passage of time. He wondered which lover had planted them or whether his mother had visited and sowed them in memory of his twin, Alessandro.

At the wide entrance to the Sibyl's cave Romeo stopped. Girding his loins before entering, he scrutinised the long, narrow, murky tunnel hewn through the andesitic rock. Deep within him Romeo understood blackness and felt afraid to cross the mystical threshold. A man's sonorous voice echoing around the passageway startled him.

"Afraid of confined spaces?" the man asked, his owl eyes boring into Romeo.

"A little" acknowledged Romeo. "I don't like being hemmed in."

"Once you're through this tunnel, there are bright wide chambers hollowed into the rock. Everyone must travel through the dark at some point. You'll come out the other side. No need to worry."

"Thanks" replied Romeo. "That's reassuring to know" but privately thought that darkness was sometimes a little too hard to endure.

"Here, let me take you beyond this passageway. I'm Arturo. Occasionally I work here as a guide." He grinned "and it's your lucky day because I'm not taking anyone to the Underworld."

Romeo looked apprehensive and forced a laugh.

"Don't worry. It was a joke" reassured Arturo. "I'm not going to murder you in the cave. Not today anyway."

Romeo offered a wan smile and despite misgivings, stepped inside.

"I'm Romeo. I'd like to know the myth which surrounds the cave and the Cumaean Sibyl."

"Oh, the Sibyl! She was quite a formidable woman, that one. Let me show you around where she lived."

It did not take long to walk the forty-metre shadowy corridor.

"Did you pass the Temple which honours Proserpina, Daughter of the Goddess Ceres on your way here? asked Arturo.

"Yes, and I saw a red fox which appeared to be guarding the Temple."

Arturo smirked.

"Proserpina was the daughter of Goddess Ceres and the God Jupiter. The God Pluto snatched guileless Proserpina and took her to live in the Underworld. When Goddess Ceres abandoned her responsibility for the harvests to search for her daughter, the crops failed. Once she found her, Pluto agreed that Proserpina could leave the Underworld for half a year. We say the crops grow when Proserpina is with her mother for six months. The fox you saw was guarding the path around Proserpina's Temple."

Arturo's voice changed to a whisper. "It's a sign from the Universe that you may be straying from your path. Be careful. You don't want to end up in the Underworld" advised Arturo.

The tunnel was hot which made Romeo sweat. Unsettled, he ignored Arturo's comment and asked, "What do you know about the cave and the Sibyl?"

"Follow me" ordered Arturo.

Romeo scuttled behind his guide into the main chamber. Along the walls he could see doorways to three small rooms. The sun's dancing rays streamed through lateral openings to illuminate silver galena crystal engravings on the walls of the chamber depicting the moon in its different phases: crescent, gibbous and full. Hundreds of stars, decorated with mazarine-blue veined lapis lazuli were scored into the walls. Blood pounded in his head. Romeo recognised this place. He knew that sunlight streamed into the space at dawn and dusk through hidden notches to represent life and death. He had been here before to celebrate Lammas, in honour of the God Sol and Goddess Luna to offer thanks at the beginning of the autumn equinox. But when?

With closed eyes and a deep breath Romeo recalled an image of a striking woman with auburn plaited hair wrapped around her head, staring at him in this room. Her warm indigo eyes sparkled as she gestured for him to sit opposite to her. She had held his hand and prophesised he would marry a queen. Romeo's pulse leapt. His eyes darted around the room, seeking answers. He intuitively knew that the woman was the Cumaean Sibyl, and her name was Cassinia. She had been the close friend of Ceres who was wife of the Legate, Titus. Shocked, Romeo recalled a vague image of living life as a highly decorated soldier in Julius Caesar's army. Was it a vision that he had once fraternised with Sybils and Queens, Vestal Virgins and Legates? Surely his memory mocked him as he recollected being acquainted with Julius Caesar in a past life. With breath tense as a violin string, Romeo demanded to know the story of the Cumaean Sibyl.

"The Cumaean Sybil isn't here anymore" Arturo said waving his arms, as if she used to live in the cave waiting for tourists to cross her palm with silver. "Some say that she can be seen here on full moon, but I've never encountered her."

"What do you know about her?" whispered Romeo.

"Only three things have been written and they are myths" answered Arturo breezily.

"Tell me" urged Romeo.

"She was a stunning Sibyl with luscious poppy-red lips and twinkling indigo eyes who caught the unwanted attention of the God Apollo. He granted her one wish if she would lay down with him. The Sibyl …"

"Her name was Cassinia" interrupted Romeo.

"Whatever you say" replied Arturo sarcastically. "The Sibyl, Cassinia, grabbed a handful of sand and asked to live for as many years as the number of grains she held in her hand. Her wish was granted but she refused to couple with Apollo, and rejected his amorous advances. To punish her, Cassinia was granted eternal life but not eternal youth. Her body shrivelled during the thousand years that she lived, until she became so tiny, she was placed in an ampulla[29] and carried around."

"There are things worse than death" replied Romeo. "She must have realised that sharing a bed, even with a God if she didn't wish to be with him, is not better than living for a thousand years. What else do you know?"

"She guided Aeneas into the Underworld."

"Yes, I have read Virgil's poem. What is the third thing you know about her?"

"There were twelve Sibyls and twelve grimoires in which the Sibyls wrote their Divine prophecies. The books included instructions on how to perform spells, charms, create amulets, invoke spirit. They were known as the Sibylline Books."

"Did Cassinia hold all twelve grimoires?" asked Romeo.

Arturo hesitated.

"The official story is that she offered twelve Sybilline Books to King Tarquinius of Rome, but he refused to pay her price. She burned three of them and offered him the remaining nine grimoires at the same price. Again, he refused. She burned three

---

[29] Round glass vessel with two handles.

more of the books, then three more, and at that point the King paid the original asking price."

"Why would she offer him the twelve grimoires?"

Arturo frowned and said, "I cannot answer that, but there is a different tale whispered by some."

"Which is?" questioned Romeo.

"That there was an additional Sibyl. A thirteenth Sibyl. There were three Sibyls in Rome at the time of Julius Caesar's assassination, not two. The Cumaean Sibyl, the Tiburtine Sibyl and the Cambrian Sibyl. Rumour has it that three of the Sibylline Books were taken from the Temple of Jupiter by one of those Sibyls."

Romeo frowned and struggled for breath. Damp air hung silently around the two men.

"Where might the grimoires be now?" quizzed Romeo.

Arturo shook his head.

"Nobody knows the whereabouts of the Sibylline Books. Or even if they still exist. The legend is that the Cambrian Sibyl escaped with the three Sibylline Books helped by one of Julius Caesar's closest allies."

His face ashen Romeo asked, "And Sibyls. Do they still exist?"

"You're asking me if I believe that some people have the power of prophecy? Can offer Divine revelations?" asked Arturo. He remained silent for a long time and Romeo did not interrupt his thoughts. Eventually Arturo replied, "Religions throughout the world can recount prophecies from Divine beings. Gods if you like. For all our education and interconnectedness, millions of people from different cultures, in every part of the world still believe in messages from supernatural entities without necessarily having physical proof. The highest religious authorities claim that messages appear through dreams or visions. Perhaps some people have the power to visit the past, present and future."

Arturo stared at Romeo and said, "Do I believe that Sibyls exist now? I think that these days most people shrink from knowing the truth about the past, present and future, so they decry divinations from the Sibyls of yesteryear and those of present-day."

Fraught with anxiety, thoughts entangled, Romeo wondered if it were possible to have lived different lives, for he felt that he had known the Cambrian Sibyl, whose name was Ceres. She had been the wife of the Legate Titus in Ancient Rome. He knew that it was the Cambrian Sibyl, Ceres who removed three Sibylline books from the Temple of Jupiter in Rome. The air closed in tightly around Romeo. Fragments of information pounded his consciousness as his mind filtered images. The Sibyls Ceres and Cassinia. Vestal Virgins. The Legate Titus. Emperor Julius Caesar. A queen. Divine prophecies. The Sibylline Books.

How did they link to him?

And that was when Romeo realised, he was the Primus Pilus Magpie … in a different life.

August 2010

Chapter 12 – Where Romans Play

We laughed and we danced.

It was a slow motorbike journey from Monte di Cuma for a long shadow followed Romeo into the sinful Ancient Roman maritime area of Pozzuoli. The problem was, since finishing at the liceo[30], he had found time and space to think and needed to fend off visions that slithered snake-like into his mind. He drank a few beers in a local café, visited a private club close to the town centre and ordered à la carte room service later that night at his waterside hotel, but it wasn't food that was served.

When he woke early the following afternoon, Romeo kissed goodbye to his overnight entertainment, and took a long cool shower. He stepped out of the bathroom with a white towel wrapped around his lower body, poured himself an espresso, lit a cigarette and sat on his balcony surveying the rocky peninsular. The gilded hillside reflected the sunshine, and soothing waves lapped around children's feet at the water's edge down below in the Bay. The sweet citrus scent of coastal lemons, cultivated locally in small orchards behind the hotel, clung to the air. The fragrance of grapes laced with olives from the trees below reminded him of happy hours spent with Alessandro in the garden at home. An assault on his senses. Romeo frowned, took long deep breaths, and felt his tension creep away to be replaced by excited anticipation. He had promised his brother to have enough experiences for them both. And he would.

Dionysus had arrived in town.

Romeo raced his Ducati through the twisting, narrow roads past white-washed time-worn captivating villages, beside zingy

---

[30] Upper secondary school.

lemon orchards. He stopped occasionally for a drink and to admire the breathtaking coastal views where white yachts skimmed azure harbours. The sun was almost tipping the sea when Romeo headed to Porto di Pozzuoli. He parked his Ducati and began to search for the yacht, Il Sole to book his next adventure. Scuba diving.

It was not difficult to spot the colourful, sleek boat which had just docked as it was a hive of activity with animated divers disembarking. Amidst the flurry of commotion Romeo spotted a woman wearing the navy-blue shorts and yellow t-shirt uniform of a crew member. He waved to catch her attention.

"Excuse me" he shouted above the melee "I'm looking for Captain Hell."

"Who are you? The police?" she challenged.

"No."

"The Tax Man?" she questioned.

"No."

"A beggar?" she said.

"No."

"A thief?" she quizzed.

Romeo blushed and said guiltily, "A thief? Why are you asking if I'm a thief?"

The woman noticed his discomfiture and probed, "Like to steal bright, shiny items, do you?"

Apprehension rose within Romeo, his heart beat hard, for he was guilty of stealing a bright, shiny aureus and the evidence lay in his back trouser pocket.

"What do you mean?" he responded.

"Magpies" she said, pointing to his neck "claim for their own anything that sparkles."

"Oh" Romeo said, relieved. He breathed out deeply. "No. None of the above. Do you know Captain Hell?"

"Yes" was her curt reply.

This communication was not going well. For the first time in his life Romeo felt discombobulated by a woman. He stared at her insightful blue eyes woven with slivers of malachite green, full lips, and golden hair which framed her sun-kissed face. Delightfully stippled across her nose and on her forehead were a few delicate freckles, he noticed.

"What do you want?" she demanded.

"Erm" he hesitated for an age.

"Nope. We don't have any erms here" she stated and turned away. He was used to women melting at the sight of his large black eyes, not to them ignoring him.

"Erm" he said again "excuse me Miss I'm looking for Captain Hell."

"Who are you?"

"Romeo" he replied.

She snorted loudly.

"Well Romeo, Captain Hell ain't no Juliet. Why are you looking for the Captain?"

Romeo fumbled in his t-shirt pocket and pulled out a business card.

"Here" he said passing the worn card to the woman. "My friend Giovanni recommended Captain Hell as the best teacher of scuba diving in the area."

"So?"

"Erm" he hesitated "I wanted to book some lessons."

"You ever done scuba diving before?" she asked.

Romeo was flailing around, completely at sea, searching for a lifejacket.

"Erm no."

"What kind of lessons do you want?"

"Scuba diving lessons" he responded.

The woman sighed heavily, almost tutted but thought better of it and refrained from shouting at him.

"A day's introductory lesson, or a first level course to acquire the basic principles, or a second level course or a tailor-made course?"

Romeo finally gathered his sensibilities.

"Let's start again. Hello, my name is Romeo. I'd like to speak to the ship's Captain. Is he on board?"

The woman stared at him, paused then finally responded by saying, "Hello Romeo. I am Captain Hell."

"Oh sorry. I presumed you were a man" he said "not that I didn't think you were a woman. Clearly you are a woman. I mean, you look womanly, so I guessed you were female. Oh, bloody hell I'm making such an idiot of myself. I made the mistake of assuming that a Captain of a yacht like this would be male. There. I admit to being a little naive."

Captain Hell smiled at him.

"And now I feel Hellish" he said impishly.

A tiny smile quivered across Hell's lips.

"Hell. It's short for Helianthus. It means sunflower. I think my parents were quite unkind giving me that name. They thought it suited me when I was born with a crop of bright orange hair."

"Not because you grew from a seed then, that finally popped out?"

Hell did not smile.

Romeo thought his quip amusing. He tried to redeem himself. "A sunflower does represent the sparkly sun which is usually orange" he said inanely. "Did you know that the helianthus has many therapeutic properties? It soothed my sore throat and tonsilitis when I was a little boy. My mother made up a tincture from sunflower leaves. That's what she does. Creates potions from flowers to help people. Also did you know that sunflowers can be used in cooking? My mother adds the seeds to bread and cakes. They're good for you. A diuretic! Or so she says. The birds in our garden love the seeds, and bees use sunflowers for pollination. I'd say you're named after one of the most useful flowers which is obviously apt because your sunny disposition shines through."

Captain Hell laughed. A deliciously zingy resonance to Romeo's ears.

"Your mother sounds cool."

"She is" admitted Romeo.

"Now you've given me your life story do you want a day's introductory lesson, or a first level course to acquire the basic principles, or a second level course or a tailor-made course?"

"All of them" responded Romeo. "Do you teach them all?" he added hopefully.

"I do, but not in one day. I'll assume you have no prior experience and you're in Porto di Pozzuoli for longer than a day?"

"Correct."

"Can you swim?"

"Like a fish" Romeo replied confidently.

"A batfish can't swim."

Flummoxed, he replied, "Like any other fish in the ocean then."

"More than a breadth of a swimming pool?"

"Yes. I've got bronze, silver, and gold swimming badges from the liceo" stated Romeo proudly.

"Your own or someone else's?"

"Mine" he replied indignantly. "And a life-saving badge. Which I haven't put to practical use yet. But I could if you were drowning. Not that I want you to drown. I'm not saying that. I'm stating that I have the practical skills if you were ever in difficulty. Which you're not. At the moment."

Hell looked irritated by Romeo's ramblings.

"I've not got all day Romeo."

"I'll shut up" he volunteered.

Captain Hell smiled.

"There are theory lessons as well as practical lessons. Think you can deal with both?

Proudly he stated, "Next month I'm going to the University of Bologna to study astrophysics."

Captain Hell gave him a withering look.

"Not that I'm boasting about my academic ability. I'm not. I'm merely trying to demonstrate that I have the ability to learn. And the skill to swim. And the power to look like the biggest ninny you've ever laid eyes upon I'll wager."

Romeo watched Captain Hell's face for tell-tale signs that she was thawing towards him. There were none.

"There's a beginners' course starting tomorrow morning at nine. We take payment in advance please."

"Ok" Romeo fumbled opening his brown leather wallet. He drew out a sapphire blue card. Hell knew this was a card used by wealthy individuals. "Will this do?" he asked.

"It will" Captain Hell responded and took payment for a beginner's course lasting a week. "Thank you." To herself she said '*spoilt, rich brat never worked a day in his life*'.

When payment had been taken and the card returned, Romeo said, "Thanks Captain Hell. Goodnight."

"Call me Hell" she replied. "Bye. See you tomorrow bright and early."

He turned to wave and tripped on the gangplank.

"Oh Romeo" shouted Hell "if you want to become a professional diver, we offer courses from Dive Master up to Instructor level."

"I'll certainly think about it" he replied before scuttling off the yacht. '*Was she poking fun at me*?' he thought afterwards.

And that was how the summer playboy Gaius Romeo Cangini began to fall in love with the Captain of Il Sole, Helianthus.

***

Last night Romeo had not gone partying for the first time since he began his summer break. Once he had signed up for the scuba diving course, he drove slowly to his hotel and swam a mile in the outdoor infinity pool. He was tempted to wear pyjamas to practise water life-saving skills, but did not have any as he preferred to sleep only in boxer shorts. Wheezing a little after his marathon swim session he vowed to give up smoking. No alcohol passed his lips that evening. He did not wish to embarrass himself any more in front of Hell.

Romeo had slept fitfully. A dream amplified the sound of rhythmic music in his mind, a woman playing a tibia. His visions projected rousing dancing in a Temple where wine flowed freely. Puzzlingly, he had observed himself laughing and dancing with a dark-haired woman. The visions stopped when the sun had barely stroked the horizon. Getting out of bed he thought '*It's easier to sleep when I drink alcohol because that makes my over-active brain switch off*'.

He showered, got dressed, ate a light breakfast of cheese and prosciutto layered in a cornetto and drank espresso. A quick drag on a cigarette helped to calm him. Before he left his hotel room, Romeo placed his treasured golden aureus in the room's safe. He did not wish to risk losing it at the bottom of the Bay of Naples.

***

There were five passengers on the Introduction to Scuba Diving course to be taught by Hell. Once the group members had met each other Hell gave an overview of the Bay area.

"The Bay of Naples is a zone of great scientific interest and outstanding natural beauty. We are in a region known as Campei Flegrei which is made up of a collection of calderas. We are in the craters of a super volcano which still has widespread seismic activity. Due to this, you may already know that Pozzuoli has been raised by four metres in the past fifty years. This is known as Bradyseism which means subsidence or uplift of the vertical ground. Just be aware that tremors may happen while we are diving. If they occur, I'll signal for us to return to the yacht.

I know that a lot of you are interested in diving to the Ancient Roman city of Baiae which is approximately ten metres below present-day sea levels. This is also due to Bradyseism."

"Is it true" interrupted Romeo "that Baiae was a wild city where rich Ancient Romans went to party?"

Hell gave Romeo a withering stare.

"Baiae was an exclusive haunt of rich Ancient Romans. They went there to let off steam. It did have quite the reputation for licentious behaviour until it sank beneath the waves. Its secrets are waiting to be unlocked."

Hell paused for a moment before she said, "But Baiae is much more than that. It's an underwater urban structure and as such offers a unique gateway to our past. Baiae is a region of enormous archaeological interest. The banks along the sea front used to be covered with opulent villas populated by rich Ancient Romans. Their homes were filled with fabulously colourful, detailed mosaics and intricately decorated statues. The spot we are going to dive is a magical and mystical part of our heritage full of undiscovered Ancient Roman ruins. It's a rich crosscurrent of life which needs to be appreciated. There are very strict rules about diving here."

Was it Romeo's imagination or did Hell stare straight at him and scowl when she said, "We are not allowed to take as our own any of the ruins, or touch the geological formations or disturb flora and fauna. If you find any Ancient Roman treasure it is to be handed in to the Archaeological Society."

Romeo shifted a little uncomfortably in his seat.

'*I'm not going to feel guilty about keeping the aureus*' he thought grumpily '*as it is mine.*'

Despite the defiant words, shame weighed as heavy as the limestone rocks of Polignano beach where he used to play with Alessandro.

"I told all of you that we needed to learn the theoretical side of diving and today will be an introduction before we do a short dive tomorrow" continued Hell. "We will learn about Boyle's law, the Valsalva manoeuvre and make time to select your diving kit. When you paid for the course, it included the price of buying the dive mask, wetsuit boots and fins. You will be measured for those this afternoon ready for tomorrow's dive. By the end of the week, we will be diving to the underwater city of Baiae."

During the day, Romeo listened to Hell, made notes, and occasionally studied the other students sitting either at his elbows or directly in front of him. All were attentive to Hell as she explained the rudiments of diving, described the dangers and thrills of the infinite depths of black water which transcended time and space. An unchartered underwater world, one in which she imbued within him an excitement to enter.

That evening Romeo propelled the Ducati away from the dock as rapidly as he could. As daylight dimmed, he stopped at a cliff top, in a damp mist of sea salt and thought Hell was like cool, clear running water. Difficult to grasp.

August 2010

Chapter 13 – Baiae

Where ghosts live.

"Are you ready Romeo?" asked Hell.

"Ready?" he queried.

"Yes. You need to get into your wetsuit. Here it is."

Wearing a yellow bikini Hell began to pull her wetsuit over her toned body. Romeo paid particular attention to the dainty sunflower tattoo at the base of her spine.

"Got any more tattoos in unlikely places?" he asked.

A sharp wind led the yacht to lurch. Romeo fell to the floor with a jolt, entangled in his wetsuit and fins.

'*Ass*' thought Hell who turned slightly away from him.

From a distance she watched his breath labour, could see Romeo was embarrassed as he pulled himself to a seat, and silently prepared for the dive. Hell settled on a place next to him, her eyes clear as glacier water.

"You'll enjoy visiting Baiae, Romeo. This is the treat at the end of our first week of diving. You've mastered the lessons. We can dive to about seven metres and visit an underwater Ancient Roman villa. You'll finally get to see where those wild Romans may have partied."

Romeo's eyes regarded Hell. He nodded in assent. What he was thinking, she would never know.

Sitting on the side of the boat Hell plunged backwards into the warm Tyrrhenian Sea alert to any danger. She watched closely as her students jumped into the roiling spray and swam downwards towards the sunken city of Baiae. Torpedo-shaped shimmering tuna fish, black seabass, and schools of iridescent silver-green anchovies slid past them. In the crepuscular water, salt-eroded marble statutes of the Roman Gods Jupiter, Juno and Minerva offered generous homes to hundreds of molluscs.

Plunging through murky water towards the remnants of a villa, Hell swept away millimetres of sand and tiny white pebbles from the seabed. She revealed an intricately designed, tessellated orange, red, white, and blue mosaic of dolphins swimming under a bright sun. The divers ventured further into the home, swam along worn marble steps to view remains of a gym, sauna, and swimming pool before they turned upwards and entered an atrium.

Romeo passed through a gateway which reminded him of green glowing luminous plasma. Straining his eyes, he jolted as a surge of emotions rose through his body. He hovered over a boisterous mosaic of an eagle, which represented the Roman Empire and a bull which acted as a permanent reminder of the indomitability of Julius Caesar's Legio Ten. Romeo recognised this image and the room in which he floated, for he had danced happily on the finely plaited pattern with the married woman who lived here. The Cambrian Sybil, Ceres. When he was entwined in a different life, in Ancient Roman time.

Romeo shook, surrounded as he was by translucent green shimmering ghosts floating in the miasma where the delicate, ethereal cobwebby veil between the spirit world had thinned in the dim underwater light. He felt a wave propel him as he witnessed parts of his Ancient Roman past through the spectrum of colours bleeding in the water before him.

Breathing deeply, Romeo's unyielding gaze revealed a muscular man cloaked in a white linen, purple edged toga brandishing a tattoo of two magpies on his neck. Himself! An Ancient Roman Primus Pilus named Magpie. Startled, Romeo observed as if watching the flickering reel of his life, as Magpie sprinted through the cobbled alleyways, into the Forum towards the dreaded Gemonian Stairs where traitors of Rome were persecuted. Magpie stood helplessly as three Vigiles from Rome's night-watch mercilessly whipped a young slave whom they barracked '*the lover*'. Heart-red blood seeped from every broken pore. With shivering skin, Romeo recognised this man as Magpie's brave Hispanic slave, Feliciano, a celebrity in Rome due to his stupendous charioteering skills. Horrified, Romeo watched the Vigiles drag screaming Feliciano to the top of the Tarpeian Rock before flinging him unceremoniously to the pits below where his smashed body lay, unmoving in the Forum. His crime? Loving a young Vestal Virgin named Diana.

The water pressed heavily upon tense Romeo. Head bowed he closed his eyes and watched a different scene. A young woman, clad all in white silk led by the Pontifex Maximus, and followed by her family through the narrow passageways of Rome. Savage observers spat, and jeered '*Diana the whore*'. She stared straight ahead into the dark night, travelling at an unbroken pace. Dignified. Resolute. The procession streamed away from the centre of Rome to a deep cave set in a remote hillside. Sharply shoved in the back, Diana stumbled into the murky, dank grotto. The Pontifex Maximus followed her, placed a lit white candle onto the floor alongside a piece of bread and a small cup of water. He called upon Destiny to decide the Fate of this eighteen-year-old Vestal Virgin for the sin of fraternising with a slave. If only the Pontifex Maximus had realised that love is ignorant to the transient societal values placed on the masses.

Romeo stared through the twilight as Diana inhaled deeply, held her breath, exhaled loudly then knelt and beseeched a Priestess of the God Apollo, the Cambrian Sybil, Ceres to help guide her out of the cavern. A white stone boulder was heaved over the entrance leaving Diana alone, waiting for death. Romeo heard her entreaties and continued to watch his movie, willing Diana to find an escape.

Finally, the sun arrived gently reflecting pale yellow onto the limestone rock surface. Romeo spotted the Sibyl Ceres and two burly men outside the cave. He heard the Sibyl utter a spell which enabled the men to push aside the boulder sealing the cave's entrance as easily as if it were a beach pebble. Three people entered the dank grotto and in the passage of short minutes, silently four people emerged. They resealed the cave, mounted fractious stallions, and rode towards the caves of Cumae, where freedom lay and Cassinia, the Cumaean Sybil waited. Magpie, Titus, and Ceres, part of Julius Caesar's trusted entourage had rescued Diana. The golden threads of life had not been severed by Morta, the third Goddess of Fate … yet.

With open horrified eyes Romeo scrutinised the film reel depicting his past life. Blinded by the light, he jolted, blinked, and shook his head. Could he really see a lembus, the small agile ship of pirates in confused battle with a Roman naves gallicae? Romeo observed closely. A legionary dived from the Roman ship and dragged another soldier from the cold, swirling sea towards the Roman vessel. Thick ropes were thrown overboard. Treading water, the legionary coiled a line tightly around the unconscious soldier who was slowly hoisted aboard. The rescuer dragged himself up the ship's side steps and lay exhausted on the deck. Romeo recognised the saviour. Himself, Magpie.

On the bow stood the Sibyl Ceres who leaned over the unconscious warrior. She put her amber ring to his forehead, directly on his third eye to draw disease from him, but his swollen face was already grey as sea fog, and his body cold as ice. Ceres placed two denarii over his closed eyes to pay the blazing-eyed ferryman Charon for his passage to the Underworld and on to the glorious Elysian Fields. The Seer could do no more.

On the deck Magpie had staggered to his feet when Ceres spun around and spoke to her husband.

"Titus, Gannicus Po has gone to the Underworld. This young legionary has been as brave as any lion."

"Yes Ceres" replied Titus "I saw Magpie jump into the murky waves and enormous swell to save Gannicus Po. In recognition of his bravery, he will take over from Gannicus as my trusted Primus Pilus and receive my special gladius for his act of bravery in the freezing waters. The gladius is a unique weapon which has saved me in many battles. Forged in Segontium, inscribed with SPQR, a golden spiral and Legio X below the ivory hilt, its powers are renowned throughout Cambria. It was created at the same time as the amber handled pugio I gave you when we met on the Vardre under a Full Moon."

Ceres replied, "Then it must be known as the Segontium Gladius. Your generosity is renowned Legate, and I shall offer a spell of protection for it and Magpie.

'By the power of the sky
By the power of the sea
By the power of the earth
By the power of the trees
May my circle of protection
always be around
he who carries the Segontium Gladius.'

In an unusual display of affection in front of his legion, Titus wrapped his arms around his Prophetess wife. Romeo's brain whirred and churned when he spotted tattoos of an eagle and a bull rippling on Titus's muscular arms. The same colour and design as he had witnessed on the floor of the underwater villa. His intuition told him that Titus was his friend and Legate, commander of the feared Legio X and he, Romeo was Magpie, a Primus Pilus in Julius Caesar's army. The villa in Baiae had been built for Titus and his Prophetess wife, Ceres, the Cambrian Sibyl.

She was the married lady he had danced with at a party to celebrate the birth of her twin daughters. Over two thousand years ago.

August 2010

Chapter 14 – Chess

Welcome to Hell.

"O Romeo, Romeo, wherefore art thou Romeo?" joked Hell.

Bursting to speak to him, she was sitting on a red leather chair nearby as he lay in bed.

"You gave me quite a scare when we were diving. How are you feeling? Want anything to eat? Drink?"

Romeo felt grim. He looked worse.

"Ice cold water would be great … to drink I mean" replied Romeo. He knew that Hell would be truth-seeking when she returned.

"There you are. From the fridge" said Hell as she passed him a bottle of Acqua Panna.

"Why am I in bed? Am I on your yacht?"

"You had a strange turn when we were diving around Baiae. Looked like you were in a trance for a while, so I had to take you out of the water and bring you here, to Il Sole. Thought it was a good idea for you to rest. Too many wild nights perhaps? Too much drinking? Or drugs?"

She was fishing, Romeo knew that. He had better throw her a suitable catch.

"I feel grim. My waywardness is probably to blame" he said, but by the way he did not meet her eyes, Hell knew he was lying. Silence passed between them as air travels lightly through a void. Hell felt the need to explain, "The other divers helped me to undress you and put you to bed".

"Good. Good" replied Romeo. "That was kind of them … and you." He smiled wanly.

"You can stay the night if you like. It would be better if someone kept a close eye on you. My brother Giovanni, your tattooist friend, said you were alone in Naples."

Hell laughed at the expression on Romeo's face.

"Giovanni didn't tell you I was his sister, did he?" she asked.

"No!"

"He's spoken a little about you and I'm happy for you to stay here for a few nights. Until you feel a little stronger. I've got a couple of cabins on board."

"Thanks Hell. I do feel washed out."

"You looked like you'd seen a spirit in Baiae, and not your usual alcoholic option."

Hell was still trawling. Like a frogfish, Romeo outmanoeuvred her by remaining motionless. Taciturn. His eyes fixed upon a Murano glass chess set placed on a walnut side table. She followed his gaze.

"Play chess with me" she suggested.

His eyes were steady on hers. "I don't play chess" he replied. "My brother Alessandro was a Chess Master. He played chess with my father. It was never my game."

"You have a brother?" she asked.

"A twin brother. Alessandro. Very talented, funny, pedantic, adorable. He used to torment me to play chess with him. He loved to challenge me, but I knew I'd never win."

"Why didn't he come with you to the Bay of Naples?"

"He's not around."

"Do you still see him?"

"I do. From time to time. Usually immediately before I go to sleep, or just before I wake up."

"What?"

"I see his spirit."

"His spirit?" she laughed. "What do you mean? You see his spirit?"

"From a young age I've been able to predict events that will happen. I see people who have passed over. I see past, present and future."

"No-one can do that. Why would you lie to me?"

"I'm telling the truth, but I know it's difficult to believe." Romeo paused and smiled to himself. "When we were diving. I saw spirits in Baiae. The essence of people I once knew. A long time ago."

"You saw your brother?"

"No. Not when we were diving at Baiae. But" he paused for a while as if debating whether to explain himself to Hell. "I do see him. He visits me, particularly when I meditate."

Hell stood up. An odd feeling rose within her. A nervousness.

"Has that dive addled your brain?" she asked crossly.

"No."

"No?" she quizzed.

"He died when we were eleven. My brother. His name was Alessandro. An illness took him away."

"Oh" whispered Hell not knowing how to console Romeo. A thought immediately surfaced. "You too are sick then? That is why you took a turn under water?"

"No. I told you. I saw the past. In Baiae's chaos of subterranean colours, the veil between this world and other dimensions thinned and revealed Baiae from two thousand years ago. Showed me Ancient Roman friends who once shared my life."

"Are you sure you're not bonkers?" Hell asked.

"I'm unlikely to tell you if I am!"

"Giovanni said you were normal. Well. Mostly normal. He didn't say anything about you being able to see the past."

"And the future" Romeo reminded her with a wry smile.

Remnants of her recent conversation with Giovanni processed noisily through Hell's mind. *'He can be a bit strange sometimes*' was how her brother described Romeo. She thought he meant by drinking too much and womanising, not by seeing spooks.

"Now listen Romeo. I don't believe in any of this crap. What happens in the here and now, that's life as we know it. That's real. Not some spiritual mumbo jumbo about visions. Cut out the nonsense. You fainted during the dive. You can't remember what happened. There. It's easily explained. You're simply too embarrassed to admit it. It probably makes you feel less … manly. I've seen it before with men."

"If you say so" responded Romeo, shocked by her outburst.

"NO! Not if I say so. That's what happened. There are no such things as ghostly entities, past, present, or future. You're not bloody Dante Alighieri journeying through Hell, Purgatory or Paradise."

"Ok. Ok. Calm down!"

Unnerved, Hell shouted "I AM CALM. DON'T PATRONISE ME. STOP TALKING ABOUT HALLUCINATIONS. THEY'RE JUST THAT. NOT REAL. HELP YOURSELF TO FOOD. I'M GOING TO BED."

Romeo wanted to share with Hell the details of his visions in Baiae. He wished to explain what he had seen so that she would realise he was normal. But he had taken an irrevocable step. One move too many for Hell. Pity, because he liked her.

There was time to ponder once she left the cabin. '*Did I say normal? What is normal?*' he thought since he had seen this same terrified reaction in his parents. '*Better to keep quiet*' he decided '*as usual.*'

***

At breakfast the following morning Hell was planning to apologise for her outburst. When she entered the galley, Romeo surprised her.

"Welcome to Hell's kitchen. Here's your food. I made it myself" he said proudly.

She grinned. "What do we have here?"

"Fresh espresso, cornetto, ciabatta, parmesan, ricotta and mascarpone cheeses served with grapes."

"You made the cornetto yourself?" she queried "and the cheeses? And the grapes? Amazing!"

"Of course not. I bought the cornetto from the local bakery, the rest from the local delicatessen and placed all of it with my own hands on this food board. Especially for you."

"Lovely." Hell paused. "I see you're feeling stronger. Romeo, I need to apologise for my behaviour last night. I didn't ask you about your twin brother and that was unforgivable."

"I took you by surprise. No-one knows how to react when they hear a child has died."

"You're right. I didn't know what to say. Don't know what to say, other than I'm sorry your family went through that trauma. Forgive me for over-reacting about your visions. But I still don't believe in ghosts."

"Thanks for your condolences. Listen. It's fine. We're at opposite ends on the ghost-thing, that's all."

"No more talk of spirits then?"

"No. I promise."

Romeo was checked. '*Checkmate*' he thought. Right there. Right then. With this vow, once again he shut off speaking about an important part of himself.

Having spent his childhood experiencing revelations, they did not stop for Romeo simply because he had made a declaration never to discuss them with Hell. In the second half of that night a thunderous, startling scream woke Hell, echoing as it did around the boat. Quivering, she ran to Romeo's cabin and found him in bed, curled in a ball, shivering cold with terror, black eyes staring wildly, drops of sweat visible on his forehead. In a concerned voice she called out to him, "ROMEO."

A shadow passed over Romeo's face for he could still see the image in his mind's eye. The semblance of a man slumped in a filthy alleyway, saturated in blood, dark red as Hell's lipstick and a woman standing over him, bloodied knife in hand.

"A nightmare. Probably too much red wine after dinner" he replied by way of explanation.

In the shadows of the cabin, Hell moved towards the bed where Romeo's shape looked curiously fragile. Delicately she removed her bra and panties before she lay behind his long, lean naked body. With strong hands, she massaged his shoulders, stroked the contours of his damp skin, caressed his back, held him tightly until the spirits dispersed and his trembling subsided.

***

Fourteen days later Romeo was still living on Hell's yacht. The two young people had established a warm affinity; she taught diving courses during the day which he attended. In the evening, they drank wine, laughed, and danced on the boat under the light of the moon. During the night, occasionally in the day, she led him to her bed where he would embrace the golden helianthus at the base of her spine. A simple life.

When Romeo asked Hell if she would keep in touch when he was at university, she responded, "Personal doesn't last". And that was how it was. No strings attached. No long-term expectations of each other. Except, a deep attachment had formed and without any encouragement from her, Romeo was in love with Hell. The twenty-four-year-old wild woman, fearless and enigmatic had captivated an eighteen-year-old romantic, who was unsure how to fit into his adult skin.

Staying with her for a short while was enough for Romeo to realise that Hell was forthright and uncompromising. She angered easily, and Romeo recognised that Hell needed to find a way to relax. Meditation had begun to play a part in his life, and he wished to teach her how to pay attention to her thoughts and feelings so that she could better manage her reactions. Initially reluctant, as she had never been encouraged to control her temper before, Hell voiced objections, but Romeo persisted.

"It'll be a positive experience Hell" he persuaded. "Meditation slows your heart rate and decreases stress hormones. Here. C'mon. Let's try it. Sit upright on your favourite chair."

Warily Hell obeyed Romeo's instruction.

"Take a few deep breaths. In through your nose, out through your mouth."

Initially she had peeped out through half-closed eyes.

"Close your eyes" ordered Romeo. "Focus your awareness on the middle of your chest. Concentrate on your heart. Remember to breathe deeply. Pay attention to the sensation of clear air moving in and out of your body. Exhale slowly. Visualise a golden light around you. Breathe this golden energy into your lungs, in through your nose. Feel that energy moving around your body. Exhale slowly through your mouth.

Beginning at your root chakra, the base of your spine, imagine energy moving gently through your body, extending into the sacral chakra in your abdomen, into your solar plexus above your belly button and resting for a while in your heart chakra."

Hell concentrated, not knowing what he meant by chakras.

"Breathe in again and exhale gently. Feel the energy moving up into your throat chakra, continuing up to your forehead and third eye chakra. The energy will finally settle at the top of your head in your crown chakra."

Sitting calmly for ten minutes Hell obeyed Romeo's instruction until she was finally guided to open her eyes.

"How did I do?" she asked.

"How do you feel?" replied Romeo.

"Rested. Calm. Peaceful."

"Good. We are starting to balance the energy centres in your body using your chakras. Remember, be mindful in all that you do Hell" advised Romeo. "Meditate each day to keep your energy centres open. There can be too much or too little energetic activity in any of the chakras. This may manifest negative outcomes for you."

"I've not got the faintest idea what you're talking about Romeo, but I feel serene. As you know, that's not usually how I am. I'm known as Hell for good reason."

At this declaration, Romeo smiled.

Hell sought clarification about chakras, and he explained.

"Chakras run from the base of the spine to the top of the head. Imagine them to be little coloured circles placed at different points within your body. If a circle is blocked it may lead you to experience negative physical or emotional symptoms."

When he had been in Naples, the words Stella used when she introduced Romeo to chakras resonated with him, '*You're predominantly driven by personal pleasures offered by the senses. Sex. You enjoy sex, but making love is different. It's better. You'll see.*'

Romeo shook his head as if to expel the memory. He could not be sure that Hell understood the difference between sex and making love so said, "If the orange sacral chakra, the energy located in the lower abdomen is overactive it means addictions dominate your life. If you have an underactive sacral chakra, you will feel as if your emotions are jumbled and the lust for gratification may overwhelm you".

For a moment surprise flickered across her face. Hell moistened her lips and laughed at him.

"Try to be balanced in all you do" Romeo continued, and immediately recognised he had offered Hell advice he had never taken.

***

From a notorious and wealthy Italian family, '*possibly Mafiosi*' Romeo speculated, Hell was of robust character chiselled from the luna marble of unyielding parents. That morning when they were out on a commercial diving trip in the Bay of Naples, two customers refused to pay for their diving training. Hell left them stranded on the crescent moon-shaped island of Vivara, a breathtaking nature reserve connected to Santa Margherita by a footbridge. Self-assured and bold, she would not tolerate fools or thieves.

"That will teach you not to steal from me" she bellowed as she waved a short-bladed titanium dive-knife from the boat deck. "Thieves. You're lucky I didn't kill you. You're a disgusting pair of dog fleas!"

She turned to Romeo and said, "Thanks for teaching me how to meditate otherwise I would have hacked them both to death and hurled pieces of them into the sea! My chakras would have been thrown into meltdown!"

With eyes which almost popped out of his head, Romeo silently deliberated whether Hell needed more practice at meditation. She was not afraid to speak her uncompromising truth. Indifferent to the divers' plight, Hell laughed as she guided Il Sole to the beautiful island of Procida. Discombobulated, Romeo persuaded her to moor the yacht at this smallest island in the Bay of Naples.

They sat and smoked together at the millennial Abbey of San Michele Arcangelo, visited the fortified medieval village of Terra Murata, and ate Luveri al sole, caught fresh from local waters served overlooking the Tyrrhenian Sea. Later in the evening a snaking walkway led them down to water as clear as natural blue topaz crystal in the flamboyant and traffic-free fishing port of Marina Corricella. Irrepressible Hell persuaded Romeo that they must celebrate the end of his trip by visiting Sing in Chiaia, a trendy nightclub on the mainland in Naples. If they left now, once back in port they could take his motorbike and arrive at the club before midnight.

In high spirits, Romeo sang badly in a tenor voice as he deftly swung the Ducati around twisting roads, challenging the motorbike to avoid verging over sheer cliff edges, whilst Hell clung tightly to his waist. He enjoyed the feeling. Eventually Romeo pulled over on Via Guiseppe and parked directly outside the nightclub. Once inside the bar, Hell glowed as she led Romeo towards blue up-lit tables. Beside a dancefloor which pulsed and changed colour, like a queen bee, friends immediately swarmed around her, kissing the air at the side of her face then buzzed around handsome Romeo.

It was all going so well.

The surge of women around Hell comprised golden skin, shiny hair, and perfectly made-up faces. Dazzling friends encouraged her onto the pulsating dancefloor, as they whispered and gyrated to a retro song, Donna Summer's, I Feel Love. Romeo sat at the sharp edge, an on-looker to hedonism. He maintained his distance to avoid disturbing the colony who, in their collective wisdom, continually gorged on alcoholic shots. A weird sense of presentiment overcame him when a thick hand gripped his forearm.

"Do you own the red Ducati mate that's parked outside?"

"Why?"

"There's a gang of lads around it. Looks like they're trying to steal the bike."

A tremor of anger oscillated in Romeo's stomach. He turned in search of Hell who was on the dancefloor passionately kissing an alluring dark-haired woman. Like volts of electricity, a prickle of fear and a shot of jealousy surged through his body, giving his heart an irregular beat. Greedily Romeo gulped air, rose up, brushed past onlookers, and followed the exit signs. He dashed outside into the shadowy, lonely night to confront the enemy. All six of them.

"Oi" he shouted before entering a maelstrom of awfulness.

Stupefied by a blow to the face Romeo staggered backwards. He felt the knife penetrate his left buttock long after blood had seeped to the floor. A stomach blow made him retch and lunge forward. He vomited and crumbled to his feet. Practised in atrocious attacks, the six thugs jeered. Unable to take on all of them, Romeo wrapped his arms tightly around the legs of one assailant, who overbalanced and dropped to the floor. With movement as swift as a peregrine falcon, Romeo dealt a vertical elbow chop to the throat of his prey, who began to choke. Keen night vision enabled Romeo to kick out at his next victim who fell backwards into the path of an oncoming car. Amidst the sound of screeching tyres, honking horns, screams, and shouts Romeo's highly sensitive hearing picked out Hell's voice. She was threatening a leering man. When his fat mouth sneered in her face, without hesitation Hell withdrew her titanium dive-knife, slashed the man's ruddy cheek and his distended stomach but not before she had stabbed another aggressor deep in his thigh. The two men writhed on the floor like chopped worms. Hell laughed. Blood collected around Romeo's eye sockets. From under purple eyelids, he watched as his beautiful red Ducati screeched away with two ill-tempered men astride. This was a salutary message, '*don't visit Naples again*'.

With blood on her hands Hell ran to help Romeo get to his feet. Once at eye level he looked directly at her. A shadow passed over Romeo's face for he could see two men slumped in a filthy alleyway, saturated in dark red blood, where Hell had stood with her dive-knife. Romeo realised his presentiment had been a warning. Destiny decreed that Hell was not his vivid Ariadne, the Goddess who unfailingly loved the God Dionysus and whom he cherished in return. Gently kissing Hell's flushed cheek, Romeo thanked her, and stumbled away towards the beach, grateful that his treasured golden aureus was in his back pocket. Tonight, he had lost enough. Much more than his beloved red Ducati.

It had been Hell.

November 2023

Chapter 15 – Love You To The Moon And Back

Time. Our most precious resource.

By the firelight on a chilly November morning in Conwy, nain sought tranquility which comes only with stillness of the mind. Surrounded by gold velvet cushions Moon lay across nain's lap as she sat in the living room of Beudy Bryn Gosol. Dying dull red embers in the inglenook fireplace illuminated the dog's soft, furry ears which twitched as he dreamt. Nain wondered if Moon was imagining scampering on the Vardre, accompanied by her husband Tomos. The thought was a painful reminder of Tomos's recent passing. Once raised, memories of him were hard to put down. Absently, nain stroked Moon's midnight blue fur. The dog whimpered gently.

"Come on Moon" whispered nain. "I need to get ready to meet Seren and Madoc for my birthday lunch at Dylan's otherwise I'll be late. Time waits for no-one."

The Blue Roan cocker spaniel opened one bloodshot, chestnut coloured eye. Slowly he unfurled his paws, slid delicately off nain's knees, and placed his bloated body lazily upon the stone floor.

"Oh Moon" said nain with matter-of-fact acceptance "you're not long for this world I know. Stay until the end of my birthday please, then you can join Tomos."

Once washed, changed, perfumed and ready for her lunch date, Nain checked on Moon who was sleeping quietly. She walked down the long path away from Beudy Bryn Gosol and closed the wooden gate, with its fierce red dragon emblazoned on it. The creature's presence, the lavender planted outside the back door, and the hawthorn wreath hanging on the front door, reassured nain that her home was protected. A cab whisked her away.

As Moon lounged in the inglenook, his sister and partner-in-crime Star was fearsomely chasing icy, grey-topped waves on Benarth Beach. Watching from the slope of battered and bruised Conwy Castle, Seren's beaming smile bathed Madoc in sunshine.

"You're drying the dog this time missy" Madoc shouted above the wind. "She has a foul stink of seaweed, saltwater and dog breath."

"I'm ready with the towels" replied Seren "but we'd better be quick, or we'll be late meeting nain at Dylan's. We need to drop off Star at the dog groomers. We'll certainly get our money's worth from them today. This dog is in a sorry, hairy mess."

"When we get to Wagtails, you take in Star" prompted Madoc "because she smells strongly of the sea."

"No way. It's your turn. I'll dry Star, get her in the car, the rest is over to you Madoc Thomson."

Ten minutes worth of dog drop-off debate later, Star was safely ensconced in a soft warm towel, kindly provided by her dog groomer. The little cocker spaniel was blissfully unaware that her devoted brother and best friend Moon was sucking on his last breath, alone by the fireside at Beudy Bryn Gosol.

***

Nain stepped out of the cab at the Conwy arch. A breeze tugged at her green woollen coat. Her quiet incantations floated away as she hurried across The Square towards Dylan's café. The presence of the dead was always close in this central area of Conwy. Nain delighted in seeing the imposing 13th Century castle which provided a dramatic backdrop to the quaint harbour. The castle walls enveloped the town and narrow three-storey pargeted houses encircled The Square where a charming medieval appearance belied Conwy's historical importance.

In power for forty years until 1240, politically astute Llewellyn The Great, grandson of the mighty Owain Gwynedd, was born near Conwy and ruled Wales for much of his life. In Chester he married Joan, the daughter of King John which sealed his links with the Crown. To commemorate his achievements, a statue of Llewellyn The Great had been erected in The Square. It was always in this part of town that nain felt most troubled. She hardly dared look at the icon as she passed him before she turned right into the High Street.

Of course, she blamed Queen Elizabeth I for the influx of visitors which made The Square a focal point for public entertainment. In 1576 the Queen had decreed the main postal seaport between London and Dublin would be Holyhead on the island of Anglesey in North Wales. The Queen's declaration made Conwy the ideal staging post for travellers which had increased the town's vibrancy but created an uneasy relationship with the locals. The town was listed as a World Heritage Site and nain wondered how many tourists knew that. She shuddered, aware that The Square she was about to cross was once used for public hangings, among them women who practised healing, later outlawed as witches. '*Lives were stolen in this Square*' thought nain sorrowfully '*while people looked on and enjoyed the illusory theatre of it all.*'

With its dual front windows elegantly sited within a sandstone structure, Dylan's was one of the most exciting restaurants in town. Seren and Madoc had booked a table upstairs with superb views over the castle and Saint Mary's church. They knew that nain approved of the restaurant's policy to use local seafood, meat and vegetables alongside Welsh beer and spirits. It always made them laugh when she received the menu and chuckled at the section which mentioned sourcing Welsh spirits! Nain had the ability to do that herself. Spirits with lots of energy.

Nain pushed open the glass door, walked slowly up the restaurant's stairs, entered the warmly lit large, open room peppered with day-trippers and locals, and joined Seren and Madoc at a cast iron table. As she removed her coat, nain exhaled a long sigh of relief like a deflating balloon.

"What a morning!" she exclaimed as she sat down.

"Why? What's happened?" questioned Madoc.

"I'm sorry to start off with bad news but the spark of light is disappearing from Moon" she said.

Seren stopped midway between helping herself to a warm, brown roll and swallowed a bitter lump which rose in her throat. "Oh no" she said quietly.

"If there is any help we can offer nain, let us know" stated Madoc as he moved his arm protectively around Seren.

"Call in at Beudy Bryn Gosol before you both go home please, and we can check on Moon together" requested nain.

The awkward atmosphere was pricked when an elderly man, with a greying five o'clock shadow approached the table.

"Hello Gwen. Hello Seren and Madoc. Are you here for something special?" he asked.

"It's my birthday Dafydd" said nain.

"Happy birthday Gwen. Let me buy drinks for you all" he offered.

"Thank you Dafydd, that's kind of you, we've known each other a long time."

"I miss Tomos" responded Dafydd "it's the least I can do on your special day." He moved to another table and shouted "cheers" as he left. Nain thought it was lovely to bump into old friends.

"Happy birthday nain" said Seren and passed across the table a small brown box tied with string.

"Thank you cariad tlws. I'm determined to enjoy our time together this afternoon. What do we have here?"

"Let's order food before you open your gift" instructed Madoc. "You must be hungry nain after your busy morning."

A smartly dressed waiter arrived and took the order from Seren.

"Menai mussels for Madoc, braised feather blade of Welsh beef for nain, mushroom and lentil linguine for me please."

The waiter promptly left the trio to chat. He surreptitiously watched Nain unwrap her small parcel and saw her extrude a silver card.

"I'm invited on a trip to Genova! In Italy?" he overheard nain exclaim.

"Northern Italy. We thought the three of us could go for a long weekend in March. We know that it delays receiving your birthday gift, but we thought it would be warmer at that time of year. Is that ok?" queried Madoc with concern.

Nain lavishly shared her joy. "Sign me up" she ordered "I can't wait to go. How delightful. Exciting. Remember Vincenzo, the flower shop owner I met in Rome? He told me about Genova. His extended family live there. Did you know that Christopher Columbus was Genoese, not Spanish as most people think? And he began his sailing career in Lisbon, so the Portuguese claim him as their own too."

"I know" admitted Seren "Vincenzo told me when he invited us to visit and stay at his family's home."

Madoc's eyebrows shot up almost to the bald crown of his head. Nain had the grace to blush at the mention of Vincenzo. Seren was sure that Madoc would question her closely about the trip now he realised that she had kept in touch with nain's friend.

"What's this about Moon then nain?" asked Madoc, deftly changing the subject. "If his health has deteriorated overnight,

I'll take him to the vet later" he offered. "We need to pick up Star from Wagtails in Conwy."

"Thanks Madoc. That would be helpful." Nain was pensive. "Remember the time Moon chewed my tarot cards when he was a puppy? I rescued them just in time, but his teeth marks are still on those cards."

Seren and Madoc laughed.

"I've never seen you move so quickly nain" admitted Seren "to wrestle your tarot cards from him. You were as fast as a Red Arrows' display 'plane practising manoeuvres off Anglesey."

"You try grappling a dog! Luckily it wasn't my ancient grimoire" grinned nain.

"Absolutely" responded Madoc "as that's irreplaceable, holding as it does the mysteries of centuries."

Nain chose to ignore Madoc's comment. She was particularly protective of the book's ancient secrets.

"Thank you both for my surprising and delightful gift" said nain graciously.

"Oh. I almost forgot. This is from Haf and Gareth" said Seren as she rummaged around in her battered leather handbag and extracted a golden envelope which she placed in front of nain.

"My golden ticket?" exclaimed nain optimistically. "Am I off to Willy Wonka's factory?"

"That would be great nain, but lower your expectations" suggested Madoc with a smile.

Nain unsealed the sleeve to reveal a gift voucher for Healing Hands holistic beauty salon.

"Oh, what a superb treat. A shell back massage with Haf. Has she settled into her new room at Benarth Beach, Seren?"

"Yes, she's really enjoying being her own boss. We meet for coffee once a week before work and have a catch up. Her room is beautiful. It's just down the corridor from my room."

"How's that romance of hers going with Gareth?" enquired nain.

"Ok I think" replied Seren guardedly. "Not much to report there. No engagement or anything."

"And Gareth's work colleague? The Gorgeous Gaius Romeo Cangini" said nain as she focused upon Seren knowing with certainty that Madoc would be bristling at the mention of this name. "Are you prepared for your past life regression with him?"

"I am and I'm not nain. I was hoping you would let me practise on you please beforehand. A sort of dummy run."

Nain nodded. The type of gentle nod a queen might have given before she embarked on a mysterious journey.

"Thanks nain. Have you ever had one performed before?" questioned Seren.

"No" admitted nain. "I've done past life regression with lots of people, but I've never had one done on me. Of course, I meditate, visualise, and dream, so I've seen some of my past lives, but I've never actually entered one. Should be fun … I hope. Perhaps. Maybe."

"Why don't you do it in the Temple of Mithras?" suggested Madoc "place nain on the altar Seren, like a human sacrifice."

Nain shuddered at the ghoulish image.

"I hope it doesn't end that badly" retorted Seren "but the Temple of Mithras it is."

"Nain, do you know about the myth of Mithras?" asked Madoc.

"Mithra was important to Roman soldiers" began nain "because he was the God of obligation. The kind of honourable responsibility that should occur between a leader and warriors. Sol, the Roman Sun God ordered Mithra to sacrifice a white bull in a cave, which he did with a heavy heart. Upon death, the bull metamorphosed into the moon, which led to the creation of time because day could alternate with night. To a soldier, light signifies life and dark implies death. When we die, our soul crosses a bridge between life and death and Mithra is one of three judges who decide what happens to the soul when a life ends."

"And the Roman soldiers paid homage to Mithra by way of offerings" asked Madoc "in the Temple of Mithras?"

"Yes" replied nain. "They would place gifts of pottery, wooden sculptures, wine, fruit, flowers, or their hard-earned money."

"Is it possible that there could be Ancient Roman coins buried in the secret underground passageway between Bryn Gosol Farm and the Temple of Mithras? Way below Saint Hilary's Church in Llanrhos?" asked Madoc.

"I'm sure that treasured items, those created, handled or worn by Ancient Romans will be there somewhere" assured nain.

"Why?" asked Seren suspiciously.

"We might need to use our metal detectors!" replied Madoc with a mischievous grin. "Like Jim and Allan used in the Segontium, field."

"Jim and Allan?" questioned nain.

"The two men in the newspaper article who recently found Ancient Roman coins in the Conwy Valley nain" reminded Seren.

The two women stared at Madoc. They had agreed to undertake an adventure together, a past life regression, the outcome of which would be placed in the hands of Destiny. Seren offered up a silent request for Ysbryd[31] to guide them onto their highest path, including Madoc. She could see his cogs whirring. Would Madoc choose to reveal the secrets held at Bryn Gosol Farm for the price of Ancient Roman coins? Enigmas of the Temple of Mithras and the ancient grimoire were long held by her, nain and taid. Would Madoc give them up? Surely not.

---

[31] Spirit

November 2023

Chapter 16 – Tick, Tock

Be open to the unknown.

On a mission, on the appointed day of the past life regression, nain entered the kitchen at Bryn Gosol Farmhouse as the kettle stopped boiling.

"Hello nain. You're early. Would you like a panad?

"Yes please, Seren. Where's Madoc?"

"He's working today for the Historical Society. He won't be back until late."

"Good. Then we'll be undisturbed when we do the past life regression. I'm a little bit apprehensive about it but I think that's how everyone feels when they venture into the unknown."

"It is. You're right. Here. I'll stir the tea clockwise to bring in good things. What's in this envelope?"

"Oh that? Open it. It's from the vet."

Across the honey oak table, nain passed a white envelope to Seren who held it for what seemed an age. Outside one magpie pecked nimbly at the grass, grabbed a grub, squeezed its quarry tightly then soared noiselessly into a beech tree.

'*One for sorrow*' thought Seren.

From the envelope Seren picked out a condolence card with an image of a full moon, the inscription '*smile, we walked for a while*' and a small packet of forget-me-not seeds.

"It's in memory of Moon" stated nain needlessly. "I thought we could plant the seeds in the back garden here at the Farm, if that's ok with you? There will not be a frost this winter."

Seren's eyes were fixed upon the card.

"Bryn Gosol Farm will always be your home, nain. You don't need permission to plant anything. Of course, we can place the forget-me-not seeds in the back garden. Let's do that before we go to the Temple of Mithras. It was thoughtful of the vet. Or, if you like we could plant the seeds on the side of the Vardre where we've buried Moon?"

"Let's do half and half as I don't get up the Vardre much these days Seren. We'll put some here by the back door and some on the mountain. How does that sound cariad tlws?"

Seren felt her heart crack as if she'd stepped on a delicate twig.

"It sounds perfect nain. Now, drink up we've got a lot to do. I'm glad to see you're wearing wellies. It's muddy where we're going."

After depositing seeds in remembrance of Moon, and afterwards mindful to wipe their muddy wellies in the boot room, the two women walked down the corridor to the front living room. In the inglenook, Star lay asleep on the rug. She had lost all her sparkle without Moon, her twin-flame and soulmate.

"Just pull the rug the dog is lying on Seren. Star won't wake up and we can get to the hidden staircase. I'll light the candle and grab your hawkstaff. I agree with Madoc, sometimes that piece of driftwood with its shimmering moonstone eye almost looks alive."

"It's as you always say nain, the hawkstaff is like Gandolf's staff which acts as an amplifier of magic, and feels energetic. I'll remember to stomp it on the floor to put energy into the ground and say, '*the deal is sealed*' when we've finished our ritual. Why don't we just move with the times though and carry a torch instead of a candle?"

"Two reasons. One, a candle is atmospheric and two, when the flame flickers it means our spirit guides are with us. You don't get that with a torch."

"Ok. We'll go old school."

Seren and nain heaved a stone flag from the farmhouse floor which led to a secret passageway. Struggling to carry lit candles, the hawkstaff, a thick blanket and a flask the pair clambered down the steep stone steps. They followed a long path to a musty place where the tunnel widened and revealed part of the hidden Temple of Mithras buried deep under Saint Hilary's church. Roman legionaries had secretly worshipped here. Dim embellishments of Mithras slaughtering a white bull and dining with Sol, the Sun God could be depicted on damp, rotting wooden pilings which held up the ceiling. Nain led Seren down a small dais to the central nave as shadows in the northern alcove bounced and sprang nimbly in the orange light.

Soothing in manner, Seren instructed nain to lie in the nave and wrapped her in a Welsh plaid, handstitched red and black tapestry blanket so that she would remain warm throughout the ritual. Strangely, usually brave nain felt trepidatious.

"Remember nain, we need to meditate before doing the past life regression. Make yourself comfortable. You're in control, you can stop at any time. I'll guide you. I'm going to stomp hawkstaff now" explained Seren and banged hawkstaff to put energy into the ground. "Choose a spot on the ceiling and focus upon it. Breathe deeply to the count of five, hold your breath to the count of five, breathe out to the count of five to relax yourself and enter a meditative state."

"I'm a little afraid, Seren" embarrassed nain exclaimed, with a quick glance at her granddaughter.

Seren was now in the driving seat and took control.

"Don't be fearful my cariad tlws" she soothed nain. "I'll be with you. You'll still hear my voice and feel sensations."

Following instructions carefully, Nain breathed deeply through her nose and exhaled through her mouth to calm her nerves, placing total trust in Seren. Once Seren felt that nain was relaxed enough she said, "Now we'll begin. Open your eyes nain. Continue to breathe deeply to the count of five, hold your breath to the count of five, breathe out to the count of five. I'll go from ten to one. As I say each number blink your eyes. When I reach one, close your eyes."

Nain followed instructions.

"Nain, in your mind's eye, can you see the steps?"

"Yes."

"Now I'm going to count to ten. As I count, walk up the steps, slowly."

Nain listened intently and sighed.

"Can you see a chair?"

"Yes"

"This is your safe space. You can always return to this chair. There are several doors before you. Choose one door which is drawing you to it. Tell me, what is the year on that door?"

"The year? It's 1724."

"Good. Now open the door and walk through it into a past life. Tell me what you see, hear, and feel" instructed Seren.

"I will."

Under kippered oak roof beams nain looked around her. She was standing on a stone floor strewn with hay. A freshly lit fire in an inglenook glowed brightly and the air smelled of musky burning wood. The room was familiar. Nain recounted to Seren what was happening.

The woman nain was watching had returned from meeting her lover in Marl Woods. She lifted her legs out of muddy boots, patted her mid-length heavy flannel dress woven from a red and navy fabric, and adjusted her white apron. A low-cut navy cotton blouse remained tightly fitted as she placed a white cotton cap of goffered folded fabric upon her head. She carried her black woollen cloak as she changed into grey woollen shoes, walked along a corridor, and opened the front door after a third knock reverberated around the farmhouse.

Seren watched nain who trembled as she described events.

"An elegantly dressed woman has entered the house, walked into the kitchen, and is now sitting stiffly in a carved wooden chair. She's obviously out of place at Bryn Gosol Farm and uncomfortable here. Her blue embroidered silk travelling coat trails around her leather clad feet."

This is what unfolded before nain's eyes.

"You must help, Angharad" said the woman, her eyes bleak in the sunlight which streamed through the open window. "Although you are only twenty-two, I know that in Conwy you are revered as a wise woman. You connect to nature and the Divine. You have created potions which have helped others."

Nain knew the woman was addressing her in a past life. She remained intent and relayed her inner visions to Seren.

"The lady who has recently moved into the Hall has been trying to conceive a child, without success" continued the woman. "Please will you use one of your mixtures to help her have a healthy pregnancy? She will pay you well for it Angharad. Five gold crowns."

"I don't usually charge for my help Miss Elizabeth" replied Angharad honestly.

"The lady insisted I give you money" stated Elizabeth as she looked around the sparse room at the layered kindling and the battered spinning wheel placed in a corner by the window.

"Sometimes Miss Elizabeth these events are not meant to be and that must be accepted. If nothing happens, Destiny has decreed it was never the intended way."

"Word around Conwy is that you have helped women in the past in this situation, and still do so in the present. Will you assist? I beseech you."

"I will create a concoction that may help the lady, Miss Elizabeth but there are no guarantees it will work."

"How long will the mixture take to create?"

"An hour or two Miss Elizabeth."

"I'll take my carriage into Conwy. When I return, you must come with me to the Hall, bring your potion and speak with the lady. Explain to her what she must do to help her conceive a much wished-for child. I'll be back in two hours."

With that, Elizabeth left the house.

As she lay wrapped in the Temple of Mithras, with shocked eyes nain scrutinised proceedings. Vigilantly she observed as Angharad waited a few minutes before she changed again into her muddy boots, walked to the back garden, cut leaves from rosemary, lavender, and chamomile herbs she had cultivated and returned to the house. Once in the kitchen, into a small silk bag she placed a shell from Conwy beach, a clear quartz crystal shaped in the diagonal and some of the herbs, the rest she boiled with honey, water, and bee pollen. The aromatic plants were left to steep whilst Angharad laid three white candles, a jar of thick golden honey, and the pale silk bag into a wooden box. Almost ready.

In the living room, she lifted a stone beside the inglenook fireplace and, holding a lit candle, carefully walked down stone steps and ran along a moist passageway to the nave of the Temple of Mithras. She pulled a key from her apron to open a gold box which was hidden under a stone floor tile embossed with the Ace of Cups. Angharad checked that the ancient grimoire was there, read an enchantment by candlelight, returned the book of spells to its rightful place, locked the gold box, and replaced it under the floor tile near the nave. The key she put deep into her clothing, next to her heart. Upon her return to Bryn Gosol Farm she changed into her woollen shoes, washed the floors, and hid the key in the kitchen where it did not look out of place.

When Elizabeth returned, the potion had already been spooned into a stoppered glass bottle. The wooden box was covered with a small white linen cloth. Angharad was ready for magic.

"These are the items I will take to the Hall, Miss Elizabeth."

"Good. Thank you Angharad. Bring them to the carriage. You may travel with me, but you must walk back home when you have finished. You will be well rewarded. Here are the five gold crowns as promised."

Angharad received the crowns and held them tightly in her left hand.

"Thank you, Miss Elizabeth. Excuse me for a moment while I prepare for the journey."

Nain watched Angharad walk down the corridor, into the front lounge, towards the inglenook fire. Angharad placed her hand on the floor, felt around the stone and heaved at a slab which moved just enough for her to place the gold crowns under it. The spot where steps led to the secret tunnel.

'*Interesting*' thought nain '*Angharad has just become richer than perhaps she ever thought. No wonder she's hiding the money.*'

Angharad returned to the kitchen wearing her long, black hooded woollen cloak.

"I am ready Miss Elizabeth."

Angharad picked up the small wooden box and carried it carefully to the waiting two-horse carriage. When both women had ascended and were securely sitting beside each other, Elizabeth said, "You are never to speak of this Angharad. The lady does not wish anyone to know."

"I am discreet Miss Elizabeth. I never speak of my healing. It is others that do so. Not me."

"Good. I am pleased that you understand the lady's dilemma. Her husband is desperate for a male heir. Without exaggeration he is a handsome man, but overwhelmed by his own importance and becoming increasingly angry, displeased with events. Within moments he can conjure an atmosphere in the Hall which is tense and where the lady is led to believe she is the culprit."

The two women continued their bumpy journey in silence, along narrow country lanes, past the Vardre, through Marl Woods and on to a magnificent Hall in the Conwy Valley. The carriage stopped on a gravel path where Elizabeth and Angharad alighted. They made their own way to the glittering drawing room where the lady of the Hall was writing.

Elizabeth said quietly, "M'Lady. Angharad is with me."

The lady turned to face Elizabeth and Angharad, her delicate features ashen as heavy rain clouds. A strange sense of unease rose within nain as she observed the three women. This triumvirate. This unholy alliance.

"She is here to help you. In this wooden box is the potion Angharad has made."

"What do we need to do Angharad?" replied the lady "and how long will it take as my husband is away on a hunt in Marl Woods. He will be back later this afternoon."

"I will be as quick as possible m'Lady."

Angharad pulled back the white linen cloth, removed the bottle, pulled out the stopper and passed it to the lady. The atmosphere was as strained as athletes' sinews.

"Shortly I will cast a spell and when I have finished you will need to drink this potion from the bottle" she instructed. "Every morning for seven days, eat toast smeared with thick honey as it has healing properties. There are three phases of the moon you must watch for and light one of these candles at each event" Angharad instructed.

"Which phases? What do you mean?" asked the lady.

"On the new moon, a full moon and at the end of a waning crescent moon, light one candle until it is no more" replied Angharad.

"I understand."

"Imagine yourself giving birth to a healthy baby boy. When it is a full moon bury this silk bag in your garden. Its contents of a clear quartz crystal, cowrie shell and herbs promise a successful pregnancy."

"Thank you Angharad. When will you do your magic spell?"

"If you sit here by the window, I shall do it now m'Lady. Please may I have a clean bowl filled with fresh water?"

"Yes" replied Elizabeth "I will bring one from the kitchen."

Alone together the lady's slender hand gently touched Angharad's arm. With the frightened look of the hunted, she said, "Angharad this is very important to my husband. Thank you for helping me delight him."

Elizabeth returned to the drawing room and passed the full bowl to Angharad who added a drop of frankincense oil, a magpie's feather, a small shell from Conwy beach, a tiny elder twig, and a sunflower seed picked from her back garden. Gently she asked the lady to touch the bowl and thus began her invocation, "Luna, Goddess of women, The fountain of life, Please help this woman to conceive a male baby, I ask your power of help, so let it be."

The woman looked terrified.

"Now m'Lady you must drink this potion" instructed Angharad "and return the bottle to me. Remember to light the first white candle tonight as it is a new moon, bury your little silk bag and eat plenty of honey. I will leave you now. Blessed be."

"Thank you Angharad" said the lady who smiled for the first time since they had met.

"M'Lady, be careful what you wish for" replied Angharad.

"I wish for my husband to be happy" the lady replied.

"Your wishes should be for yourself m'Lady as we never know what is in another's heart."

"I will show you out" said Elizabeth quickly.

At the end of the hallway an exquisite, vividly coloured plaster mantlepiece caught Angharad's attention. Breath quickly squeezed its way out of her lungs as she stopped in front of a gilded work of art.

"The man in the painting, Miss Elizabeth, how is he connected to this house?" she asked.

"That's the Lord of the Hall I was telling you about. M'Lady's husband, Myrick. I said he was handsome. Don't you agree?"

"Devilishly so" replied Angharad who recognised the long-lashed dashing man with a dark gaze which seemed to follow her from above the fireplace. This was her lover. Married! The father of her unborn child.

Nain visibly winced. '*Beauty without does not necessarily beget beauty within*' she thought.

***

Trembling, Angharad left the Hall and entered Marl Woods where the ground was pounded. She leaned against a wizened wych elm tree which crumbled to the touch. Raucous woodpeckers foraged in nearby ash trees. Ordinarily a walk here would offer joy, but not now. A cave close by was where she conceived the child, and her lover had promised to marry her. And what had she done? Given a magic potion to her lover's wife so that they could have a child together. The future for her own baby looked bleak. The source of gossip in Conwy for the rest of its life, and the possibility that a sibling would live the life of a Lord. Humiliation burned hot as a Welsh dragon's breath.

A decision was made in a moment. Resolutely Angharad walked the steep path. Off the beaten track, she headed for a deep well known locally as Jacob's Ladder. Her nain had recounted the legend of Jacob who had a dream about a ladder which was set on earth and reached heaven. He witnessed angels travelling up and down the ladder who encouraged him to fulfil his Destiny. This, said her nain, signified a divine connection between earth and heaven. Her nain had said that this well acted as a bridge between life and death which the soul crossed when a life ended and Mithra, one of three judges would decide what happened to the soul. Of course, what Jacob had not realised, related her nain, was that he had witnessed a worm hole in space. A different dimension of time.

On her journey, Angharad paused at the high limestone outcrop where once stood an Ancient Roman signal station, an aid to sailors who navigated the Conwy estuary. Eyes fixed on the swirling dark Irish Sea, she breathed the floating drops of sea spray, and made up her mind. Tonight Mithra would decide what would happen to her soul because her life was about to end deep inside the well. A well of souls. Or so she planned.

But Angharad did not know that the Three Goddesses of Fate control life from birth to death and even the Gods fear them. The first Fate, Nona spins the golden thread of life. She decides when souls are born. The second Fate, Decima measures the length of the thread of life for each soul. The third Fate, Morta cuts the thread of life. Only she has the power to choose how and when a person dies. The Fates, or witches weave the golden skein of life, add, or remove knots, unravel, and sever the skein at will. Not mortals.

The bright sunlight turned dim. The moon overtook the sun and forced darkness across Marl Woods. Traumatised Angharad stood beside Jacob's Ladder and sobbed until she slumped exhausted onto the boggy ground. In the early hours of the morning, Angharad's brother Brenin found her asleep by the well. He knew this place, circled as it was around his heart. They had played here as children. Made dens in caves, dared each other to climb deep into the black hole of the well, up and down until their arms ached. They had swung from tree ropes, created magic potions, slept under the stars, laughed until their sides ached and danced in the moon light. When she had not returned home, Brenin had known where to find Angharad.

He covered his sister with his thick cotton jacket and built a fire for warmth and light. From this Brenin lit a candle and foraged around the wood edges for wild, tan-coloured mushrooms, lavender, thyme, sage, and marjoram herbs. The ingredients he cooked in a small pan of water brought from Bryn Gosol Farm and patiently waited for his sister to awaken. When he pushed hair away from her thin face, Angharad's blue eyes opened. Gently he spooned the broth into her mouth.

"Eat this" he coaxed as she swallowed thirstily allowing the effect of the soup to burrow its way into her subconscious mind.

Once all the liquid had been drunk, she asked, "What are you doing here?"

"I came in search of you. The potion will make you feel better. Cure your melancholia."

"What makes you think something is wrong?" Angharad challenged.

"You didn't arrive home. I found you by Jacob's Ladder. They're clues that all is not good. It won't be long before this potion begins to work. You are always energized and excited when you eat this broth. Your visions are clearer too. We will set off home when the sun comes up. No rush" Brenin said calmly.

***

Months later, neighbours still called upon Angharad for help. As dusk fell rapidly, heavily pregnant she marched through Marl Woods followed closely by an icy north wind which promised snow. With woollen cloak clasped around her swollen stomach, her hands held firmly onto a glass bottle which contained home-made onion poultice. When she arrived at the labourer's cottage,

Evan Jones, the youngest of six children, had strenuous breathing. His life hung in the balance. Angharad gave him thyme, honey, and lavender to swallow, rubbed the onion compress onto his chest, cast a spell and waited until late in the evening until she was sure he would survive the night.

Fear rose within Angharad on the way home as she passed Saint Hilary's church where ghosts called out. With heavy legs her boots sloshed in the mud, keeping pace with the trees which swung in harmony to the wind's winter song. On the hill in front of her stood the solitary figure of the Devil's Tree, its naked branches shivering with cold. Underfoot she felt the pounding hooves of a horse long before she saw the rider, Myrick. He had no regard for man, woman, or beast. The vices of life came easily to him: wine, women, gambling. He rounded his steed to block Angharad's path at the Devil's Tree and dismounted.

"Where have you been?" he asked.

"To your labourer's cottage. I tended to the youngest child so that he did not die."

"Did you use one of your incantations?"

"Yes. It always made you smile when I created potions for us and chanted spells" laughed Angharad.

Sated with wine, he surged like a turbulent west wind, "I see you kept my child".

"I did" answered Angharad defiantly placing her hands protectively upon her stomach.

"There was no spell to rid you of it?" screamed Myrick as he dismounted.

Taken by surprise, Angharad reeled at the impact of a punch to her face and fell to the ground. Almost immediately a blue-purple bruise appeared on her skin.

"My wife is pregnant. She must never know that this child of yours is mine also, or next time we meet I will kill you" he threatened. "And the child."

'And you sir, will never know happiness' Angharad thought as she picked herself up off the floor and watched Myrick ride off towards Marl Woods and his Hall.

Within a few weeks of the fateful meeting, Myrick's wife, who suspected nothing, and his mistress who knew everything, each gave birth to a healthy baby boy.

***

He stole into Saint Hilary's church as any robber might. Cradled in his arms, with a fever his baby did not move. In the darkness Myrick knew exactly where to find the secret underground tunnel to the Temple of Mithras and Bryn Gosol Farm beyond, since Angharad had shown him. He was on a covert mission to see her and beseech her help in curing his child of a terrible fever. Stealthily he made his way past the Temple's central nave, stepped up the small dais, felt his way along the damp passageway where his search light depicted Mithra slaughtering a white bull and dining with Sol, the Sun God. Myrick lay his baby on the top step as he pushed up on the floor at Bryn Gosol Farm where he knew a gap fell. Once beside the inglenook he could see Angharad's baby asleep in its cradle.

Myrick had wept when pea-sized pustules appeared on his baby's skin to confirm the doctor's diagnosis of smallpox. There was never any original intention to harm Angharad or her baby. As he stood by the inglenook, Myrick's son drew in his last breath before his father had an opportunity to speak with or see Angharad. In a panic, Myrick removed Angharad's baby from its crib and replaced it with his dead son. Stealthily he made his way back down the tunnel to the Temple of Mithras. When he returned to the Hall, Angharad's child was placed safely in a cot beside Myrick's unsuspecting wife.

Two hours later, following a tip off from the local Lord, the police visited Bryn Gosol Farm. The unmarried mother was accused of witchcraft. When the dead baby was found in a cradle, Angharad was suspected of the murder of her illegitimate child and an indictment drawn.

When it came to a trial, under threat of losing his job and home, the labourer who worked for Myrick gave true evidence that Angharad had made a potion for his youngest son, Evan Jones. There was no mention that the boy had been cured. Despite pleading innocence, and claiming that the dead baby was not her child, Angharad was found guilty of causing death by witchcraft.

A thick rope was placed around her neck, and she was hung from a tree on The Square in the shadow of Conwy Castle. As her eyes bulged, she watched Myrick push his way through the crowd, hold up her baby in triumph just as the third Fate, Morta gently snipped her golden thread of life. This was Angharad's final image before she walked up Jacob's Ladder.

***

"Nain, find the chair" instructed Seren briskly.

Breathlessly nain replied "Yes, I've found it".

Nain looked pale and dishevelled by her past life regression. Seren offered her a cup of hot chocolate from a flask and a chocolate brownie. Both were received by nain with gratitude. Not trusting her emotions, nain waited for Seren to speak.

"You know nain that by learning lessons from each test, a person can become more enlightened, and the pathway opens to reveal the extraordinary as people aim to become their highest selves. It's all about learning lessons from the past to go forward into the future."

"Yes, the vision of the past has given me valuable information Seren. I know why I don't like being in The Square!" Nain paused. "I was naïve to believe that I was loved by a man when it was simply lust. I had not known he was married. My reputation in Conwy would have been in tatters."

Nain paced up and down the Temple. Seren tried to comfort her by saying "That's in the past. We can't change what's happened."

"We must realise that people we allow into our hearts can mortally wound us" whispered nain. "On the positive side" she smiled "my ancient grimoire was used to help others."

"I think it always was a spell book for good" reassured Seren. "Poor Angharad. "I wonder what happened to Myrick."

"Him? Perhaps he fell down Jacob's Well one night when he was drunk" replied nain unemotionally "and was never heard of again."

"And your baby?"

Nain took a deep breath.

"If I hadn't witnessed my past life, I would never have believed that I was hanged for murder. And the baby? Of his Destiny, I have no idea. Perhaps his life turned out to be useful. One where he did not let anyone down, and that's very important in life. When I met her, I sensed that the Lady would have a grief-stricken existence. She would always have been afraid that someone would reveal the truth about the boy, and her feckless husband. A woman knows her own child. Having no peace of mind means a blighted life. That's an important lesson to learn."

"There wouldn't have been any pictures of your baby?" asked Seren carefully. "To identify him I mean."

"No. At that time, no-one would ever have recognised that the child Myrick professed was his own was also mine. My son resembled his father. Quite easy to mix up one baby with another I suppose. And if anyone did suspect … they would have feared for the child's life, or their own, and remained silent. No-one would have believed the word of a woman accused of witchcraft over that of a powerful Lord."

"Oh nain. What a tragic story. The paths we choose can be dark and dangerous."

"Indeed. At least I can pinpoint when I used magic mushrooms!" laughed nain. "Have to be very careful with those" she cautioned.

"Let's go back to Bryn Gosol Farm" suggested Seren. "We can sit in the back garden, under the moonlight and be invigorated by bathing in the moon's rays. We'll moon bathe. It's less challenging."

Seren wondered if anyone ever asked nain if she needed help, instead of always beseeching her support. She decided to be mindful of this in the future.

By the time the two women arrived back at Bryn Gosol Farm they were emotionally exhausted. Seren made them both a refreshing drink of lavender tea, stirred clockwise to bring in good things. Under the bright silver rays of the moon the two women sat in companionable silence. Madoc joined them, bringing with him paper covered fish and chips from the Fisherman's chip shop on Castle Street which he had bought on his way home from work.

As he ate, Madoc innocently enquired "How did the past life regression go, nain?"

"It was perplexing Madoc. I don't want to say any more about it" she replied.

Madoc's eyebrows raised. He looked at Seren who silently shook her head to indicate '*don't push it*'.

"Anyone want some chips?" he invited inanely. "They're tasty."

"No thanks Madoc" said Seren who directed her attention to nain. "At least nain I feel prepared for the past life regression with Gaius Romeo Cangini. What will be revealed when we meet?"

"I suppose it was inevitable that one day the three of you would be together again" replied nain. "Call it serendipity or Fate. Destiny will weave her magic. What I'd like to know is, who or what brought him to Conwy?"

"Indeed" said Madoc darkly. "The simple truth is everyone has their own narrative. Wonder what his story could be?"

It wouldn't be long before they found out the remarkable details.

November 2023

Chapter 17 – Numerology 444: A Big Change Is Coming

celeriter aqua per clepxydram currit.[32]

Madoc Thomson finished his breakfast of smoked salmon, scrambled eggs and sour dough bread before he spoke to Seren.

"I'm going to meet Ozymandias today."

"Who?"

"A traveller from an antique land."

"What are you on about?" demanded Seren.

Madoc laughed. "It was my mother's favourite poem. Ozymandias by Percy Bysshe Shelley. It's the only poetry I know. It begins: '*I met a traveller from an antique land*'. Ozymandias is about Ramses II, who was a despotic Ancient Egyptian Pharaoh. As a free-range thinker, Shelley believed that science and magic combined to provide a heady potion. He considered himself haunted by apparitions."

"Did he now? You are full of surprises Madoc Thomson. Fancy you knowing a poem by Percy Bysshe Shelley! Who are you meeting and where?"

Madoc was taciturn.

"Well?" Seren demanded and waited for an explanation. Annoyingly for her, it was not immediately forthcoming. "Sometimes you can be really irritating" she said.

Madoc feigned surprise at her outburst. "What? Me? Maddening? I know. It's great, isn't it? Maybe that's why my mother called me Madoc, short for maddening. You're lovely but sometimes you're slow on the uptake" he teased.

"Come on. Tell me."

---

[32] The water runs swiftly through the water clock.

"I'm about to meet someone from an antique land, who's a scientist but also believes in the occult."

"So …?"

"I'm going to make a social connection with a certain Italian man. Come on Seren. Put the clues together."

Seren was silent. Madoc took this as a cue to slice through her thoughts.

"He died in Italy y'know" continued Madoc. "In the Tyrrhenian Sea. Not far from Genova where we will visit next March with nain. It was a boating accident."

"Who died near Genova? You've lost me. Completely."

"Keep up Seren! Percy Bysshe Shelley died in the Gulf of Spezia, near Genova. We can go there when we are in Liguria. He was out sailing, and his boat was spotted by other sailors during a storm, flying too much sail. The boat capsized and Shelley's body was found washed up on the beach days later. When he was cremated, his heart did not burn, so his wife Mary kept it wrapped in cloth until she died."

Seren shuddered. "That's a gruesome tale at breakfast."

"See your husband is full of surprises; like your boyfriend!"

"I don't have a boyfriend, you idiot."

"Well … I'm off to meet someone who you seemed quite taken with when you told me about your recent encounter."

That was Seren's lightbulb moment.

"You're going to meet Romeo?"

"Indeed."

"Don't be ridiculous Madoc. He's NOT my boyfriend" protested Seren. "Why are you meeting him and where? And how did that come about?" she blustered.

"Gareth asked if I fancied going diving and whether I minded if his work colleague, Romeo joined us. I've arranged to meet them at Moelfre Beach. We're going to search the shattered wrecks for gold."

"In November? Are the three of you insane? The water will be freezing."

"I've got my wetsuit. We won't dive for long. I'll bring you back a piece of gold if I find one among the wreckage."

"You won't find anything. It'll be too dark. Too cold. Too choppy."

"Thanks for the vote of confidence Seren. I'll be home for dinner. The forecast is clear for tonight, so I've arranged to photograph the Leonids on the Vardre with Gareth and Romeo. There's no moon so we might see around ten meteors an hour fording through the sky. It'll be spectacular" he said running around the kitchen flapping his arms and making whooshing noises.

"Ahhh, you're busy tonight observing the night sky? Where does the name come from? Leonids?"

"The constellation Leo because the meteors radiate outward from the lion's mane."

"Interesting."

"Do you want to join us?"

"I don't know. What time will the show begin?"

"From midnight to five in the morning. We're going to set up a tent, have a few beers, take some photographs."

"Will Haf be there?"

"Not sure if Gareth has invited her. I think things are a bit dark, cold and choppy on that front. I'll be back about six. Think about the invitation. See you later."

With a half-opened mouth, a preoccupied Seren watched as the front door closed behind Madoc. Once she heard his antique Jaguar car rasp its way along the drive, Seren picked up her mobile telephone and sent a text to Haf. Within moments she had arranged to meet her friend for lunch in Conwy at Pen-y-Bryn Tearooms. 'What on earth is going on?' she thought.

***

On the sheltered beach of Moelfre, Romeo's features were impenetrable as he paced along the pebbles and watched the ashen-crested waves. It was eleven years since the last time he had dived with Hell in the warm, surging, lazuline sea off the Bay of Baiae. Today a west wind whipped up the image of an enchantress, a ghostly grey-green, captivating sea-nymph, an apparition of Hell. Romeo recalled being led to the commotion of her bed, remembered touching the gentle undulations of her supple body, could taste her sweet scent on the sea spray in the air, recognised her uncontrollable passion in the rhythm of the waves. As untamed as the sea, Hell's greatest imperfection was narcissism. He knew that. Even after eleven years apart, he could see it when, with cocked head she made an unexpected approach to him recently in Bologna.

The air was fresh. The vision coiled away. Romeo stood on the shore, turned towards Moelfre town, and watched as a smiling Gareth approached him, accompanied by a brooding, balding man. Madoc. The triumvirate shook hands. Madoc noted the two impressively tattooed magpies on Romeo's neck but chose not to comment upon them.

"Morning. I've brought diving suits from the university. We can change into them at the back of the camper van" suggested Gareth. "Keep the wind off us."

The three men moved along the beach as the wind sang like a soothing siren. Gareth dragged out the diving suits, passed one each to Romeo and Madoc and they began to undress. As they changed, Romeo glanced across at the other men and stifled a gasp when he spotted tattoos of an eagle and a bull rippling on Madoc's muscular arms. The same colour and design as he had witnessed on the floor of the underwater villa when he dived in Baiae with Hell. The same colour and design he had observed in his vision tattooed on the Legate, Titus. Leader of the feared Legio X in Julius Caesar's army.

Madoc saw Romeo stare at his arms. With the bottom half of the wetsuit already stretched on his body, Madoc held out his hand to Romeo.

"Good to meet you at last Romeo, my friend. I've heard so much about you from Seren and Gareth that I feel as though I already know you. Welcome to Wales."

"Thank you, Madoc. I'm very pleased to be here and delighted to meet you. For some reason, I think we were destined to meet."

"Indeed" responded Madoc.

Gareth coughed. "Tell me. Are we going diving, or are we having a love-in now that you two have finally caught up with each other?"

Romeo raised his eyes to the heavens and Madoc grinned.

***

A sense of unease encircled Seren as she waited impatiently for Haf in the tearoom. She had consulted nain's ancient grimoire that morning before creating a potion for her agitated friend. Seren fingered the lavender glass-stoppered bottle which held a highly diluted brew. The same infusion used in Ancient Roman times to kill wolves. Extremely poisonous if taken neat.

Flushed-faced Haf entered Pen-y-Bryn, her eyes darted around the room. The reddened expression told Seren everything she needed to know. As suspected, Haf was in a high state of agitation.

"Sit next to me cariad tlws" said Seren gently. "I've ordered café latte for us both, cheese and Branston pickle sandwiches followed by an elephant's foot to share. Your favourite, I think. I hope you don't mind?"

"That's thoughtful Seren, thank you" responded Haf "but I'm not sure I'm up to eating anything. My stomach is as knotted as the back of my mother's embroidery."

"I've brought a little potion for you. It'll ease your mind and blow the storm away. Take a small spoonful of it in a glass of milk tonight. It'll calm your nerves, help you sleep, and clear your mind. You'll feel much better in a day or two. Now. Tell me all. What's going on?"

"Do you remember my reading with you last month?" quizzed Haf.

"No cariad tlws. I never remember my readings otherwise I'd go berserk." Seren laughed, then caught herself. "Why? Was something wrong with it?"

"No. Nothing wrong with the reading Seren. Everything upside down with me!"

Seren waited as Haf composed herself. Strawberry blonde hair tumbled around her pixie face as her green eyes cast apprehension.

"Tell me" urged Seren.

Registering a high pitch, Haf replied, "My life has just gone topsy turvy overnight and I don't know what to do." She paused when the waiter delivered food and drink to the table.

"For goodness' sake Haf, what's going on?" demanded Seren.

"You were right when you said in your reading that I would change jobs. I've talked things through with Gareth and I'm setting up my own business offering holistic acupuncture."

"Great. That's positive" reassured Seren. "And …?"

"My father unexpectedly gave me my nain's ring when we went out for his birthday meal. I was flabbergasted, but delighted. You said he would, and I didn't believe you."

Seren felt her stomach lurch with intensity. It never occurred to her that Haf would doubt her prognostications. She gulped to quell the butterflies bouncing around her tummy.

"I noticed the ring as soon as you walked into the room, Haf. It brings with it plenty of bling. It's gorgeous" admired Seren. "I'm delighted he had a change of heart."

Haf smiled. "Me too. My taid gave this ring to my nain three months after they met each other, so it holds their story. It's a tangible link to them. It feels great to wear it."

Seren nodded, encouraging Haf to speak more.

"Gareth and I have been invited to a wedding in Florida. My cousin, who's forty and everyone thought had been left on the shelf, is getting married to someone she's known forever. It's so unexpected. But I think that's the wedding you saw in my reading."

Haf imitated Seren's voice, '*I see a wedding over water, there are rollercoasters and boats. The chapel has purple and pink flowers at the side of it. The setting is spectacular. There is a honeymoon where the pink flamingos wander freely.*'

Seren laughed, surprised at Haf's accurate impersonation. "Cheeky madam. Carry on" insisted Seren.

"My cousin is going on a safari tour through Serengeti for her honeymoon to see pink flamingos! And whilst we're in Florida, bloody Gareth wants to visit Busch Gardens to see the pink flamingos at the park's Egypt exhibit! Why we can't see them at Chester Zoo I've no idea."

"Hang on. Why *bloody* Gareth? What's wrong there?" Seren asked.

Haf ignored the question and carried on speaking in between nibbles of food. "We bought the camper van you foresaw that we'd get."

"I know, Madoc told me. Gareth's using it to carry around the diving gear and I hear he's acquired a metal detector too. We've already bought one on the strength of the Roman find at Segontium. Next thing you know, that will become a new hobby for the four of us whether you and I like it or not!"

"It won't become my hobby Seren" said Haf, her face wan.

"What do you mean? Why not? It'll be great fun."

Flatly Haf answered, "After our holiday in Florida, Gareth is leaving Wales. '*For good*' he said. Without me."

"What? Why? When? Does Madoc know?"

Haf placed her Destiny gently into Seren's hands. "As my spiritual guide, I'm the one who needs answers from you. Despite my reservations, you've never led me along the wrong path." Then she made a surprising announcement. "It's all to do with Romeo."

"Ok. I'm trying to piece together the fragments you're giving me Haf" Seren replied good-naturedly and took a deep breath.

"You're making a fresh start. You've changed jobs. You and Gareth are going to a wedding in Florida. You bought a camper van between you, now you're splitting up, and it's all got to do with Romeo?"

"That just about sums it up" Haf responded.

"What the hell has Romeo got to do with you?" demanded Seren, then an idea sprang like cold water from Conwy waterfall.

"You've not been seeing Romeo, have you? Oh Haf, he's a lady's man" stated Seren accusingly. "He's not the one for you my dear. Someone else is meant to be with that bundle of joy."

"Don't be a complete idiot. It's nothing to do with a romance and everything to do with Gareth wanting something more than living in Conwy."

"Oh. What's wrong with Conwy?" demanded Seren.

"Nothing. To you and me. Everything to a man who wants to be '*a free spirit experiencing new-fangled ideas, fresh people, innovative food, smelling the perfume of lemons*'. That's what he said. Gareth and Romeo have swapped jobs. Gareth has stayed to introduce Romeo to his colleagues at Bangor University, during which time they will swap ideas about astrophysics, and then Gareth will live in Bologna. He has known about it since August and never said a word until this weekend. The git. He intends to take the camper van so that he can tour around Italy when he's not working at the university. It's a three-year stint but Gareth says he has no intention of ever returning to Wales. He said he's '*tired of the view*' whatever that means."

"Oh Haf. Did he ask you to go with him?" asked a startled Seren.

"Yes. But he wants different things to me. I would like to have children and bring them up here by the sea. I love living in Conwy. I don't want to leave my family or friends. Also, what I'm most afraid of is … change" Haf admitted. "He said he never promised me marriage or a family and he's right. He didn't. He aspires to be unfettered. A confirmed bachelor. No commitments."

Seren asked kindly. "And how would you like me to help you?"

Have you got your Romani cards with you? The ones used by that French woman, Mademoiselle something or other."

Seren frowned then laughed at the lack of description and waited for Haf to continue.

"You know, the Sybil you told me about who studied mathematics and astronomy as part of her prophecies and published books of her personal divinations."

"You're on the right track Haf. You mean Mademoiselle Marie-Anne Lenormand. Yes. I've got them with me. But listen. Gareth will be with Madoc and Romeo tonight on the Vardre and an acquaintance of nain's, Naomi will be visiting her. Why don't I invite Naomi and nain to Bryn Gosol and you can come too? I didn't get the chance to tell Madoc this morning before he dashed off. Naomi is going to do a sitting for us. She can do it at Bryn Gosol Farmhouse, and you can join in. Naomi knows the history of my Romani cards and you might find it interesting to talk with her. What do you say?"

"What's a sitting?" asked Haf.

"You'll see tonight if you come. Eight o'clock. Now. Are you sure you want a reading with the Romani cards" added Seren.

Haf stared at her, agog with silent expectation.

Seren said anxiously, "Haf, a Sibyl can give advice based on interpretation. It doesn't have to be taken or acted upon. You know that don't you?"

"I do" Haf nodded, her face full of eager expectation. "I'm placing my Destiny and trust in you for the next big decisions in my life Seren. Please guide me as I don't know what to do" insisted Haf.

Seren lightly tapped Haf's hand and quietly called upon a golden circle of protection. In answer to Haf she said, "There are many people who argue that there is no Divine plan, and happenstance befalls us. Others think that Sibyls, such as Marie-Anne Lenormand are only for the credulous and ignorant. I choose to keep an open mind."

Haf frowned as she looked at Seren. "Me too" she agreed.

"Now Haf. If you really wish me to read you here, the cards are in my handbag. I always carry them with me, but they're brutal" warned Seren. "You do mean the ones which offer straight advice, no holds barred?"

"Yes. Those."

Glancing over her shoulder Seren whispered to Haf, "Eyes down, look in."

Spellbound, Haf watched Seren open her worn tan leather handbag and remove a lilac velvet pouch. Gently she unpicked the silk rope tie. Across the table Seren passed the innocuous looking small pack of cards to Haf, and asked her to shuffle them. Once done, Haf returned the deck to Seren. Carefully, Seren sifted through the cards, searching for the Lady card. This would represent Haf in the divination. When she found it, Seren removed the benign card and placed it face up on the centre of the table. Seren returned the cards to Haf, who shuffled again then, under instructions from Seren, plucked out seven cards. Haf passed the cards face down to Seren.

Adroitly placing the cards in a pyramid shape, Seren's hands quickly laid three cards face down on the left of the table to denote the past. She speedily arranged one card underneath the Lady card to signify the current moment. The remaining three cards she positioned face down on the right of the table to indicate the future.

Beleaguered by a vortex of change, the trumpet of prophecy was about to be blown for Haf.

One by one Seren turned over the cards.

"These are the past cards.

The Coffin and the Tower. They show the end of a relationship which will happen quickly. There are huge blockages in this liaison, and you are not in charge of the situation. One partner, in your case Gareth, wishes to move on.

Look. Here's the Heart card. Your heart is the theme of this issue. It's all about love. This bond between you would have carried on, but choices have become the catalyst for change.

Directly underneath you, the Lady, is the Amour card. Ouch. This signifies an unpleasant surprise with a love relationship.

Haf. These cards are brutal. You must accept this change as it's Gareth's choice. The end of your attachment would have happened anyway somewhere along the line."

Anger seared Haf's stomach. Her face flushed.

"Look Haf. If something is meant for you, it will not pass you by. Let's see what these future cards hold for you."

Seren turned over the Anchor card. "You will always live by the sea. The Anchor denotes stability, and a steadfast love. A Pisces or Cancerian man will be your prospective husband. You will experience happiness in love and business. You must go through this unsettling experience with Gareth to meet a new man."

Haf frowned. A puzzled, inquisitive look. Her face showed she was beginning to untangle the knots of her life.

"Go on" she urged Seren who turned over the next card.

"House. Denotes a love of life, stability, a new love, happiness. Look at the background in this illustration, it's similar in shape to The Orme. It'd be funny if you ended up living on a farm up The Orme" said Seren pointing in the direction of Llandudno.

"Great" affirmed Haf perkily. "That's reassuring. Keep going. What's the last card?"

"Children. You will have two children with this new man."

Seren watched as Haf unfurled.

"Thanks Seren. I love Gareth unconditionally and I will let go of him, but I can't keep in touch with him. That would be too hurtful. To know what he's doing with his life without me. That would be hard to bear. The ugly truth is, Gareth doesn't love me enough and knowing that makes my guts wrench. I need time to think things through."

Seren paid attention to Haf.

"I meant what I said about tonight, Haf. Madoc will be out. Please come over to Bryn Gosol. I'm sure it will be interesting to meet Naomi, I've never met her before, and she's never done a sitting with nain. Shall I see you at eight o'clock?"

Haf eyed Seren cautiously. "Ok. I'll be there at eight. See you later. And Seren … thank you. I think Gareth might just be about to get a shock."

Haf was right. In the early evening when she told Gareth their relationship was over and she did not wish him to keep in contact, he reacted angrily. Perhaps he realised too late that Haf was good for him. But even he should realise, no-one waits forever.

***

In the kitchen of Bryn Gosol Farmhouse Seren laid out the table for dinner as a three-bean chilli gurgled on the stove. The basmati rice was already cooked, placed in a blue pot waiting to be served. Since he had arrived home, Madoc had given monosyllabic answers to an array of Seren's questions.

"You've been almost silent since you walked into Bryn Gosol. What's wrong with you?" Seren demanded.

"I'm sorry I'm not following with passionate interest the intrigue of Gareth's and Haf's love affair" Madoc finally announced angrily as he sat at the kitchen table.

"I just thought that you might have an opinion about your best friend departing Wales, packing in his job, separating from his girlfriend, and leaving you. That's all" replied Seren sniffily.

"Do not ask me again" warned Madoc.

"I just thought we could have an open conversation Madoc Thomson. On any topic. That's all" stormed Seren.

They ate their meal in silence as the day turned to evening.

"Nain's coming over later. And a woman she met at a produce fayre, Naomi. And Haf" Seren informed Madoc.

In a matter-of-fact voice, he replied, "I'm going out. As you know. I'll be back in the morning."

The oak door slammed behind Madoc as he marched out abruptly.

"Men. They can't quite seem to get the art of good communication" Seren muttered to herself. "Your mother named you correctly. You can be MADDENING, MADOC THOMSON" she shouted in the empty house. Her voice echoed throughout Bryn Gosol. "And I wonder if this new kid on the block, Romeo is like Ozymandias? If so, don't be fooled by any impressive exploits of his Madoc Thomson, because Ozymandias was also arrogant, tyrannical and did NOT make morally good decisions."

Seren went to have a shower to cool down. Had he heard her, Madoc would have diplomatically ignored this outburst for he knew his wife could not be stifled.

November 2023

Chapter 18 – The Sitting

'A riddle, wrapped in a mystery, inside an enigma.'[33]

Nobody knows the right answer about the cosmos. That's the wonderful thing about the universe, so much is still open to debate despite there being successful theories which have been collected, built upon, and used by the most brilliant minds. In short, the cosmos is an enigma.

Madoc believed it was not simply the universe that was a mystery. His friend Gareth could be defined as riddling. They had been mates since infant school and Madoc thought he was joking when Gareth said he was moving to Bologna. But it was true. An undeniable fact. And where did that leave Madoc? Without a best friend, that's where!

Out of the classic maroon Jaguar car Madoc heaved a Sony A7IV camera, telescope and stand preparing to capture, in all its splendour, the Leonid meteor shower. There was less light pollution on the Vardre than in Conwy town. He had arrived earlier than anticipated to meet Gareth and Romeo because of Seren's unceasing questions.

'*Women*' he thought '*sometimes have too much to say, especially when I want to be quiet: Are you all right? Is something wrong? Have I offended you? What's the matter? Had a bad day?'* he mimicked. *'Bloody hell. Can't a man have some peace and quiet?'*

The news of Gareth leaving Wales was a little too hard to bear. Madoc assumed his world was about to become a little greyer by the removal of his close friend. Memories oscillated of the two of them playing on the Vardre, swimming in the icy Irish Sea, surfboarding on the wild waves, pretending to be football icons

---

[33] Said by Winston Churchill, 1941

on Conwy beach or simply sitting staring at the stars together. They had never kept secrets from each other before. The salty stinging in his eyes took Madoc by surprise.

As the strained frayed border between early evening and night gently unravelled, Madoc set up a small camp around his waterproof tent. He drew his muddy-brown rainproof coat around him, dug a modest fire pit, encircled it with stones, gathered dry twigs, dry leaves, dry grass, needles, dry bark and, with the firewood he had bought in Conwy, lit a fire.

In his haste to leave Bryn Gosol he had forgotten his provisions. *'Damn'* he thought *'bloody women can be a distraction.'* Luckily, he had remembered the three blue canvas seats, like a director's chair which he arranged neatly around the campfire. The caw of rooks returning home echoed around the Vardre as Madoc sat, waiting patiently for Romeo and Gareth. *'Wonder what the next scene has in store for me?'* he questioned the west wind and inky sky. Stark silence greeted him.

It was another two hours before Madoc heard Romeo and Gareth striding up the Vardre. Their voices loud and excited carried on the wind. Madoc stoked the fire and watched shadows dance on the hills. He overhead Gareth say, "And I know that everything starts out with low entropy, but the cosmos will likely become utter chaos over time".

"Exactly" agreed Romeo "because as dark energy increases across the universe, at some point everything will be torn apart."

"But not in our lifetime Romeo, so we will still be able to see the stars and planets tonight."

Both men laughed.

"And if we could travel through spacetime at almost the speed of light we'd be able to time travel" Romeo said excitedly.

Quickly Gareth made mental calculations. "That means if we left Earth for three years, then over two thousand years would have flown by at our time of return."

"If we went forward or backward in time, we wouldn't recognise anything" exclaimed Romeo.

"We'd probably die instantly at the shock of witnessing such stark changes to what we know now" replied pragmatic Gareth. Then he reproached Romeo by adding, "Time only moves forward. It can't move backwards. As a scientist, you know that."

"Hmm. I'm not so sure Gareth. In a few days' time I'll be going back in time through a past life regression with Seren."

"I've told you, that's utter nonsense. Seren cannot possibly take you back in time. You're off your rocker. She's batty as a fruit cake and how she's persuaded Madoc that what she does for a living is a great idea, I don't know because he's a normal bloke."

"Hey, are you two discussing wormholes? The Einstein–Rosen bridges? Tunnels through the fabric of spacetime as immortalised in Blake's painting of Jacob's Ladder?" interrupted Madoc who had heard the affront to Seren and chose to deflect it. "I caught part of your conversation" he said, eying Gareth reproachfully.

"There is a scientific notion that two particles can remain connected across vast distances, but as for us being able to time travel through tunnels warped by space, well, that has never been proven" answered Gareth. "And we scientists need evidence" he announced pompously.

"Perhaps you have a point Gareth" responded Romeo. "But some of the most exceptionally gifted scientists have been guided by their imagination about space, and time. They've altered conventional beliefs about reality. Take Richard Feynman and John Wheeler as an example. One a conservative scientist, the other a scientist full of wild ideas. Between them they were able to consider contradictory possibilities about quantum physics, wormholes, and portals to the future and past. They believed time travel possible."

"So, you disagree that time is only forward in motion, Romeo?" asked Madoc.

"I do. And to prove it, I'd like to invite you both to my past life regression with Seren. What do you say?" challenged Romeo.

"I'm in" said Madoc immediately.

Gareth plucked up the courage to reply, "I'm not getting involved in witchy nonsense".

"Look Gareth. You know that Seren and I are spiritual. My wife takes these matters very seriously and you should respect her. Show consideration to us and our beliefs even if it's not what you trust to be true."

Gareth remained silent.

After a short while, using himself as an excuse, Madoc broke the tension when he announced, "As I'm the host this evening I must confess that I haven't brought any food or drink".

"That's all right, mate. No worries as we have enough for a party or two tonight" soothed Gareth.

"And some extras" said Romeo holding a few spliffs in his hand.

'*So that's how it's going to be*' thought Madoc. "I'm game" he said.

The three men sat around the glowing campfire. Alcohol flowed freely between them like amber resin springs from trees in the sun's heat. It lubricated their mouths, loosening their grip on reality. Madoc took a huge drag of marijuana and laughed.

"It's great to see that my old team Wrexham are going a storm in League Two Gareth since they were promoted at the end of last season. They've just beaten Morecambe by six goals."

"I heard that scoreline on the radio. Have you watched the tv programme about their move from non-League football? Those two American actors ..."

"You mean Ron McElhenney and Ryan Reynolds?" asked Madoc.

"*Rob* McElhenney" Gareth replied dryly. "And Ryan is Canadian American which, I think, is an important difference. The co-owners of the club have tripled its value and put the little town of Wrexham on the world map. I've heard that it's difficult to find accommodation in town when Wrexham play at home and even American fans are visiting."

"Great for North Wales, Madoc."

"Indeed" he replied and turned his attention to Romeo. "Do you follow football Romeo?"

"I follow an Italian and an English football team."

"Oh? Which?" asked Madoc surprised.

"In Italy, when I have time I watch Serie A, then my team is Bologna because that's where I'm based. Or that's where I was based, but no longer. I also observe the results of Newcastle United. They are doing well this season under Eddie Howe" stated Romeo.

Madoc looked astonished. "Is that why you have two magpies tattooed on your neck? To represent Newcastle United?"

Romeo nodded.

"Why Newcastle United? Why not the more famous Manchester United?" he added. "You could have a red devil tattooed on your neck."

"No. No. No. Definitely no devils for me. Magpies. They symbolise bravery and offer protection but having them on my neck also acts as a warning to people, that I'm no pushover and know whom to trust. The *real truth* is that the tattoo is in honour of my grandfather who played football for Newcastle United. Their emblem is magpies."

"Was he a good player?" quipped Gareth.

"The best. Of course. A brilliant shapeshifter. On the football pitch and in life" answered Romeo. "Now. Who would like another beer?"

"Me mate" agreed Madoc who saw that Romeo wished to change the subject.

"I'll have another, Romeo. And a doobie too if there is one left," said Gareth.

"You got it" said Romeo, passing marijuana to Gareth as images of his grandfather faded to sienna.

"Is Seren going to be here tonight?" asked Gareth.

"No. She's with Haf, nain and some stranger who nain invited over called Naomi. They're having a sitting."

"What's that?" questioned Gareth.

"I think it's where this Naomi woman communicates with spirits and passes on messages to the others" explained Madoc.

"Sounds like we're also having a sitting with spirits tonight, Madoc" announced Romeo boldly.

"Oh" said a nonplussed Gareth taken by surprise. "We're not doing any of that witchy stuff are we? Gives me the creeps." Unaware of his continued disrespect, Gareth turned full attention to Madoc. "How is Seren? Keeping well?"

"She's ok. But I left Bryn Gosol rather early tonight. Seren couldn't stop asking questions this evening. One after the other. I wonder if Haf's taken your news badly Gareth and that's why Seren was jabbering on."

"I'll tell you Haf hasn't taken it terribly at all" Gareth declared in reply. "She told me tonight that I should go to Bologna without her and never contact her again. She's ended it mate. She's the one who's finished with me. I never saw that coming."

"Did she call you selfish?" asked Madoc.

A shadow flickered across Gareth's face. "No. She was calm. Looked me straight in the eye. Wished me luck. Kissed my cheek. Walked away. She never looked back. How hard is she?"

"That's women for you. Think you've got them sussed and then pow … they thump you in the stomach when you're least expecting it and bring you to your knees" replied Madoc. "Then kick you in the face" he added sombrely. "Metaphorically I mean, not literally."

"Things not going too well with Seren then?" asked Gareth.

"As soon as I walked through the door tonight, she started asking me questions about my day, then telling me news about someone I vaguely know and don't care about and interrogating me about you and Haf. I like peace and quiet to unwind. I want my home to be a calm sanctuary not the Spanish bloody Inquisition" said Madoc with conviction "full of noise."

Gareth stood tall. "Women. They don't get that do they? Haf would talk incessantly about feelings and emotions and get angsty because someone said *this* to her or *that* to her" responded Gareth. "And as for text messages. Well. I found it was always safer to send a thumb up or a thumb down emoji. Words wreak havoc, mate. They can be misconstrued. Haf would often take ages to ponder '*did a text mean this or did it mean that*' when all that's been sent is the word 'ok'. Safer to say nothing. A picture covers a thousand words" Gareth concluded.

"Maybe if you'd taken the time to understand Haf, listened to her, paid her a little attention, she might have stayed with you" highlighted Madoc. "You can't have your cake and eat it too Gareth. You didn't offer her what she wanted."

Earlier that evening Gareth's sense of pride had prevented him from begging Haf to go with him to Bologna. Although he did not want marriage and children, he loved Haf and knew he would be lost without her. Now he would have to place his energies into work and exploring Italy alone. Thankfully tonight, Madoc, Romeo, alcohol and drugs were able to push away his melancholia. For now, at least. But this was to be the beginning of the downward maelstrom which would engulf Gareth in Italy. Divine punishment or his weakness?

Romeo stood by the fire, dragged on the remnants of weed in his cigarette and added to the conversation.

"Whilst we men let everything wash over us, don't we?" he laughed. "And you two have just summed up that men are from Mars and women are from Venus."

"That's right Romeo. They are" agreed Madoc. "Have you never had any woman trouble?"

"Me? Plenty of hassles" replied Romeo enthusiastically. "Possibly all self-inflicted. Except for one, recently."

Interest piqued, both men replied in unison "Go on".

Under the influence of alcohol and drugs he confessed, "It was an encounter that emotionally paralysed me".

"Great" said Madoc. "Let's sit by the fire, and have another beer whilst you spill your guts" he laughed. "Gareth, grab the lagers. Here's a burger Romeo. I assumed dealing with women would be effortless for you."

"Me? I attract trouble wherever I go" announced Romeo as he nonchalantly sucked his spliff.

"Looks like you don't care too much either?" questioned Gareth.

"Non credo.[34] Usually. But this one, I did care. Somehow, I seem to have developed the marvellous ability of straying from the path of my highest good."

The triumvirate toasted their drinks.

"To our highest good" declared Madoc.

"Here, here" agreed Gareth.

"Well. Come on Romeo. Tell us about being paralysed so we might avoid the same fate" demanded Madoc.

Romeo chuckled. "I should have known from the start that I was in trouble. Her name was Hell."

"Ouch. That was a definite, in-your-face sign mate" stated Madoc.

---

[34] I don't believe so.

"A sign? What are you on about?" demanded Gareth.

"Signs from the universe. You use your senses including your sixth sense, a gut feeling about something. You must listen to it. I'm sure Gareth that even you have sometimes heard a song which has reminded you of someone, or caught the scent of a smell, or felt someone touch you when there's no-one visible, or thought you'd seen something then persuaded yourself that it was just your imagination. That's what I mean by a sign."

Unconvinced, Gareth merely stared into the fire.

Romeo chose his words carefully.

"Eleven years ago, I left home and became wild. Mad. Bad. Dangerous to know. A beautiful woman taught me how to dive in the Tyrrhenian Sea, just off Baiae and I fell in love with her. Hell. We were out one evening and I was stabbed in a brawl when a gang stole my Ducati. Without remorse, Hell stabbed a few of the gang members. I never knew whether she killed anyone or not. I walked away. It was that night I realised she was not the woman for me.

A few months ago, I was leaving work and Hell approached me. It was great to see her until she told me she had a daughter, and that the child was mine."

"Good grief. Was that your worst nightmare?" asked Gareth.

"There are worse things than having a child, Gareth" chastised Romeo.

"What did you do?" asked Madoc.

Romeo did not meet Madoc's eyes.

"The only thing I could do. I asked for proof. A DNA paternity test."

"And?" asked Madoc and Gareth in unison.

Romeo frowned. "We went to a place in Bologna for the test. An approved clinic. It took two nerve-racking days for the results to come through."

"And?" questioned Madoc.

Romeo paused then gulped.

"Hell's daughter was not my child. She had lied to me. Or perhaps she believed it to be true and was as shocked as me. But she never considered the consequences for me. She was selfish. And I should know, because we are made of the same stuff. Egotistical. Self-absorbed."

Indelicately Gareth asked, "Why would she say the child was yours?"

Romeo's face hardened. "Who knows? Money? To rekindle a link with me? To share the responsibility of parenting? To off-load her child? I don't know the answer to your question."

"What did you do when you found out?" said Madoc, his gaze burning into Romeo.

"We met for invigorating coffee at Piazza Maggiore, spent the night together at my apartment. The following morning, I gave her the envelope with the DNA paternity test results. She dressed and left. The end."

"Is that why you're here? In Wales? You've changed your life because of an encounter with Hell?" quipped Gareth.

"I have not been a character who experiences remorse. I have been ruthless. After Hell visited me, I reflected on my life and didn't like the man I saw. There was an opportunity at work to move to Wales and I grabbed it. I wanted a fresh start in a new place. I'm sure your girlfriend, Gareth, and your wife, Madoc would not behave the way Hell did. Surely, they wouldn't?" An indefinable emotion clung to Romeo's face. He paused and looked at Madoc for an answer.

Tensely distracted by his own silliness that evening with Seren, Madoc offered another beer to Romeo.

"You let her go?" asked Madoc. Romeo was not quite sure if it was a question or an accusation.

"Yes. I let her walk out of the apartment."

"Perhaps you've paid the price for being mad, bad and dangerous to know mate" consoled Madoc.

"Seren was right" continued Romeo.

"About what?" responded Madoc.

"When she did my reading. About me. I told her that I wanted to meet her because, although I'm a scientist and usually need proof of everything, since I was a small boy I've experienced visions, images, dreams. Sometimes an event will happen, and I've known beforehand that it will occur. It's unsettling" Romeo explained. "I knew Hell would meet me in Bologna. That she had a daughter. I saw it before it happened. I'm a physicist and yet I haven't solved my own conundrum yet. I'm hoping that Seren will be the key to unlock the invisible border between this and other dimensions."

Gareth shifted in his director's chair. "The potatoes are ready" he said and passed food and condiments to Romeo and Madoc.

Romeo continued unabashed. "Seren saw that I have the choice of women, but that I pick the wrong ones in bars and clubs even though I'm waiting for my soulmate, my twin-flame."

Gareth stifled a snigger when he saw Romeo's solemn black eyes.

"She said I need someone I can connect with emotionally, spiritually, and intellectually. A woman who will happily sit and look at stars with me. She was right. That's what I'm looking for. But first, as Socrates said, my inner voice, my soul, must be nurtured and attuned. I can't wait for my past life regression as I think that will answer lots of questions."

"We've done enough sitting" announced Gareth. "Let's see which one of us can capture the best image of the Leonids" he challenged.

Madoc shrugged and looked towards the sky. "Time to stargaze" he said obliquely.

"Let the women have their sitting. Tonight, we're men of action," said Gareth.

***

Naomi beamed at Haf, Seren and nain. For a sixty-year-old woman in red flip-flops, she moved lithely around the kitchen table in Bryn Gosol Farmhouse '*absorbing the energy*'. Her long, straight white hair and vivid blue eyes reminded Seren of a female Gandolf the Wizard, but she did not dare say that aloud.

"Here's your hot water and lemon, Naomi" said Haf as she passed her a china cup. "Is that drink the secret to the appearance of your youthful skin?" asked Haf.

"I drink nothing else Haf, so I expect so."

Offering a boxful of vegetables, Naomi said, "I picked these from my garden this morning, Gwen. They'd make a lovely stew."

"Thanks Naomi" replied nain. "Are you still running your yoga classes?"

"Of course," replied Naomi confidently. "Keeps me supple and ready for sex."

Wide-eyed, Haf and Seren tittered at the thought of an aged woman still able to have sex, as if it were purely the domain of youth. Naomi cast them a cursory glance and, in a powerful Yorkshire accent, asked to be taken to the room where the sitting would take place. Seren led Naomi and Haf to the back sitting room. Nain followed.

"You should try yoga" Naomi whispered to Haf "it tightens your nether regions. Especially your butt." At which Haf reddened.

The room flickered in bright candlelight. No moon shone through the window of the farm's back sitting room. On the stone flagged floor, a black, wrought iron pot emitted intoxicating incense swirls. Gwen had placed Naomi with her back against the inglenook fireplace, where bright candlelight flickered. Blue incense smoke twirled, coiled, and curled towards the honey-coloured oak beams saturating them with the aroma of patchouli. Three women peered apprehensively at Naomi who could discern the excitement at this ritual. Expectantly the spectators waited, hardly daring to breathe. Naomi was calm, pensive.

"Bryn Gosol Farm is an enchanting place. It feels as though myth meets reality here" announced Naomi. "The lime-plastered inglenook behind me" she paused "has markings to defend the soul from evil spirits."

"Has it?" asked Seren, her mask of composure slipping away. "Did you make those nain?"

"Not me" replied nain. "How do you know they are there Naomi? We've never seen them, and you've only just entered the room. This is your first visit to Bryn Gosol Farmhouse, isn't it?"

Naomi explained. "I've never been here before. The shapes have been covered over. Remove some of the boards and you will see them. These are ancient markings known as apotropaic marks. I can see three pentangles each enclosed in a circle, three windmills and three ships."

"What do they represent?" asked Haf.

"The five-pointed stars are the pagan symbol of fire, earth, sky, water and spirit. The pentagram represents natural harmony, peace and balance. The windmills are in trust of a plentiful crop and the ships are for protection in the afterlife, to ensure a smooth journey. These symbols are in the inglenook because it was thought that evil could enter through the chimney. They are to protect the inhabitants or visitors from evil spirits. We are safe tonight" reassured Naomi.

"Oooh maybe the Historical Society might be interested in searching for them" suggested Seren.

Nain's eyes flickered away from Seren's face. "Don't want people snooping around Bryn Gosol Farmhouse" she said sourly. "Come on Naomi. Would you like to do the sitting?"

"Before we start Naomi" interjected Seren, "do you know anything about the history of Romani Gypsy cards? The ones used by the Parisian Mademoiselle Marie-Anne Lenormand."

"I do chicken because we're in the same line of business." Naomi laughed. "In the Eighteenth Century, Lenormand was supposedly famed throughout France as a Seer. In prison during the French Revolution, she is alleged to have met Marie-Josèphe-Rose Tascher de La Pagerie, whose married name was Beauharnais. It is said that Lenormand correctly predicted for Marie-Josèphe-Rose that her husband, Alexandre de Beauharnais would be guillotined in prison and that she would go on to have an advantageous marriage to Napoleon Bonaparte. The woman who received this insight would become commonly known to us as Joséphine. Through Lenormand's prophecies the two women were fated to be confidantes. Purportedly, they formed a strong alliance."

"Did Lenormand offer strategic military advice to Napoleon?" asked Haf.

"He was alleged to have an unshakeable belief in Destiny, but it is possible that Lenormand influenced Joséphine, who in turn counselled Napoleon. But legend has it that Lenormand did *read* Napoleon before he and Joséphine had met. She revealed to him that he would have more illustrious military achievements than Julius Caesar. She foresaw that success would come through a dark-haired woman. Joséphine.

Apparently Lenormand warned Napoleon not to forget that the Fates had placed Joséphine in his path and he should never abandon her otherwise he would be destroyed by a second wife, the daughter of kings. When his marriage to Joséphine was annulled, Napoleon married Marie-Louise, a member of the

House of Habsburg. He died in exile on the island of Saint Helena.

The narrative of Lenormand may be classed as fictional. We will never know the facts behind the relationship between her and the Bonapartes. Since Cuneiform script, people have considered the written word to indicate truth, but written records may not be a faithful representation of events. They may depict only one view.

There are many people who argue that there is no Divine plan, and happenstance befalls us. Others think that Sibyls, such as Lenormand and her cartomancy are only for the credulous and ignorant. I choose to keep an open mind. You see a Sibyl can give advice based on interpretation. It doesn't have to be taken or acted upon. Why do you ask Seren?"

"I have a set of Lenormand cards and wasn't quite sure about the myth surrounding them."

"That's interesting to hear the history behind Seren's cards. They can be brutal" confided Haf. "She used them for a reading for me."

"Like I say. You don't have to follow the advice of a Sybil. You have free will and only if you ask for guidance from spirit, will you receive it. You are free to choose if you will accept guidance. Now. Let's do the sitting" suggested Naomi.

"What do we *do*?" asked nain.

"Sit chicken. You three just sit here opposite me. I'll work with my spirit guides, who are here on my right and your spirit guides, who are here on my left" explained Naomi.

Haf was wide-eyed at the thought of this mystical union.

"Roman legionaries have lived in this place. I can see a high-ranking soldier with a muscular frame, close-clipped black hair, stubbly beard, and broad shoulders. His eyes are the colour of muted green. He sports tattoos of a bull and eagle on his shoulders and the mark of Julius Caesar's elite Legio X Equestris on his left calf. He is holding a gladius which I recognise as the Segontium Gladius. This fierce warrior stands behind you, Seren. His wife is with you too. Striking amber eyes, like yours, and long corn-ringed russet braids. She is a warrior in her own way."

Seren lifted her eyebrows to nain and directed a question to Naomi, "Why are they here?"

"To show that you are protected Seren," said Naomi. "Strange how everything leads back to Julius Caesar. The cards, the farm, the soldiers."

The three women were enthralled by this ethereal dimension into which Naomi led them.

"I see a man with a bible, he's wearing a blue suit as if dressed for church. He is singing in Welsh. There are links to Anglesey. He was born on the island. This man is connected to Bryn Gosol Farm and Llanrhos Church. He's telling me that the Ancient Roman couple around Seren are buried deep in the church."

"That can't be right" said Haf. "The church is Twelfth Century. Ancient Romans invaded Wales over two thousand years ago."

Without apparent concern, Naomi continued.

"This old man is holding a baby girl."

Nain smiled and whispered '*Tomos*'. It took her breath away.

Congenially Naomi spoke to Haf.

"You've been through a tumultuous relationship. Now you've broken up. Have a holiday with the girls. Do something you've never done before. Go to Ibiza and party all night long. Wildly. Your grandmother gives her blessing. She's delighted that you are wearing her ring. She says that soon you will wear another ring. You'll be happily married within the year."

In the hushed atmosphere of the back sitting room, Haf's jaw dropped before she became helpless with laughter. "That won't happen" she told Naomi.

A master craftswoman, Naomi quietly and gently closed the sitting by asking the spirits to be with the women in the room and to leave in love and light.

A year later, Haf was married to a man she met at a party in Ibiza.

November 2023

Chapter 19 – A Past Life

An energy exchange.

Seren paced ceaselessly to and from the window of the kitchen at Bryn Gosol Farmhouse. This evening, she was going to try a past life regression with Romeo. She felt surprisingly edgy, not just because he was an enigmatic man, but Madoc would accompany Romeo, and she would feel under their intense scrutiny. The back door burst open as expected, before Madoc and Romeo strode along the hallway and into the kitchen.

"Good evening. Welcome" was Seren's enthusiastic greeting.

Almost immediately Romeo noticed the commanding hawkstaff and its wonky eye. Surprised, he asked, "So hawkstaff lives here and not at your room at Benarth Beach?"

Seren explained, "We'll use hawkstaff tonight for our ritual as it acts as an amplifier of magic. I use it at the beginning of the past life regression and stomp it on the floor to put energy into the ground. When I've finished, I'll say, '*the deal is sealed*' and bang hawkstaff on the ground. That way you will know when the past life regression begins and ends."

"So hawkstaff is an important tool in this rite?" asked Romeo.

"Yes" agreed Seren. "It has remarkable powers and bends light to connect the unseen and seen worlds. Remember to use all your senses because the power of the mind is quite astonishing" she said gently and gestured to a pot of tea on the oak table. "Help yourselves to a drink" she invited as Romeo sat down and watched her intently.

The smell of warm bread and a piquant aroma of stout-filled sailors' stew bubbling on the stove floated invitingly around the room. Madoc kissed his beloved wife, as he went to mix the broth.

"Remember to stir it clockwise" advised Seren "to bring in good things."

"Are we eating now?" asked Madoc.

"No. We'll eat after the past life regression" replied Seren "but we have time for a drink."

"Your collection of images along the hallway should include the photographs of the Leonids that Gareth, Madoc and I took on the Vardre, Seren. They would look spectacular" suggested Romeo.

"I heard the three of you had an interesting evening" replied Seren. "And now you are two since Gareth left yesterday for Bologna."

"We are" agreed Romeo as he gingerly touched the spectral Hawkstaff which leaned against the kitchen table. "How was your sitting with nain's acquaintance Naomi?"

"We had a thought-provoking evening" replied Seren. "Perhaps you will meet Naomi one day?"

"Maybe. In Naples I once encountered a woman who had similar gifts to Naomi. Her name was Stella. She *read* me, but at the time I didn't realise the significance of our meeting. She declared that I'd lived before, and married a woman whose emotional, spiritual and intellectual essence linked with mine. She conveyed that the woman was a queen. Strangely she revealed that I would meet this woman again, in this life."

Seren eyed Romeo and felt embarrassed. Unabashed, he continued.

"I've also had a vision that as an Ancient Roman Primus Pilus I met the Cumaean Sibyl, Cassinia who told me that I would marry a queen. Two seers have told me the same thing. I'm interested to know what the past life regression will reveal Seren."

"We can find messages in many things" replied Seren soothingly "and everyone we meet has a significant communication of some description, if only we'd listen."

"Indeed. That's something most people fail to do. Listen. They prefer to chatter. Usually inanely." Romeo laughed. "Tonight, I'm hoping to become a new, improved version of me!"

Seren revealed to Romeo that she and Madoc would take him to a secret place for his past life regression. She was determined to take command of this situation. Silently she asked Ysbryd to guide her on the next part of the journey. It was then that Romeo chose to shock her and Madoc.

"Congratulations Seren and Madoc."

"On what?" asked Madoc.

"You're expecting a baby girl" announced Romeo gnomically.

"What? We are? I am" exclaimed an astonished Seren.

"Are we?" asked Madoc as he turned to Seren, flummoxed.

"Yes. You are" responded Romeo exuding confidence.

"No idea" stated Seren as her eyes skittered from Romeo to Madoc. "I think this is news to us Romeo. How do you know?"

"I know because I see things" replied Romeo who had drawn back the veil between the spirit world and other dimensions.

Madoc scratched his bald head. It was disconcerting being with people who communicated with Ysbryd. Those who foretold events in such a run-of-the-mill manner. He sucked in a deep breath of air and loudly exhaled.

"Well, that's some news Romeo, if it's true!" Madoc looked quizzically at Seren who shook her head as if to say, '*no idea*'.

"Romeo, finish your drink. Let's begin the magical journey of your past life regression" Madoc declared like Julius Caesar at a Triumph.

***

The underground tunnel finally widened to reveal the hidden Temple of Mithras. Romeo was astounded by what he saw. He knew that Ancient Roman Legionaries had secretly worshipped here because the setting was familiar. With his finger he traced the dim imprints on the wooden pilings depicting Mithras slaughtering a bull and dining with Sol the Sun God; amazed they had survived the test of time. He walked ahead of Seren and Madoc, instinctively stepping down worn stone steps to the central nave as shadows in the northern alcove bounced in the orange candlelight.

Romeo was excited. "I've been here before. I recognise it. I'm sure that there is a crypt to the left of the nave, quite a way below. There are bodies interred there in a sarcophagus."

"That's ridiculous Romeo" blustered Madoc before he realised that it was always advisable to remain open-minded.

Seren soothed Romeo. "Perhaps things will become clearer for us all when you've had your past life regression Romeo. Whilst it takes place, you'll still hear my voice and feel sensations. We will meditate before doing the past life regression. You'll need to lie in the nave and make yourself comfortable" instructed Seren as she wrapped him in nain's red and black Welsh plaid, handstitched tapestry blanket. "To begin with, breathe in deeply through your nose and exhale through your mouth."

Romeo was thrilled at being in the secret Temple of Mithras and the prospect of his past life regression. As he lay on the nave, Romeo's heart heaved, his body sagged. He was exhausted. Tired of running, of being angry, of not knowing what to do, then he stirred.

"Ok Romeo. Beathe deeply through your nose and exhale through your mouth. You're in control. You can stop at any time. I'll guide you. I'm going to stomp hawkstaff now" said Seren and banged her hawkstaff on the ground "to put energy into the ground. Choose a spot on the ceiling and focus upon it.

Breathe deeply to the count of five, hold your breath to the count of five, breathe out to the count of five. As I say each number blink your eyes.

You'll see some steps. When you see them, I'll instruct you to walk up them. Close your eyes. Can you see the steps?"

"Yes" replied Romeo.

Seren felt a frisson of anticipation as she caught Madoc's eye. He gently nodded encouragement.

"As I count up to ten, walk up the steps slowly" instructed Seren, who counted. "Can you see the chair?"

"Yes" replied Romeo.

"This is your safe space. You can always return to the chair." Seren paused. "There are several doors before you. Choose one door which is drawing you to it. What is the year on the door?"

"It is 44BCE" replied Romeo.

Seren looked at Madoc and smiled. Madoc's eyebrows raised to his non-existent hairline as he returned her beam with a thumb up.

"Go through the door and describe to me what is happening" instructed Seren.

"There's a commotion on the rostra, with Senators in blood-splattered white robes running in different directions yelling that Julius Caesar has been stabbed. Ahead of me, I can hear Marc Antony giving instructions to calm the melee. My Legate Titus is pushing his way through the throng towards me."

"Were you aware that day that events would unfold this way?" asked Seren.

"We had discussed prophecies from the Sibylline Books which had been divulged at the most recent Senate meeting. There had been a warning from the Sibyl Ceres, wife of Titus for Caesar to '*beware the Ides of March*'. He did not heed her prophecy.

Earlier that day a small group of us had met privately and debated with Caesar his plans. He was going to war in the

Parthian Empire to avenge the murder of Crassus in Carrhae. Caesar had asked Marc Antony to remain in Rome to lead the Empire in his absence and my Legate Titus was to return to Cambria as General. I had instructions to remain in Rome and guard Arsinoë, sister to Queen Cleopatra."

"Why was the Sibyl Ceres anxious for Caesar's welfare?" asked Seren.

"She had foretold that there were Senators who plotted against Caesar, motivated by his proposed reforms for resettling the poor and his plans to overhaul Roman governance. Some Senators had privately expressed concern to Marc Antony that Caesar appeared to have the ultimate power of a king which they resented."

There was a pause as Romeo fought for breath and a flicker of anger flashed in Madoc's eyes because of Rome's traitors.

"And now, Caesar's been stabbed" announced Romeo.

Seren asked Romeo, "What does Titus wish you to do?"

"He begged me to accompany Ceres and his three daughters to the port of Ostia where a warship would be waiting. There were enough oarsmen on standby for the war Caesar had planned the following day who were available to power the vessel. The family needed to leave for Cambria. It would not be prudent for the Sibyl Ceres to remain in Rome as she had warned Caesar about his safety" answered Romeo. "It was important that the Sibylline Secrets should not be widely known. Ceres was one of the keepers of the keys to the Sibylline Books held in the Temple of Jupiter."

Seren asked for clarification, "What are the Sibylline Secrets?"

"Three books of prophesies foretold by Sibyls. Ceres was one of the Sibyls, and highly regarded by Caesar. She was responsible for keeping the books under lock and key in the Temple of Jupiter."

"What did you do?" questioned Seren.

"The only thing I could do. Follow the instructions of my Legate. I ran through the city and to his villa just as Ceres was about to put the children to bed. I told her the divination had come true about the Ides of March and between us we grabbed the three girls. They were all in grave danger because some of the Senators knew about her foresight. Ceres would not leave the city without the Sibylline Books. She was afraid that undisclosed prophecies would become known and create further mayhem. The Sibylline Books could not remain in Rome. Ceres would take them with her to Cambria."

"Surely you would follow Titus' instructions and take his family straight to the port?" asked Seren.

"No. I too knew that Rome would be more unsafe if the Sybilline Secrets were widely revealed."

Seren forced her voice to stay calm. "What happened when you left the villa?"

"Chaos reigned. There were crowds of people openly discussing Caesar's assassination. Ceres and I carried the three children and pushed our way through the narrow alleyways. All was quiet around the Temple of Jupiter which was in total darkness save for the silver moonbeams that darted mischievously through the doorways. Ceres had the key to the sepulchre with its raised Ace of Cups insignia. Once the door to the crypt was unlocked, she pulled out the three Sibylline Books and gave one each to the three girls for safekeeping.

Like black cats we crept out of the Temple but encountered Senator Cassius on the steps who wanted the Sibylline Books for himself. He confronted us, grabbed Ceres' daughter Sabine by the hair, and threatened to kill her if we didn't give him the books. Quick as an orange fireball across the night sky, Ceres drew her amber-handled pugio and forcefully stabbed him in the shoulder. He dropped Sabine and fell to the floor. I kicked him in his hoary face rendering him unconscious. Ceres spat on him. We all escaped unhurt, with the Sibylline Books intact.

I led the family through the disorderly streets of Rome to the stables near the Campus Martius, saddled two horses, Castor and Pollux and rode with the little family to the port at Ostia. We met Titus at the naves longae[35] bound for Cambria. Beneath the full moon we vowed under no circumstances to forget our friendship. We would love each other as brothers until our dying day.

At the dockside Ceres sobbed uncontrollably but most challenging was having the three little girls peeled from my loving arms. I tried to return to Ceres the gold moonstone ring that the children had presented to me as a gift, but she refused to accept it. Ceres performed a ritual around my gladius, the one that Titus had given to me, forged in Segontium. She revealed three things to me, the Segontium Gladius would be double-edged, there was a portal at the Temple of Seti I at Abydos in Egypt to points in the universe where people could move along different timelines and that Rome would be led by a Queen. As we parted, Alesia, their eldest daughter, kissed my cheek, called me Pica and placed one of the Sibylline Books into my hand. As they left, I made a promise that we would all meet again one day.

For the first time in my life, I wept. I cried for the family I cherished as my own, and for our great leader, Caesar, who was no more.

For an age I stood at the harbour and watched the boat move slowly across the black water until it vanished on the horizon whilst exploding rays of energy shot across the Bay. Everything changed that night. I had become a keeper of the Sybilline Secrets, the Segontium Gladius had been blessed once more by a Sybil and I had sworn a vow."

---

[35] Long boat

Quivering with emotion as she listened to Romeo's story, Seren's heart ached for she did not know what had happened to grief-stricken Magpie after his only remaining family left him in Rome. A part of their soul left behind.

November 2023

Chapter 20 – Two Queens

Time dilates.

Seren could not stem her curiosity and asked, "We are still in 44BCE Romeo. What did you do once the naves longae disappeared from the horizon?"

"I had been given an important role by Marc Antony" Romeo stated simply.

"What was that task?"

"With Caesar's death it was my responsibility to protect three members of the royal Ptolemy family. My role was to return them safely to Alexandria in Egypt."

Hardly daring to hear the answer Seren asked, "Who were you guarding?"

"A woman loved by Caesar, Queen Cleopatra VIII, their son Caesarion and the Queen's sister, Arsinoë IV. All were in grave danger. Caesar had been murdered by some of Rome's Senators, it was likely they would do the same to those closely allied to him."

Seren remembered that Madoc had read aloud a newspaper article about the possibility of Arsinoë's IV's bones being found at the Temple of Artemis. Might this be the same woman? Feeling muscle-knotting anxiety Seren asked, "Why was Arsinoë IV in Rome?"

"When Caesar attacked the Ptolemies in Egypt, it was the teenager, Queen Arsinoë who raised an army and led her people against Caesar" explained Romeo.

Seren took a deep breath and said, "Are you saying that Arsinoë was Queen of Egypt and not Cleopatra?"

Romeo sighed. "Yes. She was at the time. Her army defeated Julius Caesar's soldiers. It was a humiliating loss for him. A coup for her."

Sensing that he was holding a fragile secret, Seren pushed Romeo to explain.

"Caesar had conquered Gaul and believed himself to be immortal. In Egypt when he experienced defeat at the hands of Arsinoë's army, initially he was incandescent with rage. She was a brilliant strategist. Only when Arsinoë was betrayed by one of her own people, and handed over to Caesar, was he victorious but he never defeated her. He always remembered that. The cruelty of others can be terrifying, and Caesar was ruthless, but he spared her life. She was an impressive woman."

Romeo blinked back tears.

In a whisper Seren asked, "Who betrayed Arsinoë?"

"Her sister, Cleopatra. She wished to be Queen of Egypt and formed an alliance with Caesar. It was agreed between them that a humiliated Queen Arsinoë would be paraded at the Triumph in Rome and that Cleopatra would become Queen of Egypt."

Seren asked, "What happened at the Triumph for her to be spared?"

"It was symbolic of rebirth for Arsinoë because Roman citizens cheered for her release. Caesar acquiesced."

"I wonder why?" said Seren but then she remembered nain's words:

'Like the Ancient Romans, the Ancient Egyptians worshipped many Gods who represented nature's subtle mechanisms of air, fire, water, and earth. The Goddess Artemis was linked to the moon, hunting and fertility. Her twin brother Apollo was linked to the sun, healing, and prophecy. Both twins delivered prophecies through Sibyls and Julius Caesar often consulted Prophetesses before making huge decisions. Perhaps it was a prophecy in one of the Sibylline books that Caesar must save Arsinoë IV. Or she may have reminded him of his beloved daughter Julia, who had died. Or perhaps he

wanted to remove her from Cleopatra's withering gaze. Maybe Caesar knew there was something extraordinary about Arsinoë.'

"Was there something extraordinary about Arsinoë?" asked Seren boldly.

With eyes as round as a full Beaver Moon Romeo answered, "Yes." He was silent for an age until he said, "She would die for her people. Her sister was self-serving and sacrificed the Egyptians to the Romans. Cleopatra was afraid of Arsinoë."

Seren said, "Why did Caesar save Arsinoë IV?"

"The Sibyl Ceres had told him Arsinoë IV was the Seer who would always protect his son as if he were her own."

November 2023

Chapter 21 – Insurgents

Promises are not meant to be broken.

"The boy was three when we left Rome" uttered Romeo.

"Which boy?" asked Seren.

"Caesarion. The child Cleopatra claimed was the result of her dalliance with Julius Caesar. When we left Rome to travel to Alexandria, he was a fragile boy."

"You did as Marc Antony ordered and escorted Caesarion, Cleopatra and Arsinoë to Egypt?"

"Yes" was his short answer. "I promised to deliver them safely."

Seren looked at Madoc and smiled. For the first time they might hear about Magpie's life without Titus and Ceres. His lovat eyes shining, Madoc gave Seren a thumb's up sign.

Softly Seren asked, "Romeo, do you want to carry on with this past life regression?

"Of course," he responded.

Seren continued. "Are we still in 44BCE?"

"We are" he replied.

"What did you do once the naves longae disappeared from the horizon?"

"I took the horses, Castor and Pollux back to the stables near the Campus Martius, hooked both beasts to a closed carpentum[36] and, speedily added our third and fourth horses, Callisto and Ganymede. With a feeling of foreboding, I drove to one of Caesar's homes, an outstanding villa on the outskirts of Rome

---

[36] Richly adorned state carriage with seats for three people.

where I collected three people: Queen Cleopatra, her son Caesarion and her sister, Arsinoë."

"Tell me" instructed Seren "how you escaped Rome."

"With a battle on my hands" answered Romeo with an air of triumphalism. "We left in the early hours, shortly after I lost sight of the ship carrying Titus and his family. The sky rained with long tailed golden and white sparkles, illuminating our way. Without warning six rogue legionaries, insurgents concealed in the fractures of an alleyway lined by ramshackle houses, ambushed us as our carpentum careered through Rome's empty warren of winding streets. There was obviously a spy in our midst who knew we were leaving, and our route.

The muscular soldiers on horseback encircled our carriage, stabbing at the air aggressively with their gladii. Another on foot, whose worn face displayed knotty white slash scars from previous battles, tried to grab little Caesarion as he hid among the folds of Cleopatra's purple silk dress. Hollow-eyed Arsinoë stood between her sister and the prowling legionary distracting him long enough for me to skewer his skull with the blade of my Segontium Gladius. Like a hazelnut husk, his head cracked effortlessly.

Dismounting violently from his stallion, a broad-shouldered legionary gouged my buttock with his pugio, causing poppy-red blood to seep down my leg, between my toes and into my sandals. With anger that flowed through my body I nimbly surged forward with my gladius and gored his left eye. He fell as the last of his spurting blood dripped off the poisoned Segontium Gladius and onto the cobbled path.

The four of us darted from the carpentum when the remaining legionaries descended from their mounts. Two chunky calloused hands grabbed at Cleopatra's upper arm. In a dancer's movement, she unwound her reedy tan leather waist belt and coiled it lethally around the legionary's neck until she saw his pink tongue loll upon his unshaven chin. Scowling Caesarion kicked the legionary for good measure as he slumped dead on the path.

The shouts and screams of our ferocious civil war reverberated around the passageway. In blood-splattered clothes and with nerves of steel, Arsinoë, her voice sharp and merciless shouted orders for the men to retreat. They laughed in her face. In swift retaliation, she plunged her pugio into the heart of one, and the neck of another. A few shallow breaths later, they too lay crumpled on the floor.

Violent, desperate screams from the remaining sweating legionary added to the despair of war. My clammy arms vibrated as I rained down heavy gladius blows on his thick neck and burly upper back until he fell to his knees in silence.

This brief combat over, I instructed Arsinoë, Cleopatra and Caesarion to step back into the carriage. I took the reins and rode to the southern coast as if possessed by Mars, the God of War. I thanked the God for a successful military incursion, prayed that other conspirators would be held at bay and for a smooth crossing to Alexandria. He rewarded us with a honeyed dawn over the Great Sea and the sight of moored Roman warships at the port of Puteoli, near Baiae.

Twenty days later I stood on the bow of a warship. When the lofty beacon atop the colossal white marble vision of Pharos, the beautiful lighthouse of Alexandria came into view I knew my vow to Marc Antony had been fulfilled. After all, a promise is a promise, and not to be broken."

November 2023

Chapter 22 – Banished

You'll never stop this flame.

Blood pounding in her head, heart beating wildly, Seren's inquisitiveness got the better of her. "Romeo, you said the Segontium Gladius was poisoned. Who did that?"

His voice sharp as a needle Romeo answered "The Seer, Arsinoë. She was a Prophetess who saw the past, present and future but was also a Sorceress."

"How did she make the gladius toxic?"

Romeo moved his head and answered, "With a spell and Venus's Chariot which she carried in her pouch."

"Venus's Chariot?" Seren asked evenly.

"It's a purple-blue hooded flower. Before our journey, Arsinoë extracted the black seeds from it, mixed them with honey and smeared my gladius with the concoction. It was to ward off evil spirits."

"Are you still talking about 44BCE Romeo?"

"Yes."

"Arsinoë sounds like a formidable woman. Tell me about her" coaxed Seren.

Romeo's eyes opened and darted warily around the Temple's chamber. "I was chary of collecting the two sisters because they despised each other" he whispered. "Both were highly intellectual, articulate, beguiling and determined women."

Nervously Seren asked, "What drove a wedge between them?"

"They had political differences. Queen Cleopatra had been exiled from Egypt because she favoured an alliance between Egypt and the Roman Empire. With the Queen deposed, Arsinoë was crowned Queen of Egypt. She led her country into battle with Julius Caesar's army; a fight she won. To be reinstated as Queen, Cleopatra betrayed her sister. Captured by Caesar's men, Arsinoë was humiliated by being paraded at the Triumph in Rome."

"Yet Caesar pardoned Arsinoë, and Marc Antony sent her, Cleopatra and Caesarion to Egypt, accompanied by you, one of the most trusted soldiers?"

"Caesar had been told by the Seer Ceres that Arsinoë would protect Caesarion with her life. He understood that she could call upon the Gods for help, and grasped that Cleopatra was afraid of her. He respected Arsinoë. She was a powerful, fascinating woman."

"And Marc Antony?"

"He recognised Caesarion as Caesar's son and wanted to protect his friend's family. Both Marc Antony and Cleopatra knew that cordial relations between him and the Ptolemy family might be to their long-term advantage once he was at the helm of Rome. They were both wily characters. He protected Arsinoë because she was part of the Ptolemy dynasty. The extraordinary thing was, the Ptolemy's rarely defended each other."

Romeo placed his hands behind his head and breathed a long sigh.

"Arsinoë must be the only woman to defeat Julius Caesar" stated Seren.

In the dim light of the Temple, proudly Romeo replied, "She was."

A thought Seren had not previously considered flittered through her mind: *'Had Romeo loved Arsinoë?'*

"What became of Arsinoë when you arrived in Alexandria?"

Romeo's head jolted. "Once Queen Cleopatra was safely back in her royal quarters, she banned Arsinoë from the palace at Alexandria. It was not a surprise when Arsinoë asked the Queen's permission for me to accompany her to the Temple of Seti I at

Abydos. Keen to remove her sister from Alexandria, the Queen acquiesced."

Face flushed, Seren asked, "Why did Arsinoë wish to visit the Temple?"

"On the sea journey from Rome to Alexandria I had read the Sibylline Book given to me by Alesia on the dockside at Ostia. It revealed information about the Temple of Seti I. In a rock cut chamber, there is a portal at the Temple to points in the universe where people can move along different timelines. Arsinoë knew this. She wished to absorb the energy in the Temple and use the portal to shift freely through time" explained a pale Romeo.

"Did you take her to Abydos?"

"Yes. Arsinoë explained that she needed to perform a ceremony to enter the gateway where Divine realms gently lift a thin caul between the living and the dead. She declared it was important for her to visit the Temple."

"What happened when Arsinoë was there?"

Romeo twisted the threads of his glinting gold filigree ring and the iridescent moonstone on his finger glowed in the flickering orange candlelight. Nervously he said, "she cleansed her body, mind and soul through a purification ritual where she fasted and took a hot bath".

Startled, Seren asked, "You saw her do that?"

"Yes."

"You watched her?"

"Yes" admitted Romeo. "At the Temple she meditated and then rhythmically chanted. On the altar Arsinoë sprinkled vervain for purification and laid out herbs of lavender and sage, added bread, and poured violet wine as an offering. She stood in front of a stela, but I could not read the inscription on this upright stone slab. At a tomb Arsinoë placed an exquisite, mummified doll. Later she told me the shabti had been placed in honour of one of her hand-servants who had been killed by Cleopatra's men.

She burned white candles and inhaled the spiralling peppermint incense smoke from a golden cauldron, ingested laurel leaves, and held rosemary herbs to ward off evil spirits. All the time I scrutinised her actions. She lay down and on her third eye placed belladonna leaves soaked in fat to incubate her thoughts and encourage astral travel. Those few actions were enough to enable her to enter a trance, opening a space in her unconscious mind, encouraging her to travel along the timeline.

Once the ritual was complete, Arsinoë told me of her visions. She had been channelled to witness the most astonishing occurrences revealed by spirits. She discovered that Queen Cleopatra would play a dangerous military, financial and political game which would lead to her untimely death before the age of forty. Cleopatra would dally with many men, including Marc Antony. He would have a premature death because of this liaison. It was Destiny for Arsinoë to help her nephew Caesarion to try and escape death in Alexandria but alas, he would never be King of Egypt. According to these revelations, Titus and the Seer Ceres would play an important role in Arsinoë's life.

Arsinoë asked me to protect her. I promised I would shield her in perpetuity. And I did. At the altar she cast a powerful spell over the Segontium Gladius. With her magical chant, one nick of the gladius could render anyone lifeless within moments.

There was no doubt that my flame for her glowed luminous, more intense than the sun and moon combined. She shone so brightly that her rays dazzled me."

Seren took time to digest this information, then exhaled loudly. Romeo's past life regression had turned into quite the revelation.

November 2023

Chapter 23 – The Temple of Artemis

Death in paradise.

Wrapped in a Conwy tapestry blanket, Romeo lay in the nave as if he were a human sacrifice. He adjusted his position slightly to peer into his past. Seren looked into his black eyes.

"Do you want to continue Romeo?" she asked kindly.

"Yes" he replied.

"Would you like to move forward in time?" Seren suggested.

For an age she waited for an answer, hearing only deep breaths from Romeo, the delicate murmuring of Madoc and water droplets plopping onto the floor from the mud ceiling. In a determined voice Romeo began.

"Under a high sun I am watching myself, standing with my back to the turquoise sea, outside the Temple of Artemis at Ephesus where I delivered Arsinoë, three years ago. She lived here with other Priestesses" he explained. "That day I walked around the Greek temple at least fifty times and, on each occasion, counted one hundred and twenty-seven white marble columns in a double row on all four sides. Every column magnificently etched with the image of a Greek God or Goddess, tinted black, gold, purple, red, blue, and green. Away from the horror of war, this environment nurtured my soul." Romeo sighed loudly.

"On a mission for Marc Antony, I forced myself to walk into the temple where thick marmalade sunlight strained to illuminate the way. As the heavy perfume of burning frankincense curled into my nostrils, I pounded the long and narrow passageways towards a windowless chamber and ascended stone steps.

Clad in a saffron garment, her loose ringlets black as sable delicately rested on the small of her back as Arsinoë knelt before the golden statue of Artemis, goddess of the moon, hunting and protector of women. The tall statue's legs were thoughtfully decorated with figures of wild deer, goats and bees, the top of her body was covered with breasts to symbolise fertility, a bow and quiver were slung over her shoulder and in her hand, she carried a torch to illuminate the way.

Arsinoë's slender shoulders rose and fell as she invoked the Goddess and asked for protection. I watched her place a gold votive of a bull on the altar. Without warning, Arsinoë spoke to me before our eyes had even met. She must have sensed my presence.

"You have been sent to kill me Magpie" she stated.

I acknowledged this to be true.

"In the Temple of Artemis, I pray each day with three other priestesses. I devote my life to nourishing the sick and helpless, I nurture plants and rear animals, yet Queen Cleopatra has used her wiles to persuade Marc Antony that I am a threat to my country."

Again, I acknowledged this to be true.

Arsinoë shook her head impatiently. "The Queen desires my death because she expects her son, Caesarion to be king when she dies."

"This is also true" I admitted.

Arsinoë turned to face me. Her cobalt blue eyes bright in her rich chestnut brown face.

"I love my nephew and would never harm him. Unlike his mother, Cleopatra who murdered our brother and betrayed me so that she could share control of Egypt with Romans. Sadly, I know that Caesarion will never be king of Egypt despite her efforts."

Arsinoë wept in grief for her country and her nephew. She allowed me, a Roman soldier, to comfort her. I listened to her sobs, held her tightly to my breast and could feel hers heaving against mine. I did not speak, just waited for her tears to subside and delicately kissed the top of her head. Her curls smelled of myrrh, a burnt firewood. Arsinoë angrily pulled away from me, her face streaked with black kohl.

"Cleopatra does not want me to accede and lead Egypt into war with the Roman Triumvirate: Marc Antony, Octavius and Lepidus. She is aware that I would never allow Egypt to become a Roman possession."

"Marc Antony does not covet Egypt, Arsinoë" I said. "He wishes for a partnership."

She turned to face me and spat, "Marc Antony desires Cleopatra in his bed. And the others wish to control Egypt, especially Octavian".

My face showed shock, but Arsinoë refused to stop.

"He is the great-nephew of Julius Caesar, but through his will Octavian is now recognised as Caesar's adopted son. My nephew Caesarion is a threat to the power bestowed upon Octavian. Cleopatra has been blinded by Marc Antony's attention. She does not realise her son is the target of Octavian, a sadistic murderer."

At those words I winced, for she was correct. Octavian was arrogant and would stop at nothing to wrench power for himself.

Her voice strained. "I see events others do not. As you know, I foretell the future. I have a plan Magpie, and need your help."

She did not hesitate to tell it to me.

"There are four priestesses here in the Temple of Artemis. We meditate to see the past, present and future. This temple is our sanctuary. On the full moon, our High Priestess offers a sacrifice to the goddess Artemis, a maiden from the local village. When she is dead you and I will smear her blood on the steps of this temple to indicate a struggle, we will bury her in a sarcophagus in one of the chambers and I will give you my golden ring to take to Marc Antony and Cleopatra as proof that I am dead. Cleopatra will recognise the lapis lazuli and agate inlays as she has an identical one. Our father gave them to us. For ten years I will go into exile.

For those years I will wait for you to return to me. In that time Marc Antony will lose his power and Octavian will demand the murder of my nephew Caesarion. When you come back, bring Titus and the Sybil Ceres with you. We will need their assistance. Promise you will help me. To show my gratitude I will bestow upon you the gift of seeing the past, present and future *for eternity*. This reward will never be taken away from you."

"I stared at Arsinoë. She was the sunshine in my life, my shining star. What else could I do but move my lips slowly against hers, hold her in my arms, and stroke her face, as soft as eagle feathers? I pledged a vow that I would facilitate all her demands, and return in ten years.

There was nothing but Arsinoë in my future."

November 2023

<u>Chapter 24 – Never Knew Love Like This</u>

Rare as hens' teeth.

In Llanrhos, deep underneath Saint Hilary's Church, in the secret underground Temple of Mithras, Romeo lay in the nave and wept. Madoc looked uncomfortable and asked Seren to intervene.

"Bring him back Seren" demanded Madoc. "This seems too much for him to cope with." Madoc shifted awkwardly on the stone pew. He sounded apprehensive.

"It's nothing to worry about Madoc" whispered Seren, reassuringly patting his hand. She turned her attention to Romeo. "Follow my voice, Romeo. Your soul's journey showed that you were able to protect Arsinoë and her family, and that you were planning to meet her again" said Seren tenderly. "You did your duty. You did what was expected of you and kept people safe." Seren paused. "Now it's time to find the chair Romeo. Go back to the chair."

It took quite a few nerve-racking minutes before Romeo exclaimed, "I've found it."

Madoc's eyes met Seren's. They both looked relieved.

"Good. Sit on the chair Romeo. I'm going to stomp hawkstaff now" said Seren and banged her hawkstaff on the ground. "The deal is sealed. I'll count back from ten to zero. When I say zero your eyes will open. You will return to your current life."

A pallid Romeo began to re-emerge from his meditative state. Bone cold, despite the warm blanket, he shivered as his eyes adjusted to gloomy surroundings.

"How are you feeling? asked Seren.

Romeo lay utterly still. A little concerned about the silence, Seren studied his face. "Sit up Romeo, I've got hot chocolate for you with a couple of drops of water violet. The water violet will help bring you back into balance."

Romeo's face was tranquil, but he remained immobile. Although he knew Seren had a flair for past life regression, Madoc was alarmed by Romeo's unresponsiveness.

"What's happening?" he whispered to Seren in the shadowy damp chamber. "Why's he not speaking?"

"It's ok Madoc. I didn't want to leave the Temple of Artemis. I wished to stay with Arsinoë forever" whispered Romeo.

In relieved response Madoc offered the hot chocolate to Romeo and said, "Sit up mate and sip this drink. It'll do you good".

Slowly Romeo levered himself up from the nave and sat next to Madoc. He sipped the syrupy chocolate drink and took small bites of cake. The friends did not speak until Romeo leant forward; his face illuminated by the glow of a white candle. Romeo's eyes shone and his full mouth curved into a smile. Seren studied Romeo's face carefully.

"Is there something you have learned about yourself during this past life regression?" she probed.

"I saw the love of my life" he revealed. "I held her, felt her against me, smelled her hair and knew how much she meant to me. I've been kissed, but I never knew love like this. I *am* capable of love even though I have shut it out of my life because the emotion is too painful."

"Interesting" replied Seren. "Go on. What else did you learn?"

"That I was a legitimate murderer for Julius Caesar's army. As a Primus Pilus I fought alongside Titus. I came to love him, his wife Ceres, and their three daughters Alecia, Fausta and Sabine as if they were my own family. I missed them when they left for Cambria.

It was a shock to realise that the ring I wear now may have been given to me in my Ancient Roman life. A gift from the three children. Surely that cannot happen. Is it possible to own an artefact that is over two thousand years old?" Romeo paused for a moment and thought about the many museums he had visited. They showed relics claimed to be over thousands of years old. Instinctively he touched the aureus which he usually carried in his back pocket. "If it is authentic, I wonder how the ring was passed down through generations of my family?"

"Perhaps your parents will help you piece together its history Romeo" suggested Seren. "Is there anything else you've learnt?"

"Yes." His voice was low. "I was given a Sibylline Book. Where the hell is that now? Did I lose it?"

There was momentary silence. "Maybe we will find out soon" replied Seren who was thinking of nain's secret book of spells.

Romeo frowned "And the double-edged Segontium Gladius" exclaimed Romeo "a gift from Titus and made more potent by Arsinoë. I wonder where that is now?" Romeo became agitated.

Madoc's forehead creased and his eyes darted towards Seren.

"Take time to breathe slowly Romeo, in through your nose, out through your mouth. Concentrate on the breath running through your body. This action will help to soothe your mind" advised Seren.

Romeo could not settle and would not listen. He became more agitated.

"There was a portal at the Temple of Seti I at Abydos in Egypt to points in the universe where people could move along different timelines. Is that real?"

Seren was forceful.

"Shift your focus to within yourself Romeo. Breathe deeply. We can talk about more your past life regression soon enough. It's important that you relax now."

Romeo felt his heart sink and stared hard at Seren. His voice was anxious, "Did I go back for Arsinoë?"

"You need time to percolate the past life you've just experienced Romeo. I promise we will talk it through when you've rested." Seren stood up to leave the chamber.

"Wait" commanded Romeo. "Don't leave the Temple of Mithras just yet. I told you there's a sarcophagus over there." He pointed to the left of the nave. "Is it possible to excavate the Temple?"

"Let's see" answered Madoc, giving himself time to consider the opportunity as Seren eyed him coldly.

"My own visions of my past life were never so intense. Future events that I see are more powerful" disclosed Romeo. "Will that change now Seren? Do you think I will be able to see the past clearly without the need for a past life regression?"

"I don't know Romeo. Why?"

"I'd like to see whether I returned for Arsinoë" he replied softly "and if so, what happened to us."

Seren reassured him. "We could speak to nain about it. Come over to Bryn Gosol Farmhouse tomorrow evening."

The torches on their mobile telephones lit the way as the triumvirate walked from the altar in the central nave, up the worn stone steps, past the wooden pilings which held up the ceiling and onto a muddy path. The air smelled fetid. At the end of the long tunnel, they clambered up dusty steps and entered Bryn Gosol Farmhouse, ready to eat sailors' stew.

As Romeo sat at the kitchen table he said, "It was Arsinoë who gave me the gift of divination. *Now that's a double-edged sword.* But there is one thing I now know for certain."

"Which is" questioned Madoc.

"That you two were in my Ancient Roman life. I recognise you as Titus and Ceres."

"How could you possibly recognise us from a past life?" questioned Madoc.

"Your tattoos, the shape and colour of your eyes Madoc. With Seren it was her amber ring. Ceres wore it in my visions."

"We all have a past" was all that Seren said.

Madoc smiled. "Let's see what tomorrow brings my old friend."

November 2023

Chapter 25 – Old Souls

Free will.

As the sun tipped goodbye to the horizon, effortlessly sophisticated in appearance Romeo drove into the grounds of Bryn Gosol. The brightly lit farmhouse in Llanrhos squatted neatly against thorny hawthorns and thicketed rowan trees where waxwing and redwing thrushes nipped at bright red berries. Romeo had become so tired of behaving like glassy-eyed Dionysus that he had decided six months' abstinence from his vices might be better spent in somnolent north Wales.

He strode confidently towards Bryn Gosol Farmhouse and inhaled deeply just as the front door burst open. Seren held out her arms to greet Romeo, he caught a whiff of sweet jasmine. They hugged as he lightly kissed her cinnamon-coloured cheek. In the doorway Madoc waited to greet Romeo with a handshake then led him into the kitchen. A pie of smoked haddock topped with potatoes had been baked and mushy peas bubbled patiently on the stove. Emitting positive energy and bathed in buttery light, nain rose from the oak table. She warmly greeted Romeo and invited him to sit next to her for their meal.

Romeo had heard all about nain's inherited talents of magic and power of prophecy; he knew she was the *Llanrhos Seer.* She looked at him with eyes sharp as obsidian crystals, which sparkled at the prospect of what lay ahead that evening. He calmly returned her gaze.

"I hear you found Rome interesting, Mrs Williams" began Romeo.

"Call me nain" she instructed. "Seren and Madoc were married at a former church, the Caracalla Wedding Hall. I wasn't too impressed with its unenticing brown exterior, but when we walked through the arched wooden door the interior was completely overwhelming. A hodgepodge of colour. Right in the centre of the altar was a circular floral display of yellow and orange roses, cross-stitched with dark green foliage. The array had been created by my friend Vincenzo." Romeo spotted that nain blushed at the mention of Vincenzo but said nothing. "Once Seren and Madoc were married" continued nain "I officiated at their handfasting ceremony in the Forum. It was such an emotional day."

Handfasting?" queried Romeo.

Nain explained. "It's a Pagan ritual and involves the couple's hands being tied together with coloured ribbons. Vows are exchanged as their hands are intertwined and bound."

"What do the various colours represent?"

"The couple can choose the tints they want. Blue indicates loyalty, green signifies growth and abundance, orange is for energy, purple embodies wealth, red denotes passion, white symbolises purity and new beginnings and yellow is for joy."

"I would choose yellow for joy and blue for loyalty" revealed Romeo.

Nain listened but did not answer.

Romeo continued. "And you're planning to visit Genoa?"

"We are going to stay with Vincenzo's family. He's the friend I mentioned who created the floral arrangement for us in Rome" replied nain, without divulging the nature of their friendship. Which incidentally was currently platonic thus nain had no idea why she felt flustered at the mention of Vincenzo's name. She quickly changed the subject. "How did your past life regression go with Seren? You don't need to discuss it if you don't want to" she added hastily when she saw Romeo's wary expression.

"Nain!" exclaimed Seren, fretting. "Remember client confidentiality. Romeo may choose not to speak about his experience."

Romeo appeared frozen in time. His eyes were sorrowful; he placed his elbows on the table, his chin cupped in his hands.

"At least let's eat nain before you begin interrogating Romeo" added Madoc whose eyes flittered from nain to Romeo.

"Don't worry Seren, Madoc" reassured Romeo who sat back in his chair and placed his hands behind his head, plaiting his fingers. "I had planned on speaking to nain about past life regression this evening, but let's eat first, the food smells appetizing."

After they had eaten and cleared the dishes, nain suggested moving into her favourite space, the back dining room. She missed living at the farmhouse where her memories with taid were securely stored, but she would never admit this to Seren and Madoc. Nain walked along the long hallway and pushed open the oak door, strode across the stone tiled floor to the flickering log fire and prodded it with an iron poker before sitting on an orange velvet chair which had replaced her wobbly oak table. Seren and Madoc convened opposite her on a multicoloured velvet patchwork sofa and Romeo plonked himself onto a rich purple velvet seat with green cushions.

As he sat down, Romeo was first to speak. "I'm confused nain and I trust you can guide me."

"I shall try Romeo but I'm not the font of all knowledge" laughed nain. "What's troubling you?"

"Throughout my life I have experienced visions, images, dreams which will later usually occur in real life. Premonitions I suppose you might call them. Sporadically I might experience déjà vu. You know that odd feeling you get when you think that something has already happened, but is happening now. As a scientist I know that déjà vu raises a conflict of reason between a sense of the familiar and the stark realisation that this perception might be wrong."

Nain listened in silence and surveyed Romeo's face. He looked distressed, and confessed, "Sometimes I over-indulge in alcohol."

"Many people do Romeo. They might enjoy a large glass of wine in the evening and, before they know it, they need that glass of wine every night" stated nain.

"I don't stay with one woman as I enjoy the company of lots of women nain, if you know what I mean."

She did.

"I have taken dopaminergic drugs for recreational purposes" continued Romeo.

Nain made no comment and remained in benevolent silence. Seren and Madoc moved closer together and listened intently.

"People might say that my vices induce déjà vu, or visions, or phantasmagoria but my adult actions do not account for the revelations which occurred when I was a young boy and teenager, when my life was unworldly. I suppose it could simply be confabulation."

"Confabulation?" queried Madoc.

Romeo was perturbed. "It means fabricated imaginary experiences as compensation for loss of memory."

Madoc considered this for a while. "That's feasible" he said, pursing his lips and nodding his head "but you haven't lost your memory!"

Romeo's face displayed formidable concentration as if trying to remember every detail of his youthful visions. From the sofa Madoc raised an eyebrow, Seren drew a deep breath and eyed nain.

"Have you heard of a woman named Minnie Dutton?" Nain directed her question at Romeo.

"No. Should I have?" responded Romeo his eyes wide with interest. "Does she live in Conwy?"

"Please may I tell her story?" asked nain patiently.

Romeo inclined his head. "Of course."

"Some people believe in the idea of life, death and rebirth. Whilst the evidence is not flawless, there may be some indicators that reincarnation must be considered as a serious option" began nain. "We may go through an unknown number of cycles of rebirth over many lifetimes. We may have memories of past lives or visions of future lives."

Romeo nodded and gestured for her to continue.

"Emotions, memories, and even physical bodily features may be passed on from one incarnation to another. Perhaps also tangible objects which were once treasured."

Romeo's eyes almost imperceptibly flickered to Seren and Madoc before resting on nain. His hand moved first to his neck, where he rubbed his magpie tattoo, then his fingers gently rotated his moonstone ring. He was also thinking of his gold aureus coin, still a secret, and always carried in his back pocket. He nearly reached for it but checked himself then said, "According to the block universe theory, the entirety of the past, present and future is in spacetime, but in different dimensions. Voyaging into the future is conceivable through time dilation. Journeying into the past is feasible through wormholes, via a portal."

"Let's imagine that this block theory is correct Romeo" answered nain. "It has been suggested that there is a portal at the Temple of Seti I, in Abydos, Egypt."

"That's the temple I saw in my past life regression" exclaimed Romeo.

"I don't yet know about your past life regression Romeo. I am hopeful that you will tell me all about it later" replied nain with a frown. "For now, let's concentrate on Egypt for that is where the story is based and the Temple of Seti I is at the heart of it."

Romeo smiled. Nain gracefully slipped into her narrative.

"Minnie Dutton, a cousin of mine, was born in Llyn Cowlyd, on the edge of the Carneddau mountain range. It has a mythical essence where Tylwyth Teg[37] are supposed to live. Minnie believed that in a past life she was the High Priestess Hetpet who lived in Ancient Egypt. Notes that I have read about Minnie's visions say that Seti I visited this High Priestess. When Hetpet became pregnant with his child, to avoid embarrassment for them both she ran away. Her lover was distraught."

Romeo's eyes widened.

"Let me explain" said nain. "When she was a child Minnie fell down the stairs at home and banged her head. She was unconscious, but recovered. Her accident appeared to open the gate to a different dimension for Minnie because she began to sleepwalk, experience repeated visions and speak of a visit in a dream by Pharaoh Seti I who assisted her to remember her life in Ancient Egypt. When she spoke with her parents of her past life, she described a huge columned building. Due to her 'visions' she was placed in a sanatorium."[38]

Romeo interrupted. "My parents were afraid I would be taken away from them. As a child they told me never to speak about my foresights outside my family."

"Their fear is understandable" consoled nain and paused long enough to allow Romeo to percolate his thoughts.

"As a teenager, Minnie visited the British Museum and saw her first photograph of the excavated Temple of Seti I. She claimed to recognise the temple and asked why she could not see its gardens in the image" continued nain. "She asserted that

---

[37] Welsh fairies.

[38] A place of convalescence for people with chronic illness.

Egypt was her home. Following this visit, Minnie studied ancient Egyptian hieroglyphs and worked with famous Egyptologists, who encouraged her interest."

Nain paused to have a sip of tea as Romeo urged her to continue the tale. Her enthusiasm drew him in.

"Developing a remarkable knowledge of Ancient Egypt, we were not surprised when Minnie married an Egyptian man and moved to Egypt. Whilst living there, she continued to have visions and claimed astral visits by Seti I. Following her marriage breakdown, Minnie moved to live near the Giza Pyramids."

Madoc's eyebrows rose slightly higher than Romeo's.

"Through Minnie's keen interest in antiquities, and her expertise in drawing and hieroglyphs she was able to work with Egyptologists. She quickly learned from them the techniques of archaeology."

Nain carried on her story, relentless in detail as Romeo sat up straight and swallowed hard.

"The local people embraced Minnie into their culture. They recounted mythological tales about a mystical valley in Abydos, *Pega-the-Gap*, where souls were said to pass through to the afterlife. Which is strange because there are similar folktales attributed to Llyn Cowlyd. Minnie moved to Abydos, to be near the Temple of Seti I and always maintained her past life had been in Egypt.

It was reported that Minnie's claims about her past life were checked by experts and her explanations were found to be realistic. She could identify newly uncovered wall murals, guided archaeologists to discover the hidden garden she had described as a teenager, depicted life during ancient times including rituals of a High Priestess and the information held on papyri which had been newly excavated and never read. She died as she lived, as an Egyptian and her wishes were followed, that she be buried in the valley of Pega-the-Gap."

Romeo struggled with this information. For most of his life he had hidden his visions from the sight of others. He immediately recalled his visions about the town of Herculaneum. "So, you're saying that this woman lived her life proclaiming to have had a past life in Ancient Egypt and that she could offer detailed aspects of that life previously unknown to historians and archaeologists?" asked Romeo. "She was taken seriously?"

"By some" revealed nain. "Not by everyone. Most people fear what they do not understand Romeo. You, more than most, know that" said nain softly. Romeo's faced tinged with embarrassment at her words.

"The brain holds a complete collection of everything that has happened, is happening now and will happen in the future. Our past, present and future can be accessed through the internal, timeless library held here. Meditate. Allow your mind to be still so that you can merge with the universal life force. Shift your focus to within yourself. You have freewill Romeo. Ysbryd will not intervene unless you ask for help."

"What's Ysbryd?" he asked.

"It means spirit" replied nain. "You should always ask Ysbryd for your and others' highest good, otherwise the consequences may be dire. Remember Romeo, what's meant for you will not miss you. That's known as Destiny."

Seren could see that Romeo was flummoxed. "Come on Madoc, help me prepare a fresh cup of panad. It always helps" she suggested. By the time Romeo had composed himself and considered what nain had said, Madoc had slipped into the back dining room to deposit a large blue pot of tea, four cups and four slices of bara brith.

Nain asked Romeo to tell her about his past life regression with Seren. Barely stopping for breath, he recounted every detail. When he had finished, nain said, "There is a sword dubbed the Segontium Sword Romeo. It's real. Do you know that?"

For Romeo it felt as if the world stopped turning. This news momentarily took away the breath from deep within his lungs. His face turned pale.

"How do you know?" he demanded.

"It was in Bangor, on display in the Gallery. Ancient Romans lived in Wales, Romeo. There were many Roman camps around this area. A sword was found in Segontium, which is close to Conwy and was dubbed the Segontium Sword. Madoc and Seren had an appointment to visit the Gallery today to take photographs of it, but it was missing."

"It's true Romeo," said Madoc.

At a loss, Romeo rubbed his eyes in disbelief and struggled to absorb this new information. Eventually he asked, "But how would you know if it's my Segontium Gladius?"

"We don't. But we now know what was inscribed on yours. If the missing one is found, we could check what is imprinted below the ivory handle."

"If it turns out it is my gladius, could Arsinoë have been real? The life I recalled as a Primus Pilus might be true? And the Sibylline Books may still be in existence?"

Meeting his eyes, nain said "Minnie Dutton went to live in Egypt, a place of utmost importance in her past life. Perhaps you have come to live in north Wales because it is a place that was significant in your past life. And the tangible items you recall, well, they could be apports."

"What are apports?" asked Romeo.

"Objects that appear by supernatural means" responded nain. "Spiritual calling cards so to speak. A feather might appear in an unexpected place for example. That's an apport"

"I'm sure the Segontium Sword will turn up at the gallery soon" interrupted Madoc, nodding his head.

"When it appears" said nain "it may provide evidence of a link to your history."

Romeo stifled his excitement and answered, "Would you be prepared to do a past life regression for us please, nain?" he unnecessarily indicated Seren, Madoc and himself. "I would like to know what happened to Arsinoe, Titus, Ceres and Magpie."

Seren and Madoc appeared shocked. "That is, if you both agree of course" added Romeo quickly.

"Past life memories could be responsible for the wounds people carry around with them in this life, Romeo. Feelings such as fear, rejection, control or hurt. It may be that you must learn lessons from past lives for instance, forgiveness, bravery, how to share or love unconditionally. Only you can hurt your own soul. We can all try to understand ourselves better if we witness the different lives we have led. Another past life regression could open the way to that. Let's see what happens. Shall we meet here tomorrow? Seren? Madoc? Are you in agreement?"

Both nodded their assent.

"Let's see what comes to pass" announced nain.

November 2023

Chapter 26 – East Meets West

Work to your highest good.

There was a stillness within the spacious cavern which hid the Temple of Mithras, and an air of heightened anticipation. Never had nain performed a synchronised past life regression with three people. At the outset, lit by pale honey-yellow candlelight her face had a strained expression, her tense hands reached up to Ysbryd for guidance as she chanted. Nain was astonished when Romeo, Seren and Madoc each declared they had reached the same door inscribed with the date 30BCE. The knotted ball of anxiety in her stomach, untangled slowly.

"Seren, Madoc, Romeo, open the door in front of you" instructed nain. "Walk through it into your past life. It's 30BCE. Tell me what you see, hear and feel."

Romeo began his narrative.

"As dawn broke the sweet smell of myrrh wafted through the mouth of the elongated, black cave where Arsinoë lived. At a makeshift altar she stood, preparing her ritual to the Goddess Artemis. In silence I watched her. There must have been a noise or a sense of my presence because she turned; her face shone with delight. Almost imperceptibly, as our eyes met, Arsinoë placed her left hand over her heart. A faint tremor ran through me. I had longed for this.

Thin white cotton robes clung to her body, accentuating curves I had dreamed about a thousand times. Gracefully Arsinoë moved towards me, her eyes, kohl-framed for protection, filled with joy. She placed her warm hands in mine. Our lips met before I had time to catch my breath. She tasted of honey as I pressed against her and shivered with the thrill of her touch. I had left her, hidden away on this tiny Greek island, in the safe keeping of the Goddess Artemis. For ten years I prayed she would be protected. I thanked the Goddess repeatedly for my Arsinoë.

She looked up at me, her fingers delicately brushed my unshaven cheek. "I knew you would return" she said. "The time is now."

"What is it you need me to do?" I whispered, holding her closely, touching her hair, soft as sable, afraid she might disappear in a cloud of smoke.

"Help me reach my sister Cleopatra before it is too late to save my nephew, Caesarion."

"The predictions you made are coming true Arsinoë" I told her. "In Rome, Octavian is growing in power and turning Roman citizens against Marc Antony."

"This *is* what I foretold. Octavian wishes to control all before him. He understands this cannot be done if power is shared with Marc Antony, a fellow triumvir" she answered. "It is a battle for the Roman Empire."

"Octavian is furious with Marc Antony for many supposed indiscretions against Rome" stated Magpie "and has spoken about these publicly to the Senate."

Her disposition was unruffled, her voice calm. "Explain to me what has happened since we last met" she directed.

There was a long silence as I gathered my thoughts before answering her.

"Marc Antony and Cleopatra live together in Egypt as man and wife which is against Roman convention."

Arsinoe's voice was sad. "My sister always did enjoy the company of powerful, intelligent men."

"He has publicly acknowledged Caesarion as Julius Caesar's son" I explained. Arsinoë nodded, and listened intently as she scanned my face.

She sighed. "Cleopatra is ambitious for her son."

"Caesarion is already co-ruler of Egypt, but Cleopatra intends for Caesarion to rule the Roman Empire, claiming it to be his birth right."

Arsinoë shifted on her feet. "That is enough to anger Octavian" she acknowledged. "There is more?"

"Marc Antony and Cleopatra have three children together. A twin boy and girl; Alexander Helios and Cleopatra Selene, and a third child, named Ptolemy Philadelphus."

"The children's Destiny is already set" responded Arsinoe, shaking her head sadly.

"I did as you asked, and sent a message to Titus and Ceres. They have travelled from Cambria to be with us."

"Where are they?" she demanded, and scrutinised the grotto.

"My ship is moored at the bay beyond the cliff edge. They are waiting there for us. You and I can stay here until morning. When the sun rises over the sea, we will join them and set sail for Alexandria."

"Thank you" was all she said, then laughed as she led me out of the cave. As we walked, our feet dipped slightly into the damp sand. Upon reaching the sea, Arsinoë slipped off her white gown and entered the cool, glossy blue water where she beckoned me to join her. In a moment my clothes lay next to hers at the water's edge. We splashed and swam, laughed and kissed then held each other gently until the passion became so intense that even Neptune and his nymphs blushed. We stayed on the beach until daybreak."

Nain studied Romeo's face and asked, "What happened when you joined the ship?"

"Our world changed" he answered.

November 2023

Chapter 27 – Moment For Life

Life is a prize.

Nain could smell the excitement in the chamber. Madoc and Seren stirred as if eager to be involved.

"Does anyone else remember this time in 30BCE when the world changed?" nain asked. Madoc was the first to speak.

"I do" he said and without taking a breath, began his tale. "From a wide cove, impatiently I watched the orange sun rise and tracked two silhouettes as they splashed through the white-crested ripples at the edge of the sea, Magpie and Arsinoë finally on their way to join the ship. They seemed to take an age to reach us. Legs compressed, shins vertical, triceps extended, the taut muscles of the ten oarsmen swelled in readiness for the wind to catch the purple sail for our journey to Alexandria. I willed the couple to hurry as time was short.

They boarded the scapha[39] together. Arsinoë's black coiled hair, kohl framed cobalt blue eyes and dark skin were distinctively Egyptian. I could sense a frisson of excitement among my soldiers who lustfully flashed their gaze towards her as she stepped aboard. Magpie moved closer to Arsinoë, to shield her from the warriors' stares. Regally, and without a flicker of change in her demeanour, the Prophetess's eyes scanned the ship's crew. Arsinoë needed no protection. Magpie led her to my wife, Ceres. The two women embraced, and the Sibyls sat alongside each other at the ship's bow. They were our precious cargo. A coarse woollen blanket, hooped with red was wrapped around Arsinoë's shoulders for warmth, before Magpie joined me.

---

[39] Small rowing ship.

"You lobbied me to come here Magpie to help you" I whispered. "What is the plan now that Arsinoë is on the ship?"

"Rumours abound about the agreement between Octavian, Marc Antony and Lepidus and the air of triumphalism in Rome is repugnant, Titus" replied Magpie bitterly. His eyes black as coal, burned with vengeance. "One triumvir, Lepidus has been forced to leave the alliance. Another, our beloved friend Marc Antony was humiliated by Octavian's second-in-command, Agrippa in a sea skirmish at a promontory close by here, in northern Greece. They called it the *Battle of Actium*." Magpie's anger hissed from his mouth, vicious as the whip of an adder's tongue. His knuckles turned white as he held the ivory handle of his Segontium Gladius.

"Messages reached me in Cambria of an escalation in enmity between Octavian and Marc Antony" I replied. "But conflict between those two proud men involves a war between brothers of Rome."

"Our friend Marc Antony is not an enemy of the state," spat Magpie. His grave manner emphasised authentic words.

"But his allegiance with Queen Cleopatra raises suspicion among the people of Rome" I answered. "The citizens and legionaries believe the messages spread by Octavian, that Cleopatra intends to be Queen of the Roman empire. You will need to be careful with her sister, Arsinoë. Our legionaries will not take kindly to an Egyptian woman aboard this ship" I warned.

"With this gladius, I will slay any man who goes near her." Magpie's sonorous voice carried on the breeze. I grabbed his arm, afraid that he would begin a tussle on the ship with his own soldiers. He breathed deeply. "When Octavian declared war on Egypt, he pronounced a confrontation with another Roman leader. It's not a war with Egypt. It's a battle for supremacy and Octavian intends to win at all costs. You must understand that, Titus."

"What is your plan, Magpie?" I asked.

With a formidable expression on his face, Magpie frowned, as if to consider for a moment or two whether to tell me the truth. "We are taking Arsinoë to meet with her sister, Cleopatra and our friend Marc Antony" he replied.

"But they think Arsinoë is dead" I whispered fearing she would be murdered on sight.

He laughed as if I had joked. "They are in for a shock."

Full of foreboding I cast a glance at Ceres. This might prove to be our last journey together. Some instants, some decisions, are life changing. This was a moment for life.

November 2023

Chapter 28 – Brothers

Do you dream in colour?

Titus continued his narrative.

"In the days that we travelled across the temperate waters to Alexandria, our routine was to trawl at dawn when plentiful shiny blue-black coloured fish could be netted. Magpie and I knew it was important for the crew's hunger to be satisfied. We needed to keep the men on side and optimistic about our fateful journey. The warriors were appreciative that the two Sibyls had cast spells over the water to make our journey smooth and the wind strong enough to fill our sail. It meant the men could rest for a few hours under clear, moonlit skies in readiness for any battle that lay ahead.

When the scorching sun was at its zenith, to avoid detection by Egypt's naval fleet, we dropped anchor at an island close to the huge, indulgent harbour city of Alexandria. Magpie and I agreed to send a messenger to Marc Antony to ask for an audience with him. We watched and waited as our youngest legionary, Flavius swam ashore with Ceres' amber ring, proof we were friends of the triumvir. Despite the heat, my blood ran cold as I watched Flavius' pliant body join the disarray of people on the horizon. I speculated if he would return and if so, what the message would be. We waited. We could do nothing else.

On the scapha, our legionaries entered the water, and frolicked among the fish in the cerulean sea savouring their freedom. These were happy moments. I conjectured how long the joy might last. Two days was the answer.

It was as the black blanket of sky was tugged above the horizon to reveal a slight blue fringe and a sliver of orange sun, when the lookout spotted two ships heading our way. One

Roman, the other Egyptian. Magpie ordered the legionaries to prepare for battle. They filed hooks on the end of long wooden poles, sharpened their pugios and asked the Sibyls to cover the rapier of their gladii with a spell. Once prepared, we hid the women among the deep folds of an unused sail. The warriors were most used to fighting for their lives, against all odds. An air of exuberance fluttered butterfly-light from one legionary to another. My heart beat the rhythm of war.

The Roman ship led the way, pitching against the waves. My face must have expressed genuine surprise. At the bow was our young legionary, Flavius, flanked by Lorenzo and Clemens, men Magpie and I had fought alongside in Gaul. In this current civil conflict between Romans, were we friends still, or foes, I asked myself?

The Roman ship came alongside ours. His face taciturn, Magpie lowered the gangplank to enable easy access to our vessel. A frisson of aggression passed easily from one of our legionaries to another. This was a dangerous moment, but we were armed and ready to fight.

Lorenzo spoke first. "Titus, Magpie we are here to take you to Marc Antony. He ordered the Egyptian ship to flank us to show that your scapha, and men on board, are welcome in the harbour of Alexandria."

Magpie stepped forward, gladius by his side. "Our men seek glory for Rome on behalf of Marc Antony" he said. Our legionaries cheered.

"Your warriors will be unused to the tides and currents around the harbour. We will help navigate your scapha to safety, Magpie" answered Clemens. "We know you come as brothers to us and Marc Antony. The four of us hugged. Relieved we did not have to massacre Roman men. Our brothers.

Magpie gave the order to raise the anchor. Three warships sprinted to the shore in plain sight of the inhabitants of

Alexandria. Silently we observed the city's throng of flamboyant citizens on the harbourside, where hustle and bustle wove the colourful fabric of an exotic life.

***

In a wrinkly bay near the shore of Alexandria, tall pink granite columns stood self-confidently defending the palace in which lived Marc Antony, Cleopatra, their children and Caesarion. Flanked by the two Centurions, Lorenzo and Clemens, Magpie and I stepped up a plush, rose marble staircase. Lit by enormous, burnished torches of fire, the stairway was jealously guarded by two colossal sphinx statues. Even we, used to the grandeur of Roman architecture, marvelled at our luxurious surroundings.

Ahead of us lay a long, bright hallway with its colourfully tessellated floor. This was Marc Antony's area of the palace. Muscle-ripped Clemens led the way; Lorenzo walked beside us. Gladii, sheathed in battle-worn scabbards, clung menacingly from tan leather straps around their hips. These men were used to summoning the Fate, Morta who could induce death at her will. Thankfully we were brothers in arms.

We were guided towards two latticed golden doors which gleamed in the firelight like sunstone infused with warm radiance. We paused in front them. Clemens spoke.

"Titus, Magpie, you will remember Marc Antony for his military valour, a successful, gregarious, powerful and competitive man."

We could do nothing but nod in agreement. With jaw clenched Clemens told us that Marc Antony walked alone around the palace every night. During the day he refused company.

"Our great leader has become a recluse. You are fortunate that he has agreed to see you both," said Clemens.

Lorenzo heaved open both doors and beckoned us to walk into a vast room. I scanned the space, and found it fit for a proud emperor. When I saw Marc Antony, a solid lump of sadness, bitter as any lemon, squeezed into my throat. He did not look like his old self. I felt Magpie's eyes upon me as I gulped and involuntarily moved forward. At a slight nod from their leader, the two Centurions led us to the large chair at which he sat.

The once powerful face of our triumvir was mottled red and yellow with spider veins and pus-filled skin sores. Marc Antony's bruised hands, once able to slay three men with one swipe of a pugio, shook as violently as any sapling in an autumn storm. I stared at his dishevelled appearance, looked into his sunken eyes and saw a broken man, reliant on wine for sustenance. Magpie and I knelt at his feet.

Dully he said, "Get up. I am not worthy of this. I am a disappointment. Come. Drink with me."

We moved slowly as we walked alongside him to a table crammed with unfilled grape shaped drinking pots leafed with gold, and amphorae[40] mostly empty of wine. Listing as he shifted, I was afraid Marc Antony might fall and catch his head on the granite table. I reached out to support him.

"I don't need anyone's help" he yelled.

The air reeked with the stench of his vomit. Out of place in this warm, welcoming, benevolent palace he slumped on a chair at the head of the table. We tried to propitiate him.

"Marc Antony, you have won many battles, live with the most beautiful woman in an outstanding palace in this vibrant city. We are your warriors."

He sagged under the weight of his despair. "Octavian went to war against me because he wanted total control of the Roman

---

[40] Pottery vessels.

Empire. Because of his ego my men and I had to murder Octavian's men. They were Romans. Like us. They were the same as us. I hacked at their skin, severed their sinews, nailed hands and feet to the floor, watched the blood seep out of their bodies, saw desperate eyes staring back at me. Some of the men I destroyed were soldiers who were once under my command. I am weary of violence."

It was not impossible to imagine the horror Marc Antony described. As Roman soldiers, we had defeated many, and slaughtered other Romans during our civil wars. Marc Antony placed his head in his hands and wept. I tried to comfort him, but his torment continued.

"I ordered my men to kill Roman legionaries they had fought alongside in Parthia and Armenia. We shouldn't have to execute our own brothers, uncles, fathers, and sons for one man's ego. For one man's zealous mission. For his vanity."

"What happened at your last battle?" I asked, with my heart thumping against my chest.

"The Battle of Actium they called it." His face wrinkled and he blew out his cheeks. "Cleopatra and I had more soldiers, more ships, more weapons than Octavian and his second-in-command, Agrippa."

Marc Antony took a laboured breath; his jaundiced eyes pierced my soul.

"And more cowardly deserters who told Agrippa about our battle plans. He killed my men once they had informed on us. Those legionaries got their just desserts. Trust no-one" he screamed. "We had to retreat when our supplies were cut off. Now Octavian will come to Alexandria and claim it as his own, perhaps take Queen Cleopatra and murder our children too."

The Sibyls, Arsinoë and Ceres had foretold to us Marc Antony's loss at the Battle of Actium. They said it marked a seismic shift in control of Queen Cleopatra's Egypt which only time would reveal. We allowed silence to descend as Marc Antony lifted an amphora to his violet lips. Warily Magpie's eyes darted from Marc Antony to me. His tear-stained face indicated that Marc Antony could not bear to relive the Battle of Actium. Before us, our leader fell to his knees. We sat stiffly.

"You four men are my most trusted counsel. I tell you my life is over" he muttered. "I have lost my empire, my honour and the woman I love is distraught because of it. Promise me that Queen Cleopatra, Caesarion and my children will always be protected." His red rimmed, dark eyes darted to Magpie. "I hear you have been successful in many battles." Marc Antony fingered the emerald beads around his neck. Some say you have a magical gladius. Show it to me."

Magpie carefully removed the Segontium Gladius from its scabbard. The ivory handle glistened in the torchlight; its blade danced with rivulets of ancient tears. Entranced, Marc Antony gestured to Magpie. In a light voice he said, "They tell me, Magpie that you can kill a man with one nick of this pointer. May I hold it to feel its magic?"

Magpie gently passed the Segontium Gladius to his leader. Marc Antony held the gleaming ivory handle, admired the thrust of the sword. We watched as he stroked the pitted blade, placed the pointer at his stomach and snorted. He pulled it away and I exhaled a generous sigh of relief that an alarming moment had passed. I had not expected the one swift deliberate movement which followed when Marc Antony nicked his abdomen with the Segontium Gladius.

"Let's see if one scratch of your sword will kill me" he teased "and my misery may cease."

Once the horror had subsided, we trusted that the blazing-eyed ferryman Charon would escort Marc Antony to the Elysian Fields.

Sometimes the end of life arrives too quickly.

November 2023

Chapter 29 – Sisters

Breathe and receive.

"Do you see Seren, any images from 30BCE?" asked nain "when you lived as Ceres?"

Seren seized the opportunity to tell her story.

"Yes" she answered swiftly, keen to reveal her visions. "The many chambers in Queen Cleopatra's magnificent palace held countless secrets of duplicitous arrangements. The passing of Marc Antony was just one example. His untimely death was attributed to him *falling on his sword.* The Segontium Gladius certainly was double edged.

As the wife of Titus, I was allowed into Cleopatra's chamber to commiserate with the Queen. Among the richly crafted, lustrous furniture she appeared as a sad ghost of herself. The face which once glowed with supremacy and pleasure appeared grainy, her piercing blue eyes were bright with streaming tears. Cleopatra's hands shook as she tied emerald beads around her neck, a symbol of eternal love. A present from Marc Antony, she said.

A dark veil of sorrow sheathed Cleopatra. To her, Marc Antony had the status of a God. She told me that she had placed blood-red ruby beads around the neck of his corpse to denote her passionate love for him before his journey to everlasting radiance. A hem-netjer-tepi[41] followed an ancient grimoire, the *Book of the Dead* and embalmed him, wrapped his body in lapis blue linen, placed amulets among the wrappings and wrote magical words on some of the linen strips.

---

[41] High Priest (embalmer).

To protect his body and spirit, a polished marble tomb, deep beneath the Queen's palace was prepared and decorated with rich mosaics inlaid with purple amethysts to signify power and wealth, turquoise crystals to connect Marc Antony with this world after death, and green agate to ward off negative energies. The Queen insisted that his tomb be painted with illustrations of grapes and wine, as an offering to the Gods for a safe journey into the afterlife. In his burial chamber she arranged for wine stored in amphorae to be placed around him alongside his plumed attic helmet, hammered metal body armour, scarred gladius and dented pugio.

When the time came for Marc Antony to be judged by the God Osiris and Goddess Isis, Cleopatra told me, his heart would be weighed to see if he was considered worthy to continue into the afterlife. She was certain he would not fail judgement.

"Ceres, wife of Titus" the Queen said softly "your tourmaline necklace indicates you are a sorceress. This grief is a black shadow which is suffocating me. Can your powers bring back Marc Antony?"

"He will wait for you before beginning a new life in a different realm" I explained. My answer appeared to satisfy her.

"I will share eternity with him. That is my wish."

"The Gods will grant it" I assured her. Cleopatra's eyes expressed relief; her face brightened.

"But the children" she said. "What will happen to them?"

"It depends, Queen Cleopatra, upon the decisions you make" I replied.

She eyed me with suspicion. Her head titled backwards.

"What is it you want from me sorceress?"

"That you grant an audience to your sister, Arsinoë."

I could not have shocked her more had I presented Marc Antony risen from his tomb.

"But Arsinoë died in Ephesus at the Temple of Artemis" she protested and gaped at me.

"The Goddess Artemis is a protector of young women. Under a crescent moon, when Arsinoë realised that you had issued orders for her to be murdered, she called upon the Goddess for help and was answered."

"What trickery is this?" she spat.

"Your sister wishes to see you" I insisted.

Cleopatra bowed her head, sighed, lifted her face and replied, "Very well". Her eyes burned into mine.

***

As we entered the palace, Arsinoë covered her head with a cape of teal linen which matched her long gown. Many years had passed since she had been home and walked the steps to the Queen's apartment which had once belonged to her. A handmaiden led us into a dimly lit room. The air was teeming with melancholy. Arsinoë stepped across the latticed floor. Carefully she carried an offering of compassion towards her sister, bound with a ribbon of caution. Arsinoë understood grief, loneliness and desperation. Her long separation from Magpie had taught her valuable lessons.

"Sit here" beckoned Cleopatra. Arsinoë placed herself a short distance from her sister. I sat beside the Sibyl.

"My sincere condolences for your loss Cleopatra" offered Arsinoë.

"Marc Antony was the brightness in my life" she answered. "Funny, interesting, thoughtful, brave. Now he will turn to dust as I crumble under the weight of his passing." She let out a soulful gasp of despair. "And I do not know how to face each day without him" she confessed.

"Grief can only be carried alone" answered Arsinoë. "It is a long, lonely, painful journey. You are in a sad situation."

The three of us, this triumvirate, sat side by side joined together in sorrow for a great man. I held my breath wating for Cleopatra to speak.

"Ceres said you wished to see me. You have travelled a dangerous journey, sister. What is so important?" she asked guardedly. "Are you here to claim my kingdom?"

Arsinoë looked at her sister in pitiful disbelief.

"You are a Seer, a Prophetess. Tell me what will happen now that Marc Antony is no longer here," said Cleopatra.

"You have a choice" replied Arsinoë.

"Which is?" asked Cleopatra sharply.

"You can save yourself or your children."

"I knew it. You have come to murder me and claim Egypt as your own. You are treacherous."

Cleopatra did not recognise the irony of her own words.

"Sister. You can offer yourself to Octavian. He will gladly take you and parade you at the Triumph in Rome. His prized possession. Your children will be killed."

"Or?" asked Cleopatra frowning. "My children. What do you see might happen to them?" she asked.

"The children of Marc Antony will be brought up by his wife" I said. This appeared to satisfy her.

"The son I had with Julius Caesar. What will become of him?" she asked, close to tears.

"Your eldest child, Caesarion will be rescued by a Queen."

"Do you mean me?"

Her eyes blazed when Arsinoë answered, "No, Queen Cleopatra."

"Who is this … Queen?" she demanded.

Arsinoë's voice was steady, but my stomach churned as she replied, "Me."

I had expected Cleopatra to be angry but instead silence reigned for a long time. The Queen sat in her imperial chair deliberating the possibility that her younger sister might save the heir to Rome's Empire.

"You will kill Caesarion in vengeance," she accused.

"Arsinoë is a powerful Sibyl, Queen Cleopatra," I intervened. "She is your sister and Caesarion's aunt. Perhaps now is the time for reconciliation?"

Cleopatra dismissed me with a wave of her bejewelled hand.

"You can save the children Cleopatra. Allow me to take Caesarion with me to Cambria. Octavian will stop at nothing to keep his Empire. He knows that Caesarion is the rightful heir to that throne" said Arsinoë.

An intelligent woman, Cleopatra was silent, considering this proposal. "Octavian will find Caesarion, wherever he goes" she responded.

"Not if he thinks Caesarion is dead" replied Arsinoë.

Her face was shocked, her eyes unwavering. "What do you mean?"

"Arsinoë is a powerful sorceress, Queen Cleopatra" I said. "She can create a spell which will make Caesarion appear to be dead."

Cleopatra smiled sweetly. "Fool Octavian you mean? And my son will live? And when Octavian is defeated, Julius Caesar's son will become King of Egypt and the Roman Empire. His rightful place."

Arsinoë spoke softly to her sister. "You have lost much Cleopatra. Allow me to take Caesarion as my son. He will be safely shielded by Magpie and me, Titus and Ceres. My three friends loved Julius Caesar and Marc Antony. Please allow us to help you. We will take Caesarion as our own. You and I are sisters. Let's forgive each other."

It felt as though the world stopped turning as we waited for Cleopatra's answer. How would she seal the Destiny of Egypt, the Roman Empire and her heirs? The question hung grey in the room.

"Sister, take Caesarion to Cambria" she commanded "and guard him with your life."

November 2023

Chapter 30 – Lessons Learned?

Only time will tell.

Nain's voice echoed around the chamber in the Temple of Mithras.

"I'm going to stomp hawkstaff now." She banged the rod on the ground. "The deal is sealed. I'll count back from ten to zero. When I say zero your eyes will open. The three of you will return to your current lives" nain said firmly.

The silence which followed thundered through her ears.

"Seren. Madoc. Romeo," said nain, "are you ok?"

It felt as if nain's voice was in a different dimension, floating anxiously, waiting for an answer. There was no response, only strained silence and a drip from the ceiling. Nain's dark eyes showed terror.

"Seren. Madoc. Romeo," repeated nain, "are you ok?"

"I'm as fine as a dandy's bum fluff" responded Madoc, scrabbling to find his bearings in the orange candlelight. "What about you Romeo? Are you back with us yet?" he asked.

"I feel weird. Very strange" answered Romeo uncertainly.

"Seren" boomed Madoc anxiously.

"I'm ok Madoc" Seren replied, close to tears. "It's so hard to leave where I once belonged."

"Here" said nain, passing Romeo home-baked Welsh cakes.

"What are these?" he asked, surprised.

"A cross between a scone and pancake. I baked them over my open fire. Gives them an earthy flavour. Eat some and help yourself to a cup of coffee from the flask" instructed nain "then pass the flask to Seren. Looks like she needs a drink."

Seren sat silent as an owl watching the shadows bounce off the Temple's damp walls. They created vivid images of a queen being reunited with her lover.

"Keep the blanket around you Romeo. You'll feel the cold." As Romeo sipped his drink and began to thaw, nain asked, "What lessons have you learned from your past life journey?" She watched his eyes refocus. Romeo ran his fingers through his hair to give himself time to think.

"The flow of time is a figment of our imagination so, our past, present and future is all around us, bound up in energy. We just need to use all our senses to find them."

"Exactly" replied nain. "What's meant for you will not miss you, if you open your mind."

"Time exists without the single forward arrow. That's a cool concept. Does that mean we can't change our own story?" asked Madoc.

"It's already written" replied Seren. "It's fate, or Destiny or whatever we choose to call it. Free will allows us to make choices along the road, and only if we ask for guidance from Ysbryd will we receive it to reach our highest self."

Romeo looked weary. His words floated gently around the Temple of Mithras. "We can live life making our own free will choices, doing whatever we damn well please, but it means we may not learn from the lessons given to us" he said. "And maybe that's my Destiny. Not to learn lessons! So nain, could I carry on living my selfish life? Not discovering anything from the mistakes I make? Will I have to have another life, and another life, and another one, until I learn that I need to treat others well?"

"It is that simple Romeo. It's about the relationships we have" answered nain. "People remember how you made them feel."

"That sounds a little like what we physicists call *entanglement*?" he replied.

"What do you mean mate?" asked Madoc.

"It's weird and a little freaky" replied Romeo.

"And you think that worries us?" asked Seren shifting in her seat to face Romeo. Nain and Madoc laughed.

"Entanglement." Romeo's word was deliberate as he considered his response. "The essence of it is that two particles which were once together, keep the memory of this and seem to know what the other particle is doing, even when separated over long distances and in different time zones. These particles have a special way of communicating and can transmit information to each other. It is a mystery of quantum physics how this happens. Perhaps that is what we have been able to do through the past life regression. Communicate with others even though we are separate in spacetime. Perhaps, as people we are entangled until we have learned our lessons."

"Thanks for the physics lesson, Romeo. I wasn't much for science when I was at school" admitted Madoc.

Romeo was pensive. "When I was eleven, I saw Arsinoë in a dream" he revealed. "I also dreamt about Julius Caesar, Titus and Ceres. I told my brother Alessandro about the visions because they made such an impression on me. Felt so vivid and real. That means their essence has stayed with me throughout space and time. That is, if time exists," he laughed.

"Our past life regression revealed that it was not the bones of Arsinoë IV found buried in the Temple of Artemis" responded Seren. "You must feel relieved about that,

Romeo. Instead, it was the body of a maiden from a local village. Poor girl. A human sacrifice. Terrible really. But knowing that, makes me wonder what happened to Arsinoë."

"In my past life regression, Cassinia, the Cumaean Seer said I would marry a queen. When I visited Naples, the Seer, Stella told me I married a queen" answered Romeo. "I must have married Arsinoë at some point. Interesting."

"Have you learned anything else Romeo, from your past life journey?" asked nain.

"That some men do not cope with grief" he whispered. "Instead, they follow risky behaviours like excessively drinking, or taking drugs, or womanising. Or even all three. It blots out what they cannot face." He floundered. "My feelings for Arsinoë were so intense, as was the love I had for my twin brother."

Nain urged him to carry on.

"I know after my past life regression that some friends can be called upon in times of need. They have a timeless presence." Magpie looked at Seren and Madoc, his mouth loosened into a smile.

"Anything else?" asked nain.

"It is possible to love people enough to be prepared to die for them. But, if that happens, the ones left behind have the heaviest weight to carry and the wobbliest of roads to follow."

"Grief is hard to bear" agreed nain, her shoulders sagged as she thought of her husband, Tomos.

"Despite my avoidance tactics" added Romeo, "I have been shown that I can love someone, truly, madly, deeply, receive their love and treat it with respect. I had been afraid to love." He considered for a moment and added with a smile, "Up until now. In this life."

Madoc could scarcely look at Romeo for disbelief. "You've met someone?" he asked.

Romeo was a little cagey. "Kind of" he replied, looking down. "It's a woman I've been working with. She's sweet but it's early days and I'm not rushing anything so please don't ask me any questions about her. Time will tell."

Seren bobbed her head and raised her eyes at Madoc as if to say, '*I told you so*'.

Nain kindly changed the subject. "You are learning important lessons Romeo."

He laughed, as soulful as the sound of a rich saxophone. "You have been very welcoming to me nain. Thank you." Romeo took a deep breath. "I realise now that I was the keeper of a Sibylline book when I returned to Wales. I wonder what became of that significant relic? I also had responsibility for one of the most important people in the Ancient world, Caesarion. I trust I lived up to expectations."

Nain smiled knowingly.

"And I was given the Segontium Sword, or should I call it Gladius? You have told me that it is here in Conwy but that it is missing from the gallery. I am anxious to see it. When it is found, I will know if it is the one presented to me by Titus as it has the inscription SPQR, a golden spiral and Legio X below the ivory hilt. Madoc and I would recognise it at once."

"Do you remember" began Madoc, then hesitated. "No, you may not recall, but I do."

Seren was surprised by Madoc's stumbling words. "Madoc, you're not making sense."

"This might be a wild goose chase," he said "but I remembered that Magpie buried his Roman coins at the Ancient Roman Fort of Segontium when we returned to Cambria after rescuing Arsinoë and Caesarion. He did it in thanks for a safe journey. That's where you were stationed Romeo, at Segontium. I wonder if the Segontium Sword might be found there now?"

"Why would it be there?" asked nain "and not in the gallery? Don't be ridiculous Madoc. It was already found in a field at Segontium. Remember? Do you think it will have soared through the air as quick as a red Welsh dragon, flying to its home on the mountainside?"

"Why would it disappear nain? I don't know the answer. But we could visit Segontium as we do have metal detectors now," said Madoc.

"You're just looking for a reason to use our metal detectors Madoc Thomson" maintained Seren, "hoping we will find any kind of treasure."

Madoc's eyebrows lifted slightly.

"Before we go racing away to find the Segontium Sword" reasoned Romeo, "I would like to look around this Temple to see if I can find a sarcophagus. I am sure it is close by."

Seren, who was holding nain's arm, felt her stiffen at the prospect of anyone disturbing the harmony of the Temple of Mithras. "Nain looks tired. A warm bath would be most welcome. Come on, back up to the farmhouse. Please don't go snooping around here you two."

Seren had an irrational belief that Madoc and Romeo would follow her instructions.

December 2023

Chapter 31 – Life Begins And Ends With You

Real love

While Romeo's reality was being pummelled ferociously by the laws of quantum physics and revelations from his past life, Seren's and Madoc's lives were also in a maelstrom of change. Expecting a baby can do that to a couple. Nain had been delighted about the forthcoming new addition to their family when they shared the news. Of course, she pretended to be shocked, but her visions had already revealed they would have a baby girl. Information Romeo too had already *seen*!

Much of Romeo's time in Wales had been spent grappling with chasms in the scientific world's understanding of quantum physics. '*There are vacuums in our knowledge as huge as any black hole*' he would joke.

"It wasn't funny the first time you said it Romeo," declared elegant Esther.

He enjoyed that his peer challenged, without damning him when she was underwhelmed by his humour, or his academic work. They had shared lunch in the staff canteen on occasion, and once or twice met for coffee after work. Moments he had discreetly enjoyed.

***

Over the past few weeks an academic paper had proved a thrillingly, intellectual challenge for Romeo to complete.

"You are working too hard" Esther had warned as the lights burned in his office. "The beautiful things are difficult, or is it the difficult things are beautiful?" she had asked one evening on her way home. Romeo shook his head, bemused.

For a few days he had been waiting for Esther to return his blue folder holding his research on quantum entanglement. In his investigations he had observed light from stars and used the data to determine whether entanglement between photons existed millions of years ago. It did! The conclusion was that throughout space and time (if time exists) two particles had always been able to keep the memory of being together, knowing what the other was doing and communicating with each other even when in different dimensions. Quite remarkable! Romeo was elated by his findings and had asked for Esther's professional opinion on his report, unsure why her judgement mattered to him, but it did.

Romeo beamed when he found his blue folder placed neatly on his desk one morning, just as the sun rose. Esther's endless energy fizzled through the green handwritten comments she had made on each one of his neatly typed pages. Her enthusiasm for his work was infectious. She pushed him to be better than he thought he was. At the back of his folder in a plastic sleeve, Esther had placed a ball of red silk thread, which puzzled him.

"Why the thread?" he had asked.

"It was exactly what the Goddess Ariadne did, you know, the wife of Dionysus. She gave a ball of red thread to help Prince Theseus find his way out of a maze. It's to help you navigate the labyrinth of entanglement" she explained. "I thought it might tickle you. Tata for now."

The name Dionysus and Esther's infectious laughter made the hairs on the back of his arms rise. Romeo rubbed his neck as her words reverberated around his mind long after she had left for home.

***

Esther's office desk was beside a window. A few days later, he had interrupted her as she gazed outside, daydreaming.

"Hey Esther. We know that matter around the stars and galaxies accounts for five percent of the universe. Here's a question for you. How do you know *dark* matter exists?" probed Romeo.

Esther shook her head, as if to dispel shadowy images. "Erm" she began. "Well, we can't see dark matter."

"I know that."

Esther arched her shapely eyebrows. "Dark matter makes up almost thirty percent of the universe and appears to be associated with the vacuum in space."

"Yes, but how do you *know* it exists?" Romeo persisted.

"As scientists we can only infer the existence of dark matter from the gravitational effect it seems to have on visible matter. So, I would say through reasoning, I know that something I cannot see, or explain is at work in the universe" responded Esther. "Why do you ask?"

"It doesn't matter" replied Romeo who smiled as he walked away from her desk.

Esther shook her head. '*Strange man*' she thought. '*Wait, was he making a joke about matter*?'

Romeo turned around. "Esther. Would you like to come stargazing with me on the Vardre tomorrow night?"

"Ok" she said nonchalantly with barely a consideration. "Where shall we meet?"

"Outside Llanrhos church, Saint Hilary's. Leave your car in the car park there. I'll pick you up around nine, we can drive up to the Vardre and park close by."

"Great. See you there in a spooky car park surrounded by ghosts. Sounds divine." She laughed and her interesting face creased into smile lines.

'*Is she mocking me*?' thought Romeo. He quietened his whirring mind enough to reply, "See you there."

"You will" she promised. And he did.

That is how astrophysicist and augur Romeo came to date astrophysicist, Esther. Not his usual type of woman at all. More like studious Velma from Scooby Do than siren Daphne. Mind you, had she known, would Esther have agreed to date a Seer?

***

It was a new moon night. Owl hoots from bare-armed trees had accompanied their boggy walk up the Vadre. On an untidy edge of grass at the top of the hill, Romeo and Esther had placed two directors' chairs facing the Irish Sea. They were ready for a night's stargazing before welcoming the Winter Solstice sunrise. Expertly they set up two stands, telescopes, and their wide-angle lens Nikon cameras. The moon was shyly hiding from sight.

During the night, meteors hung tantalisingly as bejewelled necklaces between the Vardre's two delicately uneven humps. Romeo and Esther watched as shiny green and pink sploshes rained upon the sky's dark inverted canvas. Both astrophysicists clicked, whirred, snapped their cameras with individual élan when rings of light seductively curved around star clusters or flashed across the sky. When heavy-eyed Esther yawned more than once, Romeo suggested they sat and drank strong coffee.

"Did you know I'm a putrid casserole?" he asked.

That made her sit up and take notice.

"I thought you were going to offer me a biscuit, not make a scary statement when I'm alone in the dark in the middle of nowhere with you, Romeo" quipped Esther panicking slightly.

It had all been going so well.

"You told me recently that something you cannot see or explain is at work in the universe. Do you believe that?" asked Romeo.

"Of course. My job is to be open-minded. Why?" For the first time, Esther was suspicious of Romeo.

"Do you believe in the occult?" he pursued.

"Do you mean magic?"

"I suppose I do. Let me explain. Then make your judgement of me" asked Romeo.

"You've already told me your own verdict of yourself so I might be a little biased in my response, but ok. I'm all ears. That's why they call me Dumbo" joked Esther, still a little afraid.

Romeo smiled. "Since I was eleven, I have undertaken the Sisyphean task of trying to ignore that I can see the past, present and future. I'm an Augur, a Seer so to speak. My twin brother died when we were eleven. I used to chat to him about my visions which began when I was a young child."

Esther's tired eyes opened a little wider. "I'm sorry to hear about your brother" she consoled.

"Thanks. As an adult I've not treated people very well in this life" admitted Romeo. "I shut them out, use them, so that I don't get hurt. As I said. Putrid casserole."

Esther remained quiet.

"Anyway. Visions of my past life have shown me that I lived a brutal life as a soldier in Ancient Rome" he announced briskly and winced. He waited for Esther's reaction. She remained silent, listening and watching. Romeo paused, wondering momentarily whether to tell Esther the whole story. The story of his life. His lives. He did and she paid rapt attention.

When he had finished, Romeo said, "I felt it was important that I showed you the real me. The reason I'm telling you this Esther is that recently I have been tortured by visions of the Seer Ceres and her husband Titus.

The recurring nightmare began with an image of Ceres, held by Titus until the last ray of bright life shone out of her. Lifeless in bed Titus, aided by me, Magpie, carried her from the farmstead to an underground sarcophagus in the Temple of Mithras.

I watched as Titus and Magpie gently laid Ceres on a slab of expansive white marble inside a casket ornately decorated with pink scallop shells. Her head rested on a green pillow of sage and thyme, a pale blue and purple silk gown covered her frail body.

As I observed these images, Magpie moved away to light more candles as Titus kissed his wife's grey-stone cheek. Arsinoë, who was already in the Temple of Mithras preparing for the funeral ceremony, walked down stone steps, approached the sarcophagus and performed a ritual of purification around Ceres' body. Once she had done this, I saw Magpie and Arsinoë step aside to allow Titus to have time with his beloved wife. Within moments, Titus had carefully laid beside Ceres, and nicked his finger with the point of the Segontium Gladius which fell noisily to the floor. Horrified, Magpie and Arsinoë watched as life quickly ebbed away from Titus. There was nothing either of them could do to resuscitate their beloved friend.

The anguish of heartbreak is challenging to watch and more difficult to bear. Unless Titus had said how he felt, it would have been impossible to know how to help him.

Shocked, Magpie and Arsinoë moved slowly away from the sarcophagus and back up the stone steps. Upon reaching the nave, Magpie dropped onto the stone floor near the altar, both hands delicately fingering each of the tiles until he reached the one finely embossed with the Ace of Cups. He lifted the tile, gently withdrew a gold box, pulled a key from his white silk tunic and opened the lid. Magpie checked that the rolls and rolls of papyri, which made up the three ancient grimoires, were there. By candlelight he read aloud the Sybils' prognostications about what would happen next. When he finished reading, Magpie spoke to Arsinoë.

"It is our Destiny Arsinoë to care for the four children, Alesia, Fausta and Sabine alongside shepherding Caesarion. There are enormous challenges ahead for the six of us."

"You and I oversee Cambria now, Magpie," advised Arsinoë as the skein of life vigorously twisted around them.

Magpie tenderly replaced the grimoires in their rightful place, locked in a gold box. The couple revisited the sarcophagus, kissed Titus on his wrinkled forehead, caressed Ceres' soft cheek. Magpie picked up the Segontium Gladius and held it tightly until Arsinoë had purified the area around Titus. As they left the tomb, deftly Arsinoë sealed the entrance. "Now their spirits can cross the river peacefully from the living world to the spirit world" she said.

Magpie walked across to the nave. He placed the sword in a hidden recess within the same deep void as the gold box which held the Sybilline Books. The floor tile was carefully replaced."

Romeo's eyes, black as soot, had widened as he relayed this story to Esther. His visions had shown him that the sarcophagus, Sibylline books and his Segontium Sword were safely stored in the Temple of Mithras. The lacunae in his story were beginning to fill.

Esther shivered. "We could always go in search of the sarcophagus, your sword and the gold box in the Temple of Mithras" she suggested. "You told me there was a covert entry and escape point on the other side of the Temple in the grounds of Saint Hilary's church. We could find the entry point and search the Temple. No-one need know that we've been into it. Depending upon what we find, you could guide Madoc and Seren to do what you think is the correct thing."

"What? You believe the sarcophagus, Sibylline books and Segontium Sword still reside in the Temple of Mithras? That I am telling you the truth?"

"Yes. And searching for them sounds like a brilliant adventure." Esther's mesmerising peacock-blue eyes shone with excitement. "Let's do it."

For a moment Romeo's eyes flashed guilt.

"What about Madoc? He'd be annoyed I'd left him out of the search."

"If, and it's a big IF, we find something of significance in the Temple, then later you could ask Madoc to search with you and *you* will know it's not a wild goose chase" replied Esther. "Up to you" she said with a mischievous smile.

"What about the Segontium Sword that's missing from the Bangor Gallery?" he said. "That might be *my* Segontium Sword and not in the Temple at all."

"Or" responded Esther "it could be a different sword found in Segontium, or a replica which has been taken out of its box for cleaning, or for repair, or sent to another gallery for an exhibition. There are lots of reasons why a sword might be absent from its case. There could be a simple explanation. Anyway. We are about to find out."

"Esther" said Romeo, staring at her. "You don't think I'm crazy, do you?"

"No Romeo. I think you're open to possibilities and that makes you an exhilarating man, not a putrid casserole."

Romeo grinned. He had experienced this same heartening feeling when, on their first date, Esther told him her name meant star. Immediately Stella's words resounded, '*You will feel a spiritual bond with this woman. You will not understand why you connect, but it will be at a deep level. Follow the star*'. Stella had been correct. Romeo did feel an emotional, spiritual and intellectual bond with Esther. He intended to follow her for as long as possible.

Romeo held out his hand to help Esther from the director's chair. He wrapped his arms around her for a lingering time as they kissed. When their lips finally unlocked, he said, "Come on, Esther. No time like the present. Let's go to Saint Hilary's churchyard."

Their eyes met. "Spooky" replied Esther lightly. She did not feel afraid.

***

Their momentous journey from the Vardre to Saint Hilary's church took exactly four minutes. Romeo parked his car on a dark country lane. Silent as rats the couple opened the lychgate to the church, scurried along the yew tree walk and into the gloomy churchyard.

"Now what?" asked Esther.

Using the torch on his mobile telephone to light the ground, Romeo replied, "I think the steps are over here next to this main path. It's centre leads to other paths, like a spider's web, straight in all directions."

"How will we find the entry?"

"It's winter so the vegetation has died back, holes and burrows are quite easy to spot. Let's start at the centre and work our way around. You stab at the ground with my Swiss army knife, I'll dig around with my hands" instructed Romeo. "Watch out for badger holes though, they're quite wide and shaped like a sideways 'D'. Badgers will defend themselves if disturbed."

"Great" replied Esther "what have I got myself into?"

"I know you're enjoying yourself" Romeo answered buoyantly.

"I am" she confessed.

Almost an hour later a small hole had emerged into a pit which revealed one dirty stone step, then another. Excitedly, Romeo and Esther continued to dig until they found a boulder which they managed to move to the side. More steps were uncovered.

"Here Esther, I'll go down the steps first" instructed Romeo and his feet were the last part of his body to disappear underground.

Esther felt a surge of excitement.

"Come on" Romeo shouted impatiently.

They entered the nave of the Temple of Mithras two hours after their initial quest had begun.

***

Face, hands and clothes smeared with dirt Romeo's eyes were alight with anticipation as he looked at Esther. In the half-light, her lips curved into the brightest smile.

"Wow. Look at this place. It's awesome."

"I know. Here. Hold my mobile telephone and shine the light on the floor near the left of the altar. We can look around for the Ace of Cups etched onto a floor tile."

On hands and knees, Esther did as instructed.

"It's there, it's there, it's there Romeo" she said excitedly, her eyes filled with joy as she pointed to a worn stone tile with faint scratchings.

"Pass me the Swiss army knife, I'll try to lever the tile" he said.

Esther held her breath. She did not know what to say. Shaking, she passed the knife to Romeo. He scraped at the edges, which came away easily as if the tile were used to being lifted. Before he raised the tile, he glanced at Esther, who gently nodded approval.

"Do it" she instructed.

"As I pick up the tile Esther, shine the mobile telephone into the space. You'll be able to see if there is anything there."

They were both silent. The only sound was a faint plop of water as, on hands and knees, Romeo and Esther waited nervously for their world to change.

"Well?" asked Romeo, with closed eyes as he held the tile in both hands.

"Romeo" she answered. "There's a gold box here" she paused to gulp. "You feel around carefully for the sword."

Romeo gently placed the tile to his side, lay on the floor and scrabbled around with his hands, feeling the recess in the void.

"Shine the torch in the hole Esther, just here to my left whilst I look in." Romeo's head disappeared into the cavity. When he finally lifted his head, Romeo's eyes were bright with tears.

"My Segontium Gladius is in this space, Esther. It's here. I'm not going crazy. And the sarcophagus is over there" he pointed, "but before we search for it, I'll text Madoc and ask him, Seren and nain to join us in the Temple. They might be angry with me. They might not. We shall see."

"We can't open the tomb, Romeo. We might be cursed" whispered Esther.

His eyes anxious, Romeo asked, "Do you sense that we will be cursed?"

"My *spidey* sense is tingling" Esther teased, but Romeo knew from his father that extra senses are incredibly important when deciding upon the right path.

Romeo inhaled deeply until his lungs expanded his chest. He blew out gently.

"Nain will know what to do" he replied as he bent over his mobile telephone. "Does this text sound ok Esther? '*Hi Madoc, Seren, Bump, and nain. I failed to follow Seren's instructions. I am in the Temple of Mithras with Esther. Please join us asap. Bring your metal detectors, Welsh cakes and smelling salts. Romeo*'."

"Yes, it's fine, said Esther. "Fancy it being true that something I cannot see, or explain is at work in the universe."

Romeo half-laughed for he found it difficult to believe himself.

"While we wait for them, we can have a cup of invigorating coffee from my flask. I'm thirsty as an elephant. Esther, let's savour our moment together before this life changes completely."

Out of his backpack, with grubby hands Romeo cautiously pulled a small silver box tied with a blue wire bow and placed it on his lap. He thought Giovanni's handmade silver torque necklace with an asp's head on either side and sapphire eyes would make a perfect gift for Esther. He was impatient to tell her that it was a symbol of wisdom, temptation and power, but conversely also fragility. He trusted it would attract her attention.

He watched Esther. She poured thick, aromatic coffee for them both, sighed as she looked around the Temple of Mithras before passing Romeo his drink. With her beaming smile, flushed skin, mesmerising turquoise eyes and authentic opinions, Romeo knew the Fates had finally stopped taunting him.

Destiny had manifested him a woman whose character he could love. Truly. Madly. Deeply.

She was his North Star. Polaris.

Reliable, bright, constant.

Si vis amari ama[42] x

Until The End Of Time

xxx

[42] If you want to be loved, love. x

Acknowledgements

Some of the inspiration for this novel has come from the life and times of real historical events or people, several of whom may be considered interested in the mystical side of life, or claimed to have past lives. This is a fictional story.

For giving up precious time to help us, heartfelt thanks are extended to: An Idiosyncratic Dreamer whose essence ignited, illuminated, infuriated, and inspired; Historian Gill Richards for her generous insights; Illustrator and Designer Amy Turrell for expertly crafting the stunning cover design; Inspirational Nain and Taid Williams, whose lives were well-lived with love and honour. *Na'i dy garu di am byth*; John and Diane Elphick who eagerly read the final draft; Linguist and teacher Angela Shafiq who patiently, carefully, and repeatedly checked the manuscript to offer a friendly and literary critique; Martin Thomson for his extensive knowledge of Ancient Rome, the night sky, and always demonstrating an unfailing belief in his wife; Philip who loved paragliding; PJ^2 for the magic of entanglement; Storiel Gallery for information about, and images of the Segontium Sword; The current owner of Bryn Gosol Farm, Jackie Horgan for allowing us to use its name in our work; Twin souls throughout infinity, Alwyn and Ian; Ysbryd for gentle guidance when crafting the narrative.

***

Acknowledgements

Ceris would also like to acknowledge her family and friends. "For my stargazer husband Martin, we will always reach for stars together. For my grandchildren Lydia Haf, Dexter Martin, Juno Cariad and Luna Tlws, you all make me smile. Alfie Moon and Lacey Star, Martin and I still walk on the beach with you."

The universe works in strange ways. An ancient relic, we saw the Segontium Sword on display at the Storiel Gallery in 2014. We were already suffused in Ancient Roman history through living in the Conwy Valley with its connections to the Ancient Roman Forts in Caernarfon and Canovium. Little did we know that ten years later we would have the magical fiction of the Segontium Sword permanently in our lives through this book.
Ceris and Martin Thomson

Forged from the fire of ancient dragons
Dipped in magic, passion in its blade
Blood, sweat and tears from which it is made
This Sword can give and take life away
A queen, a priestess, a seer, a girl
Have all touched this double-edged sword
Once lost in the mists of time
Found again to change Destiny
Ceris Thomson

***

Printed in Great Britain
by Amazon

53561347R00148